WRATH

ROBERT SANTORO

SterlingHouse Publisher, Inc. Pittsburgh, PA

WRATH

Pero thrillers

ISBN-10: 1-56315-457-9
ISBN-13: 978-1-56-315457-7
Trade Paperback

Library of Congress #2009922486

Requests for information should be addressed to:
SterlingHouse Publisher, Inc.
3468 Babcock Boulevard
Pittsburgh, PA 15237
info@sterlinghousepublisher.com
www.sterlinghousepublisher.com

Pero Thrillers
is an imprint of SterlingHouse Publisher, Inc.

Cover Design: Brandon M. Bittner
Interior Design: Kathleen M. Gall

Printed in U.S.A.

TO MY SEVEN YEAR OLD TWIN BOYS
JAKE AND CHASE

ACKNOWLEDGMENTS

WHAT AN EXCITING YEAR! *WRATH* WAS AN ABSOLUTE BLAST TO write—a fun and amazing journey. Thank you to all who endured the summer I decided to become an author.

I am forever indebted to my new buddy and fellow author Michael Balkind for introducing me to the wonderful people at SterlingHouse. There aren't enough cigars and rounds of golf to repay you for that one, Mike!

Thank you to the truly amazing group at SterlingHouse Publisher: Lisa, Jennifer, Megan and Brandon. You all made the process an exciting learning experience. And, of course, to Dr. Cynthia Sterling for taking a chance and believing in my unproven abilities. You're awesome!

To my new friends at the Brooklyn Bar Association for all of your support in helping to promote my work. Thank you: Avery Eli Okin, Esq., Diana Szochet, Esq., Gregory Cerchione, Esq., Jeannie Costello, Esq., Sydney Cherubin, Esq. and Jessica Spiegel.

To my first editors: my caring and "well read" wife Cristina and my patient and loving mother Geraldine. Cris, this book would only be a dream without your undivided support for me and our little boys, Jake and Chase. Your literary knowledge and utter command of words has proven not only to be invaluable but unparalleled. Mom, you have always been there for me (unconditionally). You are one of the kindest and smartest people in my life. Thank you both for knowing where to place the commas.

To my dad, Philip Santoriella; Your generosity and knowledge of business and finance are unmatched. *Wrath* wouldn't be half the book it is without your contributions.

To my friends, family and first readers; thank you all for taking the time to rumble through my work in progress. Your input has without doubt made *Wrath* a much, much better novel! So, thank you to Tania Rodriguez, Stefanie Iennaco, Carol and Joe Grieco, Carolyn Marie Carlin, Joanne and Craig Roffman, Diane Spinelli, Eddie and Lisa Krycerick, Joanie Spota, Jim Erlanger, Frank Audino and of course, my law partner, Marc DiTomaso.

To my cousin, Michael Spinelli; the *Wrath* web site is awesome because of you. You rock!

To my talented, bright paralegals, Lisa Harris and Kathy Murphy; Thank you both so much for helping to put this project together.

To my grandmother, Mary Antonacci; Gramps' death was a big loss. Somehow I think he would have gotten a kick out of this.

Stephanie Costa, special thanks goes out to you for tirelessly reading out loud to me; chapter by chapter, page by page and line by line. Wow!

CHAPTER 1

F.B.I. AGENT JAKE CHASE COULD HEAR THE GUNSHOTS ECHOING off the buildings on 42nd Street. People ran for their lives in every direction, taking cover from the hail of ricocheting bullets flying overhead.

"Get down, get down!" he screamed as he chased three men, all dressed in expensive suits, down 42nd Street in the direction of the United Nations.

It was lunchtime on a sunny Friday afternoon and the streets were packed with hundreds of businessmen and women on their lunch hour. On any other day, the three men he was chasing would have easily blended in with the suit-clad business crowd; except for the fact that these men were top-ranking members of Al Qaeda and were firing automatic weapons in his direction, spraying the street and sidewalk with bullets.

Trying desperately not to lose sight of the men amongst the throngs of panicking bystanders, Jake listened intently through a tiny earpiece as Deputy Director Ken Devasher strategically positioned four teams of F.B.I. field men into a one-block circumference surrounding the fleeing terrorists. From a chopper hovering above the city, Devasher called out coordinates and closed the gap on the three men, like a coach planning the winning plays in the Super Bowl.

We're finally going to get these bastards, Jake thought as he charged down 42nd Street with his Glock 9mm semi-automatic clenched tightly between his fists. *After a year and a half we're finally gonna bust these guys.*

"Ken, this is Jake. I have positive ID. These are our guys!" Jake shouted into the small microphone positioned inches from his mouth as he charged across 42nd street. He slid across the hood of a yellow cab and landed in front of another, causing it to screech to a stop.

"Hey asshole, watch where you're going!"

"Roger that, Jake. What's your twenty?"

"Heading east on the south side of 42nd Street, approaching 2nd Avenue," he huffed.

"Jake, do they have the device?"

"All three men wearing backpacks. Repeat, all three wearing backpacks. The bomb could be in any one of them."

"Roger, Jake. Stay with them. Repeat stay with those men!"

Kicking it into high gear, Jake could hear Devasher through his earpiece coordinating the other field teams to tighten the gap on the terrorists; much like a master chess player closing in on his opponent's king. It was a work of art, a thing of beauty and listening to it gave Jake a huge burst of adrenaline.

Deputy Director Ken Devasher was the number two man at Quantico. He reported right to the Director and on certain cases to the President of the United States.

"Field team two, this is Devasher, do you copy?"

"Field team two, we copy, Deputy Director."

"Field team two, what's your twenty?"

"Heading west on 42nd Street. South side."

"Team two, do you have visual?"

"Affirmative, Deputy Director, we have visual. They're headed right for us."

"Ok, gentlemen it's "Go" time!" commanded Devasher. "Remember, in one of those backpacks is a bomb capable of taking out most of the block. Shoot to kill!"

Black king's knight, take pawn!

"Fuck, they spotted us!" screamed one of the field men from team two. "This is the F.B.I., put your weapons down," he ordered.

The three men didn't seem the slightest bit concerned that they were now cornered in the middle of the block. In fact, they appeared a bit amused by the situation. As both field teams closed in, Jake repeated team two's order. "Place your weapons to the ground and get your hands in the air or we will shoot!"

No response. Instead the three men formed a tight circle, backs pressed against one another, automatic weapons fully engaged and ready to fire. Team two was to the east, Jake was to the west, a row of parked cars formed a border to the north, and the Daily News Building prevented any escape to the south. They were completely boxed in.

"You are completely surrounded," yelled Jake, with his 9mm pointed directly at the head of the terrorist who was facing him. "The choice is yours. Lower your weapons or we will take you down."

"No, Agent Chase, the choice is yours. Lower your weapon and allow us to go about our business or we will take you down," said the man positioned directly in front of him. Then he smiled.

The two other F.B.I. field teams had taken up positions, one just behind team two and the other behind a row of parked cars on 42nd Street.

"This is your last chance. Put down your weapons!" Jake shouted.

"No, Agent Chase, that was your last chance!"

Suddenly the three men opened fire, sending a flurry of bullets in every direction. The sound of gunfire and shattering glass was deafening. Jake quickly dove underneath a parked box truck as shards of broken glass fell down upon him like jagged rain. Devasher was demanding status and innocent people were running frantically for their lives.

A woman and two little girls, who had ducked for cover in the doorway to the News Building, were grabbed by one of the gunmen, who was now using them as human shields. The two other gunmen each grabbed a child and lifted them up to block any gunfire.

"Hold your fire! Hold your fire," Jake screamed into the headset microphone.

"I told you that was your last chance, Agent Chase. Now see what you have done?"

There was an eerie calmness to his voice, and even with his hostage frantically struggling to get to her daughters, who were now crying hysterically for their mother, he never lost composure.

"Come on, Momar, let the little girls go. We can talk this through," said Jake, trying to get a clear shot at the bastard's head.

Okay sweetie. Move your head just a little to the left and let me cap this prick.

"No, Agent Chase, the time for talking is over. Now you must pay. Now this city will pay, and at exactly 1:00 PM your government will pay dearly," he replied, making sure to keep himself well protected by his human shield.

Mohammed Momar was a key man in Al Qaeda. He was one of Bin Laden's deadliest henchmen and had been on the F.B.I.'s ten most wanted list since September 11th. The F.B.I. had been tracking him for over a year, and INTEL believed he was in New York City to blow up the Summit meetings being held at the United Nations. Among the world leaders speaking at the Summit that day was the President of the United States.

"Look around you, Momar. It's over. You've lost. Even if you could detonate the bomb, the explosion will never reach the United Nations building from here. And, God as my witness, you will not get any closer to the UN than where you are standing now."

"You do not want to play that game with me, Agent Chase. I've read your profile. Sooner die yourself than to watch an innocent woman or child be harmed." He scowled as he rubbed the nozzle of the semiautomatic across his hostage's face. "That is the difference between us, Agent Chase. A woman or child is killed in my country and it is merely collateral damage."

Come on, baby, just move your head...just a few inches.

"That may be, Momar, but from where I sit, I count ten other F.B.I. Agents, all with their sights locked on you. And trust me, we have some crazy motherfuckers just itchin' to be the one getting high fives back at Quantico for takin' you down."

"What if I told you, Agent Chase, that we do not have the device? We are merely a distraction, you fool. While you waste your time negotiating for hostages, the actual bomb is already in the lobby of the United Nations."

"You're bluffing, Momar. See, I read your profile, too. You wouldn't allow that bomb to be set off by anyone but yourself. You want to be the martyr; you need to be the martyr. Have ever since the World Trade Center. You wouldn't pass up the opportunity."

"Of course, Agent Chase, but I already am a martyr. You see, I can die right here on this street and I will still be greeted in paradise by seventy-two virgins. Let me prove it to you. Azzam, Mekev, kill the little girls!" he said smiling.

"No no, please no," screamed the children's mother. She began flailing about, kicking and screaming, allowing for a clear shot at Momar's head.

BANG!

The bullet hit Momar on the bridge of his nose and knocked him backwards off his feet into the two other men. His hostage, now free, raced to her daughters. One of the terrorists raised his semiautomatic and began firing in the direction of the frantic woman. Immediately, two F.B.I. agents dove in front of the gunfire as a third agent pulled her to safety.

"No, please, let me go. I have to get to my daughters," she pleaded, as the agent pulled her behind the wall of parked cars.

Jake raced in the direction of the two men, with his gun pointing at both of them. They both appeared very confused and began yelling at each other in Arabic.

"Take it easy. Calm down," Jake said as he cautiously approached the two men who were holding the little girls tightly against their bodies. "It doesn't have to go down that way for you two," he said forcing a smile, as the two men backed toward the entrance of the Daily News Building. The girls, who were crying hysterically, couldn't have been more than five years old. With their feet dangling about mid-waist, they barely covered the terrorists' upper bodies.

"Ok, everybody be cool," Jake said, in the direction of the terrorists; although, he was more concerned about the army of trigger-happy F.B.I. agents behind him. "Mark, check Momar's backpack."

"Empty, Jake. Just some crumpled newspaper."

"Fuck!"

The clock was ticking and Jake had about half an hour to find the device and get Malone and the boys from the bomb squad to disarm it. He was quickly running out of time.

"Ok listen, if you guys don't want to end up with your brains all over the street like your friend Momar over there, let the girls go and hand over the backpacks."

"I don't think so, Agent Chase," replied Azzam, as he and his cohort Mekev, made their way into the lobby of the building.

"Okay, people, everyone sit tight. We can't risk the lives of those little girls by all piling into the building," said Jake. "Mark, Donny, you two come with me. Jeff, scatter your men around the United Nations building in case that bomb isn't in one of those backpacks."

"We're on it, Jake."

Cautiously, Jake, Mark and Donny followed the two men, still toting their human shields, into the lobby, around a huge world globe statue, to the elevator banks.

"Going somewhere, Azzam?" asked Jake rhetorically.

"The roof. Best place to watch the collapse of your United Nations building. Just like the World Trade Center. You remember that day, don't you, Agent Chase? Lost your father in the tragedy, right?" said Azzam with a smile.

As the elevator doors opened, the two men got in with their human shields crying hysterically for their mother.

"I will see you again!" said Jake through tightly clenched teeth, pointing deliberately to the terrorists as the doors closed, leaving the three men alone in the lobby. "Mark, come with me! Donny, stay here and watch where that elevator stops. Radio us when it does!"

"Got it, Jake."

Charging up the stairwell, Jake listened as Donny called out the floors. "10, 15, 20…Jake, they stopped at the top floor. They're on the roof!"

Jake burst through the roof door to see the two men dragging the girls to the edge. They were chanting praise to Allah and to Osama Bin Laden.

"Freeze!" Jake screamed, with about as much breath as he could muster after running up thirty-eight flights of stairs.

"Agent Chase, you are persistent, I will give you that."

"Put down the girls and hand over the backpacks," yelled Mark, his gun tightly clenched between his fists.

"Ah, the backpacks. Sure, here ya go," said one of the terrorists as they both tossed the satchels to Mark's feet. "You see, more newspaper. Just as we told you."

"Yes," said Mekev. "While you two waste your time trying to save these little girls, the real bomb is already inside the lobby of the United Nations. How do you say? Oh yes, class trip."

"Mekev, you fool!"

"Do not worry, Azzam. They will never find the bomb in time. There are only 20 minutes left."

Without taking his eyes or his gun off either of the two men, Jake said to Mark, "You see the shot?"

"Absolutely, Jake."

"Azzam, you know the best thing about five-year-olds?" asked Jake.

"What is that, my friend?" replied Azzam, with a curious look.

"They're so darn short."

BANG, BANG.

Simultaneously, Jake and Mark fired shots into each of the terrorist's kneecaps. As they fell to the ground grimacing in pain, the agents repeated with two more shots to the head.

Checkmate!

"Mark, get these girls to their mother. I'll radio Devasher. We need every man available searching childrens' backpacks. We've got to get that bomb!"

CHAPTER 2

WHEN JAKE ARRIVED AT THE UNITED NATIONS BUILDING THE place was swarming with NYC police and F.B.I. agents all frantically searching backpacks. Children were being quickly ushered away and everyone from bomb techs to teachers were carefully unzipping packs and spilling their contents onto the courtyard. Jake looked down at his watch: ten minutes to one. This is gonna be close!

"Hey, over here. Over here, I found something!"

About midway between the row of flagpoles that fly along First Avenue and the UN building was a uniformed NYC Police Officer who was slowly backing away from a torn open satchel.

"Get back!" Jake shouted in the direction of the officer, as he ran to the device that was now protruding from the remains of the plastic backpack.

"Hey, no problem, man," he replied, as he ran in the direction of First Avenue.

"How bad is it, Jake?"

Jake looked up momentarily from the device. It was the Deputy Director. "Not sure yet, Ken," he said, as he carefully removed the device from the backpack, revealing a small LCD clock.

"Does that answer your question?" Jake said, pointing to the twelve minutes and thirty-four seconds remaining till detonation.

"Okay, Jake, time to go. Let the bomb squad take it from here."

"Yeah, Jake, move over. Let's take a look at what we're dealing with here," said Eddie Malone, as he put on a pair of wire-framed bifocals and knelt down in front of the bomb.

Eddie was the Bureau's top technician. He had been with the F.B.I. for about 40 years and was due to retire in the fall. He had been called in on thousands of assignments for the Bureau, and he'd seen and disarmed just about every device out there.

"Wow, this is real high tech stuff," he said, as he undid the velcro on his tool kit and set it on the ground in front of the device. "Very cool," he mumbled to himself, as he checked out the bomb from all angles. "These guys really mean business."

As he carefully undid the screws on the face of the device, he looked up at Jake and Devasher. "You know you two guys don't need to be here, right?"

"But I get such a thrill out of watching you work, Eddie," Jake said, with a boyish grin.

"Well, as long as you're along for the ride, make yourself useful and hold this steady," he said, as he carefully handed Jake the faceplate from the device; which was still connected to the base by several wires. "Hold it very steady. Whatever you do, don't let the metal from the faceplate touch the metal on the base."

"Or what?" Jake asked, trying to keep his hands from shaking.

"Let's just say it would be a very bad thing."

"Right. Don't let the metal touch. Got it."

"Ok, here we go gentlemen. Like you've seen in the movies a thousand times: a red wire and a green wire. Ken, hand me the wire cutters."

"Here ya go, Eddie," Ken said, as he handed him the cutters with a very shaky hand.

"Relax, Ken," said Eddy, "we're almost home. Now Jake, what's you favorite color: red or green?"

"Come on Eddie, quit fucking around. We're down to one minute forty-five seconds."

"So you'd better hurry up and choose," he said, giving Devasher a wink.

"Fuck, green. Green is my favorite color, all right, ya maniac? Now turn this fucking bomb off."

"Okay," he said, as he put the cutters on the green wire but at the last second moved them to the red wire and snipped it in half. Instantly, the clock stopped counting with eight seconds left.

"Wow! That was a close one. Good thing you're not on the

bomb squad, Jake," he said, laughing as he gathered up his tools.

"You're a goddamn lunatic, you know that, Eddie?"

"Well, you kind of have to be to do what I do for a living."

"Eddie, you son-of- a- bi...."

Suddenly there was someone screaming. "There's another bomb. Here by the building!"

Without wasting a second, the three men ran in the direction of the screaming woman. There, in a torn backpack, was another bomb. Eddie quickly removed the device from the remains of the pack and slowly turned it over. Jake's heart nearly stopped beating when he read the LCD clock: *four minutes twenty seconds.*

Opening his tools again, Eddie said, "Okay fellas, now it really is time for you both to get the fuck out of here."

"But Eddie, it took us over ten minutes to disarm the last one. There just isn't enough...."

"I said get the fuck out of here and let me work."

"Eddie, it's suicide."

"Jake, the more you keep distracting me, the more time we waste," he said, motioning to Devasher.

"He's right, Jake. Let's get out of here; he knows what he's doing." Devasher grabbed Jake's arm and started leading him away from Eddie and the device.

"Yeah, I guess you're right, Ken," said Jake, as he began to follow Devasher's lead. But just as Ken loosened his grip, Jake quickly turned and knocked Eddie over, grabbed the bomb and started running with it tucked under his arm like a football.

"What the fuck are you doing? Jake, get back here!"

As Jake ran for the helipad at the far end of the UN building he looked down at the timer: *three minutes fifty-one seconds*. "Jake, what the fuck are you doing?" he screamed out loud, as he approached one of the helicopters.

It belonged to the Prime Minister of Japan. The pilot, who was taking a nap in the cockpit, had missed all of the earlier commotion.

"Hey, sleeping beauty, rise and shine," Jake said, as he jumped into the co-pilot seat and put the device carefully on the floor in front of him: *two minutes ten seconds.*

The pilot woke up completely disoriented. "Hey, you no belong heah!"

"Just fly," Jake yelled, as he pulled out his 9mm and pointed it in the pilot's direction.

"Whatever you say. Where to, boss man?"

"Fly out to the middle of the river."

"You got it, boss man!"

When they got to the middle of the East River, they were hovering about 20 feet above the water. Jake looked down at the device: *one minute fifty-eight seconds.*

Think, think, think.

"Hey whatcha got there, boss man?"

"It's a bomb!"

"It's a what!"

"Look, can this thing ascend vertically on autopilot?"

"Did you say a bomb?"

"Hey, I don't have time. Straight up. Can this thing go straight up without you on the controls?"

"Oh yes. Dis very sophisticated aircraft. Just press autopilot button and...." Before he could finish the demonstration, Jake reached over and unlatched his door, pressed the autopilot button and dove out of the helicopter with the pilot in his arms.

As the two men fell twenty feet into the East River, the helicopter carrying the bomb headed straight up. It climbed well beyond the city skyline, over a thousand feet into the clouds. When the bomb finally detonated, the sound of the explosion was enormous. The aftershock made waves in the river and caused buildings to rattle. But no damage!

"You did it, boss man, you did it," the pilot cheered, trying to hug Jake, as they bobbed up and down in the now turbulent water, nearly drowning him.

Looking back at the United Nations building, Jake could see the Deputy Director, and he didn't look happy.

"Yeah, I did it all right."

CHAPTER 3

STILL COMPLETELY DRENCHED, JAKE HOPPED INTO HIS ASTON Martin DB9 coupe and headed north on the FDR for Westchester County. He thought about calling his wife Diane but decided to hold off.

Don't want to rush into that call, he thought to himself, smiling, as he rubbed the wetness out of his hair with the towel provided to him courtesy of the NYPD.

He needed more time to process what had just happened and somehow tone it down to a version that she could handle. Diane was cool. But not that cool.

It was really amazing how much his life had changed since marrying Diane. In fact, pretty much nothing he did or owned would be possible on his G-man's salary. Even the car was an early birthday present from her.

Had Jake stayed the course and actually made partner at Devon, Reif & Reed, his first and only law job out of NYU Law, he still wouldn't have come close to the kind of life he was now living in snooty Mount Kisco. Correction; snooty Bedford Hills. Such a faux pas he had once made at a dinner party to the alarming dismay of just about all of the guests and most of the wait staff. Even the family's Golden Retriever had looked up from his mat in the corner and given him a disapproving stare.

Little did Jake know, or care for that matter, that the good folks of Bedford didn't wish to equate themselves with their Mount Kisco neighbors; who probably only paid a meager two million to live just down the block in paupersville.

Either way, none of that really mattered much to him. Diane was the socialite of the family. After all, it was her money. Actually it was her daddy Jack Shepard's money, all left to her, his only child, in a tidy little trust carefully drafted by an arsenal of attorneys to avoid paying a penny more than was necessary in estate taxes. Knowing Jack, he probably paid the IRS a few pennies short.

Old Jack really cared about his family though, in life and in death. The one thing Jack could never understand, though, was why the IRS was able to extort so much of his money while he was building his empire and then take another bite at what was left when he died in estate taxes.

The real kicker was that some years ago The President revamped the Federal Estate Tax regulations. In an effort to slowly diminish Federal Estate Taxes, an exemption was put in place, which increased in value each year and topped off in the year 2010. So if you were lucky enough to die in 2010, the first $3,500,000.00 of your estate passed tax-free to your family. Jack had spent three times that decorating the interior of his Gulfstream.

That's why guys like Jack hire armies of estate planners and tax attorneys to find every loophole possible to minimize the amount paid to the government and maximize what was left to family members.

So along with more than 100 million dollars, Diane inherited the 15,000 square-foot Bedford Estate (once owned by some Vanderbilt, which was now home), the apartment in Manhattan, which takes up the entire floor in some Donald Trump building, the West Coast beach house in Malibu, the East Coast beach house in Southampton, and a Gulfstream G5 to dart between them in record time.

Before his untimely death, Jack Shepard was listed as one of Forbes Magazine's 100 richest Americans. One of the original junk bond traders of the eighties, he used to joke that he had taught Mike Milken everything he knew except, how to stay out of prison. With the millions he made on Wall Street, Captain Jack made wise investments that sent his net worth skyrocketing. He invested in everything from the real estate market to munitions. He even produced a few Hollywood movies and was involved in several lucrative deals with Barry Diller, the former CEO of Universal Studios.

In under a year, old Jack made tens of millions for himself and Diller and both men instantly became recognized as Hollywood movers and shakers. Good old Jack absolutely had the Midas touch. That was, of course, until they found Jack murdered in his Malibu Beach house two years ago. Shot in the back of the head, execution style. Diane, who was extremely close to her dad, was devastated beyond words.

In the beginning the case drew huge media attention but, when no weapon and no murder suspect turned up, the Malibu Police shelved the case and turned their attention to more important matters of business; like arresting Mel Gibson on DWI charges.

Diane's mom had died of cancer when Diane was still in high school. Jack never remarried. Thus, the entire family fortune was now all theirs. Not bad for two 37-year-olds.

With a classic Van Halen tune blasting from the car stereo and the wind blowing in his still damp hair, which, unlike most of his friends, Jake still had plenty of, he couldn't help thinking how happy he was since leaving his short-lived legal career at Devon, Reif & Reed. Smartest move he ever made, actually.

God, the expression on their faces when he told those pompous jerks he was quitting his position at the almighty DR&R and taking a job with the F.B.I.

"You're leaving The Devon Firm to take a government job?" asked Reed in utter disbelief. "A civil servant?"

"Civil servant, my ass; I am an F.B.I. Agent, fluent in six languages, and I am in charge of the Bureau's Anti-terrorism Division," he said out loud, as if reliving once again the ego-crushing partners meeting. Even during the intense training program at Quantico, Jake knew he had made the right decision. It was hard to believe that was ten years ago; it felt like another lifetime.

As David Lee Roth bellowed out the words to *Beautiful Girls,* Jake slowly rolled the DB9 up to the wrought iron gates at the bottom of the driveway and punched in the 4 digit code on the security panel attached to one of the stone pillars. The gates slowly opened to allow for his passage, revealing a long tree lined drive which led up to the main house.

The House was an old Tudor which sat on about fourteen acres, all very secluded. That was the way Captain Jack liked things: extremely private. In the backyard there's a black bottom infinity edge swimming pool, clay tennis courts and a pool house bigger than the home Jake grew up in. There were two other buildings on the property, which house some of the help, including the caretaker and his wife.

Although the house is over one hundred years old, it had all of the modern amenities: Wolf stoves, oversized Sub Zero refrigerators, Bosch dishwashers; though neither Diane nor Jake did much cooking or cleaning. In the basement, Jack had installed a 20-seat home theater that is actually the original prototype Sony had designed for its IMAX movie theaters. He also put in a fully stocked Irish pub with a one thousand bottle wine cellar and walk-in humidor, a gym that rivals any of the local sports clubs, a virtual golf course simulator featuring 50 of the world's best golf courses, and a home office equipped with a T1 connection to the Internet.

Diane often referred to the basement as "Man-land" although she too enjoyed working out in the gym and smacking a few golf balls around Pebble Beach or Augusta National.

She had graduated at the top of her class from Columbia University and went on to get her medical degree at Johns Hopkins. For a short time she was on staff as a pediatrician at the Mount Kisco Medical Group which was close to the house, but now spends a good deal of time volunteering at the Blythedale Children's Hospital.

She was 5'11" to Jake's 6'3", had a swimmer's body, tall and lean and in her younger days had done some modeling for Calvin Klein, who now happens to live a few houses away. She had dark brown hair that falls just below her shoulders. And, her face had an innocent look to it, but when she smiled a certain way it seemed to reveal a hint of wickedness about her.

Little Miss Proper at a charity banquet or fundraiser who would think nothing of spicing things up by going down on Jake on the drive home from the event.

The perfect chick!

As he approached the house, Jake pulled the car under the porte-cochere and around back to the carriage doors. He opened the glove compartment and put his BlackBerry PDA and Glock 9mm inside. Both tools of his profession, Diane couldn't decide which she hated more: the Glock, because it constantly reminded her of how dangerous Jake's job actually was, or the PDA, which always interrupted the limited time they had together with emails and phone calls. Either way, Jake made a conscious effort to keep them out of his home life as best he could.

It was a beautiful spring afternoon, warmer than normal for this time of the year, and Diane was outside taking advantage of the perfect weather. Jake spotted her in the garden. Her hair was pulled back in a pony-tail and she was wearing a faded pair of ripped jeans which revealed ever so slightly her perfect little bum. Her top was a short-sleeved New York Yankees tee shirt with the NY emblem on the front and the number 2 displayed prominently on the back directly below the name Jeter; her favorite Yankee. She was tending to the rose vines she had trained to grow over the pergola at the far end of the pool, and was so focused on her gardening that she didn't notice Jake as he snuck up behind her. Without warning he wrapped his arms around her and began to kiss the back of her neck. He could taste the saltiness of her perspiration and it excited him.

"Carlos, please! I told you Jake will be home soon."

"Carlos?" Jake replied, as he swung her around to face him. He knew perfectly well that Diane was kidding but decided to play along.

Carlos is the full time maintenance man who attends to the heavier landscaping and household needs.

"Oh my God, Jake, I am so sorry I thought you were someone else," Diane said, revealing that wicked little smile of hers.

"Carlos, huh? Well, I suppose that's fitting, since I have had a thing with his wife Maria for the past few months."

"Wow, Maria, huh? I am impressed; she's a cutie," Diane quipped as her hands reached for Jake's already stiffening member, her grin becoming wider and wickeder.

Jake knew there was no winning these little bantering sessions with Diane, so he decided to quit while he was ahead...well, almost ahead anyway. So, he decided to kiss her. After 10 years of marriage, he still loved kissing Diane. Rare for most married couples. Following his lead, Diane began unbuttoning Jake's dark blue Armani shirt and unzipped his trousers, letting them fall to the ground.

"Jake, you're soaking wet. What happened?"

"It's a long story."

CHAPTER 4

AS THE SUN SET BEYOND THE SWIMMING POOL, THE CLOUDS were reflected in the dark, tranquil water. The pool was designed to appear to be spilling over into the hills of Westchester County from its infinity edge. From where Jake was sitting on the stone patio, he could see the Byram Lake Reservoir and, as the sun quickly sank into the horizon, it cast a purple hue over the black water. It was the perfect setting.

"So, what's on tap for this weekend, baby?" Jake asked, as it was usually Diane who was in charge of the weekend festivities.

"Well, I thought we could go out East and open up the beach house for the season. After all, Monday is Memorial Day."

By "out East" Diane was referring to their summer home in Southampton, a small, very affluent town nestled along the Atlantic Ocean on the South Shore of Long Island. From the Hampton Bays to Montauk and every beach town in between, weekenders, as they were referred to, would flee New York City on summer weekends and head for the beaches on Long Island in throngs.

They would ask questions of one another like, are you heading out East this weekend? Or will you be summering in the Hamptons this season? It all seemed a little pretentious to Jake. He'd spent most of his summers working construction to pay for college.

Of course, Jake knew Diane wasn't trying to sound snooty; it was just a part of who she was, where she had come from. Now it was becoming a part of who he was, no matter how hard he tried to fight it.

"Sure thing, baby doll, sounds like a plan. We should leave early tomorrow morning and hopefully miss some of the traffic on the Long Island Expressway."

"Um, and sweetie…would you mind very much if we invited Mike and Anita for the weekend as well?"

By the way she was asking Jake knew Diane had already spoken to Anita and the deal was all but done. "Sure, sounds like fun."

Mike and Anita Dumont were Jake and Diane's closest friends. Mike and Jake started at DR&R together. Mike was a workaholic and the best way to impress old man Devon was to bill hours. Lots of them! As a young associate, Mike clocked upwards of 80 hours a week for his first eight months at the firm and then tempered it down to about 60 when Anita threatened divorce. He was their golden boy, their moneymaker. It's no wonder he made junior partner in his third year at the firm, which under normal circumstances was unheard of.

If anyone was on the road to a full partnership, Mike Dumont was certainly the forerunner, which was good, because all Mike wanted was to become full partner at the prestigious DR&R, while all Jake wanted was to run as far from the law business as he possibly could. It seemed both men had gotten what they wished for.

Anita and Diane had met at a firm function and immediately hit it off. Though they came from very different backgrounds, they seemed to have so much in common, namely the Devon Firm's control over their husbands' free time. It's no wonder they became so close. They really had no one else for companionship. Such was true of Diane. Anita always seemed to have her own agenda.

With the sun completely down, the night air brought a chill that quickly reminded Jake that it was still early in the season. Diane came out of the house wearing an oversized NYU sweatshirt and carrying a plate with two rib-eye steaks she'd been marinating all day.

"I hope you like spicy?" she said, as she handed Jake a plate with the two steaks completely smothered in Cajun seasonings. "And remember, I like mine bloody."

"They smell great, Di Di," said Jake, as he carefully placed them side-by-side in the center of the barbecue.

Referring to the grill as a barbecue was like referring to The

Great Wall of China as a fence. The barbecues Jake remembered were round metal canisters set on wobbly legs and required charcoal and lighter fluid. The 52" cooking surface set in the middle of Jack's outdoor kitchen was designed like a giant L-shaped pool bar.

The long section of the granite "L" faced the pool and, in addition to the oversized grill, had a sink for cleaning vegetables, a keg cooler with a beer tap (which in the spring and summer months always had iced cold Sam Adams flowing), a wine refrigerator, an icemaker and a pizza oven. The smaller section of the "L" was the sitting area with 6 custom-made, high-back barstools.

The backyard would have been a terrific place for family gatherings, except that neither Jake nor Diane had much family left. Jack used it mostly to entertain clients and business associates. Said he liked having the home field advantage.

Everyone from high profile politicians to Hollywood executives and movie stars had been through the house at one time or another. In fact, old Jack used to have a weekly tennis match with Henry Kissinger.

Now it was just the two of them. Very quiet and very peaceful. This was the beginning of a perfect three-day weekend. Or so it seemed.

CHAPTER 5

NATALYA PAVLOVA COULD NOT BELIEVE HER GOOD FORTUNE. What a great week she was having. Finally landing a job as an extra with a small speaking part in the newest addition to the Mission Impossible franchise and now bedding down her own real live producer. This was how it worked, wasn't it? Fuck your way to the top. That's how they all make it out here in Hollywood. Isn't it?

As The Producer lay sleeping on Natalya's small bed in the tiny one bedroom she rented on Sunset Boulevard, she sat by the window, still naked from the incredible sex she had given him several hours ago. She was 22 years old, 5'9", with a perfect tight little body. Her olive complexion made her look tan all year round and, since she only allowed herself one meal a day, she was thin as a rail. Plus, she had a perfect set of perky little tits, if she did say so herself.

As she sat gazing at the streetlights on Sunset, she reached for the opened pack of Marlboro Lights, lit a cigarette and inhaled deeply. With her face inches from the window, she blew a stream of smoke that crashed angrily into the glass and then dissipated into the already stale room.

She had come to LA two years ago from her small town in southern Uzbekistan. Just a few miles from the Afghanistan border, her town had become increasingly unsafe.

Her parents had taken every precaution to protect her and her younger brother from the perils of the Taliban. How ironic it was that one evening she had refused to go to Mosque with her family, and instead insisted on going to the disco with her friends.

"The discos are prime targets for the terrorists," warned her father, but Natalya would have none of that nonsense. Mocking him for his paranoia, she fled the house.

She never saw her family again. A Taliban terrorist had fire-bombed the Mosque where her parents had taken her 4 year old brother that evening. Everyone in the Mosque had burned to death.

As she finished her cigarette, she noticed that it was 5:30 in the morning. The studio would be sending the car for her soon. This was it. This was her big break, and she didn't want to screw it up.

She had to wake up the mysterious man in her bed, take a quick shower and get into the limousine sent by the director to take her to Paramount Studios. Movie studios like Paramount would often send cars to pick up actors that had an early call to ensure that everyone was on the set when they were required to be. This was extremely important when the director needed a shot to take place during a certain time of the day, like dawn or dusk, or when they had some party-girl actress who just couldn't be trusted. The main actors in a movie were sent their own private car. Extras like Natalya were squeezed in with eight or ten others and the ride was only one way. They had to find their own transportation home.

The studios often looked like Grand Central Station with all the limousines and town cars coming and going, but the system seemed to work.

As Natalya looked at her handsome guest curled up in her sheets, she decided to wake him with some soft baby kisses. "Wake up sleepy head," she whispered, as she playfully nibbled on the bottom of his ear. She desperately needed to get things moving along but she didn't want to seem pushy. She had just enough time to give him a little head and still have him gone before the studio car showed up. Anyway, if she pleased him, maybe he would put her in his next movie like he had promised the night before.

It didn't take very long for The Producer to finish. As she watched, he sat up in bed and searched for his pack of Marlboro Lights. "Look, baby, I have a car coming. I have that early call at Paramount I told you about," said Natalya, cautiously.

"Sure, Princess, let me throw my clothes on and I'll be out of here before you can say cherry pie," he said, flashing her that same smile that had made her knees weak the night before when he had bought her and her friends drinks at the Polo Lounge in the Beverly Hills Hotel.

His Hugo Boss suit was neatly hanging on the back of a chair in Natalya's kitchen/living room/bedroom. As he dressed, Natalya couldn't believe how attractive he was. He'd told her his name was Alisher Nurmatov, Ali for short. He was from the Middle East. He said he came from some fabulously wealthy oil family. He was 6'1" with dark eyes and jet-black hair which he wore combed back like a Wall Street investment banker.

"Okay, Princess, here's my card. My cell number is written on the back." Natalya took the card and looked it over intently. "I'm signing contracts at Paramount this afternoon. Call me and I'll buy you lunch after your shoot," he said, kissing her on the cheek.

Could this be? Was he actually asking her out on another date? Was a Hollywood producer actually interested in Natalya Pavlova?

The Producer shot her that amazing smile again and made his way out to the stairwell leading to the street. As the door closed behind him, Natalya leaned against it with her back to it shut completely and once again looked down at the business card.

EASTERN BLOCK PRODUCTIONS,
ALI NURMATOV, CEO.

There were addresses and phone numbers for offices in Beverly Hills, London and The United Emirates of Dubai. On the back, handwritten in pen, was his cell number.

Natalya looked up from the card and let out a scream of excitement as she skipped to the bathroom to get ready for her big day. Possibly, the biggest of her life.

CHAPTER 6

EVEN THOUGH THE ALARM CLOCK WAS SET FOR 5:30 AM, JAKE'S eyes were already open as he lay in bed staring at the ceiling. His internal clock had him up five minutes ahead of time, as usual. Quietly, he turned the alarm off so it wouldn't wake Diane, who was still peacefully sleeping on her side of the bed.

The sun was just about coming up as he made his way downstairs to the home gym. For as long as he could remember, sunrise workouts had become a way of life for Jake. Every morning he would make the ritual journey down to the basement to begin his day, stretching, lifting and running until his clothes were drenched with sweat. Every day, pushing himself a little further.

A few years ago Diane had completely renovated the entire room. She had installed all new his and hers exercise equipment, two of everything. It's what the ark would have looked like if Noah was a health nut. Jake grabbed a bottle of Fiji water from a small refrigerator and began his usual workout: thirty minutes of cardio, thirty minutes of weight training.

Running on the treadmill at a pretty fast pace, Jake turned on the 60 inch plasma television mounted on the far wall in front of the cardio equipment. He clicked onto ESPN just in time to see that the New York Yankees had lost to the Los Angeles Dodgers 6-5.

"Fucking A-Rod!" he said shaking his head in disbelief, as he clicked over to CNBC. Joe Kernen, the host of "Squawk Box" was conducting some interview…of some CEO…of some company… somewhere.

With the volume off, Jake watched the stock ticker scroll across the bottom of the screen and thought how different his life had become since the death of Diane's father, and how the choice of his two cable stations was symbolic of that in some screwed up sort of way. He often wondered if his lower middleclass upbringing would ever put a strain on his relationship with Diane. It was like they came from two different planets.

"Who the fuck clicks between CNBC and ESPN?" he mumbled to himself. Certainly not his old friends back in Jersey City, that's for sure. Although, his friends from Jersey City would probably like watching "The Closing Bell" with Maria Bartiromo, he thought with a smile as he chugged along on the treadmill, which was now set at full speed for the final 2 miles. As he crossed the finish line, Jake downed the last of his Fiji water, threw a towel over his shoulder and headed upstairs for a shower.

Truth was, Jake was always secretly bothered by the notion that he might not be in Diane's class of people. As ridiculous as they all were, they did have an awful lot of their own money. But that was one of the things that Diane said she loved about him, he wasn't like those pompous asses. Wasn't it?

Jake could smell the fresh-brewed coffee Diane had made the moment he stepped foot into the kitchen. He spotted her leaning over the limestone countertop, sipping from an oversized mug. Her hair was pulled back in a ponytail, still wet from her shower, and she was wearing an old pair of jeans and a blue cotton knit sweater. She was facing a small television mounted on the wall in the breakfast nook, and there was Joe Kernen speaking to some Internet giant about his company.

As Jake walked over to the coffee pot, Diane looked up at him shaking her head and said, "Yanks lost last night 6 to 5. Fucking A-Rod!"

Jake smiled affectionately and said, "You know, Di Di, I really love you, baby."

CHAPTER 7

IT WAS ALMOST 6:30 AM AND THE SUN HAD COMPLETELY RISEN on what appeared to be a picture perfect spring morning. Jake carried Diane's Louis Vuitton garment bag out to the Range Rover Sport and carefully secured it along with his Glock 9 into the SUV's rear storage compartment. As he closed the hatch on the Rover, he spotted his golf clubs in the corner of the garage. Well, hello there. I haven't seen you in a while.

I'll bet Mike is bringing his sticks, Jake thought, as he grabbed the golf bag from the spot where he had left it to hibernate for the winter.

Since both Jake and Diane kept full wardrobes at the Southampton house, packing was rather light. With the back of the Rover pretty much empty, Jake figured it couldn't hurt to take the Callaways along for the ride even if he didn't make it out to Shinnecock for 18.

Shinnecock Hills is a golf course in Southampton. It's been around since the 1800's, has hosted four U.S. Opens and was one of the first private clubs to allow women to become members. Jack had been a long-standing member at Shinnecock and some years ago decided that it would be fun for Jake and Diane to belong as well. Although there was a seven-year waiting list to become a member at Shinnecock, Jake and Diane were full members two days after Jack had suggested it. That was just the way things seemed to work with old Jack. He got pretty much everything he wanted, when he wanted it. No questions asked.

With the Range Rover packed, Jake slowly pulled through the carriage doors and around to the front of the house where Diane was waiting. She hopped in the passenger side and gave him a kiss on the cheek. Jake immediately knew what she was thinking. "Starbucks?" he asked, peering over the top of his Ray-Bans.

Diane smiled. "You read my mind."

With two Venti Vanilla Lattés in hand, Jake headed south on Interstate 684 toward the Throgs Neck Bridge to kick off the unofficial start to summer. Getting an early start had paid off. Traffic was rather light, especially for the LIE, and, by 8:30 he was cruising along Sunrise Highway in Southampton.

"Smell that?" asked Jake, grinning in Diane's direction.

"Mmm, smells like summer," she replied with a smile.

Jake always liked the way the shoulder of the road turned sandy and the smell of the air, salty when you reached Sunrise Highway. Both lattés long gone, Diane gave a huge stretch, looked over at Jake and said, "Think it's too early?"

"Not for us it isn't," he replied, as he turned onto North Sea Boulevard and pulled the Rover up in front of 75 Main, which was one of their favorite Southampton restaurants. For as long as Jake could remember, he and Diane would make the ritual stop at 75 Main, which was the street address as well as the name of the restaurant, for morning margaritas and a toast to a great weekend of sun, sand and sex. Not necessarily in that order.

As they approached, Jake saw that the huge sliding glass doors to the restaurant were fully opened with the tables spilling out onto the tree lined sidewalk. The owner, Alfonso Antonacci, (The Fonz to his friends) was chewing out a bunch of the new summer help for not having enough ketchup bottles on the tables during last night's dinner shift. Apparently, Paul McCartney, who was in town promoting his newest album, had come by the night before for a late night dinner with Eric Clapton. From what Jake could gather old "Slow Hand" had issues when his burger arrived without a nearby ketchup bottle.

When he saw Jake and Diane entering the restaurant through the open sliders, The Fonz immediately ended the barrage on his noticeably hung-over morning crew and came to greet them with a huge smile. "Ah, my two favorite weekenders," he exclaimed, giving Diane a big hug and a kiss on each cheek, and then extending his hand to Jake.

Alfonso Antonacci was as local as they come. Although he was born in the "old country," he had lived in Southampton all his life. His father, who had started the restaurant when The Fonz was a boy, owned a modest home off Elm Street by the train station. When his dad passed, The Fonz inherited the house, the restaurant and all of the grief that came with both. "Let me guess. Two top shelf margaritas, salt on the rim for Diane, none for Jake."

"Perfect," replied Diane, with a hint of that wicked little smile of hers.

The Fonz snapped his fingers at one of the waitresses, who immediately scurried over to the table. She was a pretty blonde girl, probably a college student on summer break, whose bloodshot eyes suggested she had gotten only a few hours of sleep the night before.

"Two top shelf margaritas. Pronto!" barked The Fonz in the direction of the tired waitress.

"Right away, Mr. A," she said, as she turned and headed for the bar.

"I'll leave you two alone," said The Fonz with a smile. "Please come by for dinner tonight. We have that lobster bisque that you love so much."

"Sounds wonderful," said Diane.

"Here ya go, two top shelf margaritas," said the waitress as The Fonz made his way back to the interrogation. She carefully placed two overfilled margarita glasses in front of Jake and Diane. "Can I get you anything else?"

"No thanks," said Jake, as he and Diane both picked up their glasses, trying helplessly not to spill them onto the tablecloth.

"Here's to a wonderful summer," Jake smiled, as he gently tapped his glass against Diane's.

"Yes," replied Diane. "And to a fun weekend with Mike and Anita, without any interruptions from the Bureau."

"I'll drink to that."

CHAPTER 8

WITH A TOWEL WRAPPED TIGHTLY AROUND HER HEAD, NATALYA Pavlova opened the door to her tiny bathroom as the steam from the shower poured out into the rest of the apartment. Instantly, the entire room looked and felt like the inside of a dark rain cloud. She sat down at her makeshift vanity, lit up her last Marlboro Light, took a big drag and perched the cigarette in an ashtray on the snack table in the corner of the room. She watched the smoke as it curled up the wall and followed the path of a long brown stain which ran from the ashtray to the ceiling.

Too many cigarettes, she thought silently, shaking her head in disapproval. She exhaled. Then, through the smoke and fog, she noticed it. "What's this?"

Under the snack table was a big, black case. It reminded her of the bags she saw on Geraldo Rivera. The ones the attorneys lugged in and out of court during the OJ Simpson trial.

Her beautiful producer had forgotten his bag and it was all her fault, she thought. She had kicked him out so abruptly that he had forgotten his bag in the spot he had left it the night before when they had torn each other's clothes off. She grinned.

She placed her hand on her lips and thought for a moment. Although…this could be a bit of good fortune if she played it right. Her grin becoming so wide that in crinkled her nose. Yes indeed. It was the perfect opportunity to call him without seeming desperate. The last thing she wanted to do was appear too pushy and scare him off. Although he had promised her lunch that afternoon, she had learned through experience to take nothing for granted. She had been down that road too many times.

As Natalya put on her makeup, she smiled. She hadn't been this happy in years. "This is a good sign," she said to her reflection in the vanity mirror. Her luck was finally changing, and this time she wasn't going to let anything get in her way.

CHAPTER 9

JAKE AND DIANE POLISHED OFF THE LAST OF THE MARGARITAS and waved goodbye to The Fonz, who was in the middle of berating a bartender for not having enough ice on the beers. "These Coronas haven't been this warm since they left Mexico!"

Exiting the restaurant through the same slider in which they entered, Jake reached down and took Diane's hand. He began to gently stroke her fingers with his thumb. She smiled and rested her head on the top of his shoulder. They walked silently along Main Street, holding one another affectionately, and watched as the small town began to wake up for the day. It was almost 9:00 AM and most of the shops along Main were just opening. A police officer was directing traffic at a pedestrian crosswalk as a gaggle of small children with their moms in tow ran for the sidewalk. The sun was now shining brightly and the smell of fresh baked bread and muffins billowed from the artisan bakery and hung in the air like a delicious warm edible cloud. Southampton was truly a wonderful place.

Once they arrived back at the Rover, Diane thought it best to give Mike and Anita a call to see what their ETA was looking like. She reached over and pushed a button on the underside of the steering column and announced to the Rover, "Call Anita's cell." Moments later the Rover was dialing Anita's cell phone.

"Hey, you two." Anita's voice echoed through the speakers.

"Hey, baby," said Diane. "Are you two close?"

"Just turning onto Meadow Lane," Mike's voice said.

"You guys are about five minutes ahead of us," Jake chimed in to the four-way conference (five-way if you count the Rover).

"Ok, great. And guys, when you get to the house, the code to open the gate is...."

"9447," replied Mike and Anita in unison.

Diane smiled. Looking over at Jake, she announced that she wanted to make a pit-stop at Schmidt's Gourmet to pick up some salads for lunch and asked if there were any preferences. Both Mike and Anita, who were not very fussy eaters, left the menu choices completely up to Diane.

"Right-o, see you both in a few," Diane said, as she pushed the disconnect button.

Schmidt's is a gourmet market located on the north end of Main Street in Southampton. The south end of Main is Gin Lane and the Atlantic Ocean. In addition to the normal groceries, Schmidt's has the world's best salads, meats, seafood and cheeses. Jake particularly liked the provolone stuffed olives. Although, thanks to their caretaker, the house would be stocked with enough food and drink to feed a small army, Diane liked to stop at Schmidt's for specialty items.

The parking lot looked like a Range Rover Dealership. Of the 6 parked cars, 5 were some type of Range Rover and the sole holdout was a Porsche 911 Cabriolet.

"I'll wait here for you, baby," Jake said, as he fiddled with the satellite radio in search of Howard Stern.

"Okay, wheel man, keep it running and facing the border," joked Diane, as she reached for her bag on the back seat and headed out of the car.

Just then, the 911 sped off and was replaced by two more Range Rovers. Everywhere Jake looked people were loading up their SUVs to the hilt with bags and bags of gourmet food for the weekend feasts they would be having. Whatever happened to a good old-fashioned hot dog on a bun?

About 10 minutes later, Diane came out of the shop and approached the back of the Rover. Jake pushed a button on the steering column and the rear gate slowly rose to the opened position. Diane put two bags of food in the back and then came around and hopped into the passenger seat. He then gave the same button a double click and the gate slowly shut closed.

Diane raised an eyebrow. "I bought you a present," she said handing him a plastic bag with the Schmidt's logo on it.

He pushed his Ray-Bans to the top of his head and peered inside the bag. It was a giant container of provolone stuffed olives and they looked delicious. So much for a hot dog on a bun.

As Jake drove south on Main Street, the quaint little village of Southampton turned into the fabulously wealthy Estates section of Southampton. The cute little village shops were now replaced by huge hedges that created walls of privacy for the enormous homes concealed on the other side. Occasionally you could catch a glimpse of the sprawling lawns and enormous houses set far from the road. Nothing less than 10 mil would get you one of the least expensive homes on Main Street.

As Main Street came to an end, Jake left the lower income families behind and turned onto Meadow Lane; which is a small two-way road that runs along a narrow stretch of land with the Atlantic Ocean on one side and the Shinnecock Bay on the other. Meadow Lane is world-renowned for being home to the most exceptional beach houses anywhere: nothing smaller than 10,000 square feet and nothing less than $35,000,000.00. Captain Jack's was no exception.

The beach house, or "Viewpoint," as Jack had dubbed it, sat on three acres on the ocean side of Meadow Lane. It was a 15,000-square-foot Georgian estate with over 400 feet of ocean frontage. It had seven suite bedrooms, a garden room, a library and a screening room; each with fireplaces and breathtaking water views.

There were also indoor and outdoor swimming pools, a clay tennis court, separate staff quarters and a seven-car garage where old Jack kept a set of his and hers dune buggies and his Ferrari collection. Jake collected baseball cards.

As they pulled down the gravel driveway, Jake noticed Mike's BMW 5-series parked at the far end by the house. "Ten bucks says they're already changed into their whites and are playing tennis," he said, pulling up behind the Beamer.

Diane was looking at him coolly, one eyebrow lifted to form an impressive arc. "Sweeten that bet and you're on."

Jake smiled as he switched off the ignition. "What did you have in mind?"

"The loser must be the winner's slave for the whole weekend, and when I say slave, I mean in every way imaginable," Diane replied, with her eyebrows poised to accentuate the undertone of naughtiness in what she was alluding to. "Bet?" she quipped, with her pinky extended tauntingly.

"Bet," said Jake, clenching her pinky with his own and then pulling it free.

Exiting the Rover, Jake walked to the back of the truck and opened the hatch with the remote control on his key ring. He grabbed the Louis Vuitton bag, his PDA and his Glock 9. Diane frowned.

"So then, where are they?" he asked. "Beach? Outdoor bar? Having sex on a dune?"

"Nope. Knowing those two, they're both lying by the pool, sunning themselves like movie stars."

Jake pressed a button on the bottom of the Rover's hatch and it slowly lowered and locked itself closed. He placed the gun inside the leather garment bag and swung the strap over his shoulder. "Like movie stars, you say?"

"Like movie stars," replied Diane, confidently.

The house was set high on a dune with the ocean just behind it. It looked rather magnificent with its massive stained glass front door separating two rows of upper and lower balconies. The morning sun glistened off what seemed to be endless stark-white spindles, and a neat line of palm-leaf ceiling fans gently spun in the warm spring breeze. Off to the right, where the driveway brushed up against the house, sat a sandy staircase constructed of railroad-ties and bluestone. It curved around the side of the home to the top of the dune, and then continued down the other side ending at the swimming pool and tennis courts, which were nestled between the back of the house and the beach.

The sand crunched beneath their feet as they made their way up the stairs in the direction of the dune's summit. Jake decided to switch on his BlackBerry. Mistake! It hadn't been on all morning, so he was a little concerned at the amount of emails that were awaiting him.

Diane gave a disapproving stare. "Yeah, play with that thing now 'cause when I win this bet you're throwing it in the ocean!"

"Fuck. Twenty-five emails, all from the Bureau," said Jake, shaking his head in frustration. "Maybe when I win I'll have you respond to these while I golf with Mike," he retorted sarcastically.

"Very funny, Jake."

As they approached the back of the house, Jake's smile vanished instantly. There was old Mike, barefoot, shirt off, khakis rolled to his ankles, pacing and speaking to someone on his cell phone. Probably law related. Anita, on the other hand, was lying on a teak chaise lounge. She looked very relaxed with her dirty blonde hair up in a scrunchy, wearing only a turquoise bikini bottom.

Diane peered over the top of her Armani sunglasses. "You realize the bet includes Monday too," she said, as she skipped down to the pool to greet their guests. She looked over her shoulder. "Oh, and Jakey, once you take the groceries in from the car, bring the blender and the tequila down to the pool. Thanks."

CHAPTER 10

"WHERE IS THAT FUCKING CAR?" SCREAMED NATALYA, AS SHE frantically paced the inside of her apartment. Five steps in each direction was all the small room allowed for.

They were over an hour late and she had already called the dispatcher several times to curse them out for their incompetence. She had an 8:30 call at Paramount Studios and it was already 8:05. So much for her luck changing.

She hadn't even uttered her first line in her small speaking part and already Natalya Pavlova had become a Hollywood diva. Dying for a cigarette, she searched the whole apartment but found none.

Just then, she heard the sound of a car horn. She looked down to the boulevard and sure enough, there was the studio car, pulling up in front of the building. She sighed with exasperation, and then quickly grabbed her purse and the mysterious case left behind by her overnight guest, and bolted for the door.

"Jesus Christ, what does he have in here, a dead body?" she said, struggling to get the strap over her shoulder.

Making her way down the stairs and into the car to join the other nine extras being herded to Paramount that morning, Natalya tried to reassure herself that everything was going to be fine. She was going to do great today and then her beautiful, rich producer was going to buy her lunch to celebrate. After all, she now had an insurance policy, she thought silently, as she gazed at the huge black case on the floor between her feet.

As the car left the apartment complex in the direction of Paramount, Natalya reached into her purse, pulled out her cell phone along with The Producer's card and stared down at the number he had written on the back.

She looked uncertain as she worried her lower lip between her teeth. What if he'd given her a phony number? He wouldn't. After all, he offered her his card. She didn't ask for it. Why would he do that at all if he didn't want to see her again?

You're just being paranoid, she told herself, as she continued to stare at his phone number for reassurance. She then took a deep breath, dialed the number and waited for her new boyfriend to answer.

CHAPTER 11

THE BLACK MERCEDES BENZ S600 SAT WITH ITS ENGINE RUNning in one of the studio parking lots on the corner of Melrose Avenue facing Paramount Studios. The morning had started out sunny enough, but now the smog, which loomed heavily over LA, put an abrupt end to any hope of sunshine. The lot had quickly filled to capacity with cars and SUVs, mostly belonging to studio employees, and Melrose Avenue had become quite busy. But, with all of its windows tinted black, it was impossible for passersby to see if anyone was actually inside the car.

From where he sat, The Producer had an unobstructed view of the security booth located at the studio's historic Melrose Gate entrance. The booth looked more like a tiny shack with barely enough room for the guard inside to move about. It was constructed of tan colored stucco with an orange terracotta roof, and had one small window that slid open and closed on the side facing traffic.

"Security guard, that's a joke," The Producer said mockingly. *Rent-a-cop was more like it,* he thought, as he looked at his watch and then at the cell phone sitting next to him on the passenger side seat.

Thanks to a little research on the Internet, he knew everything there was to know about Paramount Studios and, with a little help from Google Earth, he had a perfect aerial map of the entire place.

"These Americans are so fucking ridiculous," he mumbled, shaking his head as he reached for a cigarette from the pack on the dashboard. They think they are so superior, don't they? Hah, what a fucking joke that was. Paris Hilton and Britney Spears are on the cover of every magazine in the country while there are American combat soldiers dying in Iraq. Pathetic. He scowled as he lit the cigarette from the car's lighter and inhaled the smoke deep into his lungs.

Pulling a piece of tobacco from the tip of his tongue, he watched as yet another town car was waved through the gates and allowed access under the great white arches in front of Paramount Studios. He had witnessed the same routine every morning for the past two months. It was tedious, but it had to be done in order to be sure.

Like clockwork, the studio would disperse a barrage of town cars and limousines to chauffeur its precious actors to work, and not once had he seen a thorough security check of the vehicle as it passed through. Just a smile and a friendly wave in. Sometimes even a first name hello to the driver.

You certainly have let your guard down since September 11th, thought The Producer, as he watched another studio car drive through the gates onto the Paramount lot. That is going to cost you. That is going to cost you big!

CHAPTER 12

MAKING HIS WAY DOWN TO THE POOL WITH THE BLENDER AND Cuervo 1800 Diane had requested, Jake noticed Mike was still on his cell phone and was waving his free hand in the air in frustration; confirming Jake's first assumption that the call was indeed job-related.

Diane had joined Anita on a nearby chaise lounge and dangled her feet in the turquoise blue pool water. She was wearing a tasteful black one-piece bathing suit and had her hair pulled off her face in a neat ponytail. Both women had terrific bodies, except Anita's was the result of some very costly plastic surgery.

"Hi, Jakey, I hear you're going to be our slave for the weekend," teased Anita.

Jake smiled. "Sure am," he replied, taking the banter in stride. "Let's start by making a round of my signature margaritas and we'll see where that takes us, shall we?" He then placed the blender and tequila down on a circular glass table that was covered by an oversized umbrella next to the pool. He looked out past the dunes and noticed how pretty the ocean looked, and with the morning sunlight reflecting off it, it appeared to sparkle. In the distance he spotted a 3-mast sailboat tacking aggressively toward the horizon. No wonder Jack liked this house so much.

"Hey, guess what?" said Diane, rubbing in a handful of suntan lotion she had borrowed from Anita. "Mike made full partner."

"Wow! That's terrific," Jake replied enthusiastically, holding up the bottle of tequila in an abbreviated salute. He then poured its contents over the ice cubes at the bottom of the blender and covered the top. He switched the toggle to the "crush" setting, and suddenly the sound of mashing ice filled the air. It sounded like summer. At that moment a shadow fell across the table and Jake felt a hand on his shoulder. It was Mike.

"Yeah, full partnership and all the headaches that go along with it," said Mike, as he switched off his PDA and tossed it onto a nearby lounge chair.

"And all the money," volunteered Anita, squinting against the sun.

"Well, I'll drink to that," Jake said, as he poured the frozen concoction he had just created into four decorative margarita glasses. He then carefully passed an overfilled glass to Anita and then one to Diane. "Did they move you into one of the corner offices up on Devon's floor?" he asked, as he slid Mike's glass across the table.

"Not sure yet. They just told me yesterday. It's all still pretty new."

"Well, hear, hear," Jake said as he raised his glass offering a toast to Mike for all of his success. Following Jake's lead, both Diane and Anita raised their glasses in Mike's direction. "To Mike," they both said in unison.

"Let's head down to the beach and you can fill me in on all of the DR&R action," Jake said as he refilled everyone's glass with the remaining margarita from the blender.

"Honey, turn on the outdoor television. The Yankees are playing at one o'clock today," Diane said as she reached into her bag and pulled out the newest James Patterson novel.

"What are you reading?" asked Anita, nearly polishing off her second margarita in one gulp.

"Double Cross," Diane said, holding up the book to show Anita the cover.

"I love Patterson," said Anita. "Especially the Alex Cross stuff."

"Oh, me too," said Diane, giving Jake a wink.

"Here it comes," Jake mumbled to himself.

"Doesn't Alex Cross remind you of Jake?" Diane asked.

"Absolutely, or Jason Bourne," volunteered Anita, sounding almost serious.

"And a lot cuter," replied Mike, who had been dying to get into the conversation.

"All right, all right, we'll see you girls for lunch," Jake said, shoving Mike toward the wooden ramp that led over the dunes and down to the beach.

"Bye, Alex," chimed Diane and Anita, both sounding a bit giddy from the tequila.

CHAPTER 13

AT EXACTLY 8:30 AM WEST COAST TIME, THE PRODUCER'S CELL phone began ringing from where it sat on the passenger's seat of the Mercedes Benz. He took a final drag on his cigarette, lowered the car window and flicked its remains across the parking lot. So fucking predictable, he thought, allowing the phone to ring several times before answering it. He closed the car window and then pressed a small button on his hands-free earpiece which was firmly clipped around his left ear. "Ali Nurmatov."

The sound of his voice made Natalya's heart pitter-patter like a young school girl with a crush. "Hi, Ali, it's Natalya. Am I catching you at a bad time?"

No, actually your timing is spot on, you fool! "Hello, Princess, I was just thinking about you."

"Really?"

"Oh, yes. Are you at the studio yet?" he asked, although he knew that she wasn't.

Natalya sighed in exasperation. "No, the fucking studio car was an hour late! We should be there in ten minutes though." She looked down between her feet. "Um, and Ali…," she said nervously, as if it were somehow her fault he had forgotten his case. "You left your bag at my apartment this morning."

The Producer closed his eyes and rubbed his temples with the tips if his fingers. "Do you have it with you, Princess?"

"Yes, I have it here in the car with me."

"Good girl. I'll pick it up from you at lunch today. We are still on for lunch, aren't we, Princess?" he asked, again already knowing the answer to his question.

Natalya smiled. "Sure, I'm really looking forward to it."

"Perfect. Ring me back after your shoot and we'll celebrate."
"OK Ali, see you then. 'Bye."
"Yes, goodbye, Princess."
Forever!

CHAPTER 14

THE PRODUCER REMOVED THE EARPIECE, TOSSED IT ONTO THE seat next to him and watched as the studio car carrying the bomb turned onto Melrose Avenue and approached the Paramount gates.

As the driver signaled to turn into the studio, The Producer reached into the car's glove box and pulled out a small radio transmitter. The device could not have been more than the size of a TV remote control. It had a small telescoping antenna, a toggle switch that was set to the "off" position, and a small red button in the center. It looked harmless enough, but with the touch of a button, it was capable of causing devastation beyond all belief. *His own personal "weapon of mass destruction,"* he thought, as he switched the toggle to the "on" position and raised the antenna.

The limo made a right turn, cruised into the studio's entrance and then slowly came to a stop in front of the security booth. The guard leaned his head out of the booth's small window, said a few words to the driver and then waved him through. The Producer smiled. Just like that, enough explosives to level six city blocks rolled past security and entered one of the world's premier Hollywood studios, completely undetected.

Could they really be that careless?

Once the limo passed through the wrought-iron gates, The Producer looked down at his watch. He had calculated this precisely. Given the studio's 20-mile-an-hour speed limit, 30 seconds would put the car in the most heavily populated section of the studio and, more importantly, ensure that it was a safe distance from where he was parked.

As the seconds ticked away, The Producer found himself subconsciously gripping the transmitter so tightly that his hand began to ache. He took a deep breath and watched as the second hand approached the 30 second hash mark. He closed his eyes, pressed the button and silently waited for the mayhem to begin.

The sound of the explosion was deafening. Like ten 747 airplanes all roaring their jet engines at once. Even from where he sat, The Producer's ears began to ring from the noise. He watched as a fireball roared into the sky, with heat so intense that he could feel it on his face from inside the car.

The initial blast of fire was soon replaced by plumes of dark, black smoke that seemed to reach up to the heavens. Eerie screams and cries seemed to be coming from everywhere. Everything seemed to be moving in slow motion. He could see people running frantically, bodies fully engulfed in flames, then dropping to the ground, still ablaze. Sirens from inside the studio were blaring as one of the taller buildings suddenly crumpled to the ground. It all seemed so surreal but at the same time so perfect.

The Producer shook his head solemnly. "That will show them," he said, as he slowly drove the Mercedes past the fiery hell he had just created and headed for LAX, where a private jet awaited him.

CHAPTER 15

PATROLMAN HANK PETERSON HAD JUST RETURNED TO HIS workstation at police headquarters with his usual large cup of coffee, extra cream, extra sugar and two blueberry muffins, when the explosion rocked Paramount Studios.

Although the headquarters building was at least three miles from Paramount, the explosion was so intense that it rattled the entire police station. It knocked pictures from the walls and books off shelves and threw from his desk a framed photo of him and his son on a fishing trip with the caption "world's best dad," smashing it to pieces.

"What in the fuck was that!" screamed Captain John Danzinger, as he came running from his office.

There were gasps and cries from inside the precinct as everyone rushed to the windows to see the dark smoke pouring from behind the tall buildings in the direction of the studios.

Almost immediately every phone in the room was ringing and for a brief moment no one seemed to notice. Everyone was transfixed by what they were witnessing. Even Danzinger stood almost paralyzed staring out at the black smoke rising over the city.

His city. Then suddenly, as if coming out of a trance, he shouted, "All right people, back to your desks. We need to find out what in God's name just happened out there. Bonny, get me the Mayor's office right away!"

"He's already holding on line two for you, John," she replied, as he slammed the door to his office and went for the phone on his desk.

Shaking the loose pieces of glass from the broken picture frame into the garbage, Hank Peterson took a deep breath and tried to process what was going on. The entire office was still in an uproar and the constant ringing of the phones didn't help the situation much. As he took his seat, Hank picked up the phone on his desk and dialed his brother-in-law at the Bureau.

"F.B.I., this is Agent Grieco."

"Joey, this is Hank in Los Angeles. Something horrible has just happened!"

CHAPTER 16

IT WAS 11:30 AM EAST COAST TIME, AND JAKE HAD TAKEN ABOUT two steps onto the beach when his PDA and pager both went off at the same time. He looked down at the caller ID and saw that both calls were coming from the Bureau.

Jake's shoulders dropped. "This can't be good," he said in Mike's direction, as he shut off the pager and answered his PDA. "Agent Chase here."

"Jake, this is Ken Devasher. Something has happened in Los Angeles. We need to get you out there immediately."

"What's going on?" Jake asked, sensing the urgency in Devasher's voice.

"There's been an explosion, possibly a terrorist attack. I'll fill you in when I see you. Where are you?"

Jake immediately turned and started back over the dune in the direction of the house. "I'm at the summer house with Diane."

"Fine, get yourself to Road G; we'll send a chopper."

Jake knew the helipad on the bay side of Road G all too well. The Bureau had interrupted far too many weekends with Diane and this weekend would be no different.

"I'll meet you at LAX and, just so you know, Jake, the President is all over this one!"

As he hung up with Devasher, Jake was already back at the pool. Both Diane and Anita were wrapped in beach towels and were watching the breaking news on CNN. Diane had tears in her eyes. "Jake, please tell me they didn't call you on this one, please tell me that," she pleaded.

Jake looked at the television and could not believe what he was seeing. Los Angeles looked like a war zone. The words "Breaking

News" were scrolling across the bottom of the screen in bright red letters. Buildings were ablaze, people were being carried out on stretchers and gurneys, fire trucks and ambulances were everywhere. A CNN news chopper was filming overhead; and seeing the devastation from above made it look even more frightening. Jake turned to Diane and gave her a hug. "You know I have to go, Di Di. They're sending a helicopter."

"No, Jake, no, please," Diane pleaded, sobbing. "I can't live through this again. I really can't."

Jake looked back at the television. His brain had already switched into F.B.I. mode and was watching intently, searching for clues. He scrambled for something to say to make her understand, but could think of nothing. He knew he had to get out to LA, and he had to get there fast. "It will be fine, Di Di, I promise. Devasher is going to meet me in LA. I'll call you as soon as I land."

"Oh, Ken Devasher, that's just fucking great! Is that supposed to make me feel better? He almost got you both killed in Tehran last time you were in the field with him!"

"I know, I know," Jake said softly, as he gave her a hug and wiped a tear from her cheek, not for a moment taking his eyes off the television. "Di Di, I have to get ready. Mike is going to drive me to the Road G helipad, and I thought...."

Before Jake could finish his sentence, Diane ran into the house sobbing uncontrollably, leaving him standing there with Anita and Mike who both appeared speechless.

"I'll go talk to her, Jake," volunteered Anita, in a tone of voice that was unusually sympathetic for her. "She will be fine. Mike and I will take care of her while you're gone."

Jake nodded. He was still completely focused on the CNN reporter who was now being forced to move across the street by the local authorities.

Leaning over, she gave him a kiss on the check. "Be safe, Jake. Really, it looks pretty bad out there." And then she rushed up to the house to find Diane.

As they waited in the BMW on Road G, Jake and Mike listened to the news starting to unfold from the car radio. Several terrorist groups were being suspected of the bombing but nothing had been confirmed. The death toll was in the hundreds and rising fast. There were reports that several well-known Hollywood celebrities were missing and presumed dead.

As the two men sat silently listening to the reports, Jake stared out the car window amazed at how busy Gin Lane had now become. The sleepy road had quickly turned into a parade route for exotic cars and expensive SUVs. From where they were parked, Jake could see the roof-tops of the enormous mansions peering over the myriad of high sand dunes that lined Gin Lane. He reached inside his blazer and removed his Glock from its leather shoulder holster. Detaching the clip, he checked his ammo and then forced it back into position with the palm of his hand. It made a loud metallic clicking sound.

Jake sensed his friend seemed uneasy, searching for something to say. Mike cleared his throat and looked in Jake's direction. "Listen man, I don't...."

Just then the loud roar of the Blackhawk helicopter coming in for a landing cut Mike off mid-sentence and startled them both. They gave a nervous laugh and Mike reached over, grabbed Jake's shoulder and said, "Look, take care of yourself. It really sounds pretty awful over there."

"Always!" Jake replied with a cocky grin, exiting the car. He grabbed his garment bag and briefcase from the back seat, lowered his head and ran for the chopper.

"And don't worry about Diane," Mike called out over the loud noise of the propellers. "Anita and I will look after her until you come back."

Jake gave his old colleague a wave and climbed into the Blackhawk. He was immediately greeted by Dr. Doris Sinclair, Devasher's contact in the F.B.I.'s New York City office.

"Good morning, Agent Chase," she said, with about as warm a smile as she could summon given the circumstances. "Would you like some coffee?"

"Thank you, Doris, no. Maybe just a bottle of water."

As the chopper took off, Dr. Sinclair handed Jake a bottle of Evian and a very thin file. "Here is what we have so far, Jake. I am afraid it's not much."

Jake smiled politely and started reading through the file. Not much was an understatement. Truth is, they had no idea who was responsible for Paramount or why. What he did know was that people expected him to find out, and those people just happened to be the Director of the F.B.I. and the President of the United States.

As they cruised to Easthampton Executive Airport, where a Gulfstream was fueled-up and ready to take them to LAX, Jake thought about his father and how he had died that horrible morning of September 11, 2001. He was a well-respected New York City police officer and had earned two Purple Heart medals in the Korean War. But more than that, he was a family man and a terrific father. He would take Jake and his brother Matt to see the New York Yankees every chance he got. He knew everything there was to know about baseball, and he made sure Jake and Mattie did as well. Jake could knock the stitches off a hardball, and Matt could throw a 90 mile an hour fastball.

Jake really missed his dad.

He wasn't even on duty the morning the planes hit the World Trade Center. It was his day off. He was home with his wife watching the reports on CNN, but he just couldn't stand by and watch as innocent people lost their lives. That was Jake's dad.

They said he had rescued ten people before being crushed to death by falling debris from Tower Two moments before its collapse.

As Jake listened to the hum of the Blackhawk engines, transfixed in his thoughts, he wondered if his mother had pleaded the way Diane had to keep his father home, safe and sound, the morning of September 11th.

CHAPTER 17

THE GULFSTREAM G5 TOUCHED DOWN AT LAX, 2:00 PM WEST Coast time. Jake unclasped his safety belt, stood from his seat and gave a huge stretch. The flight attendant shot him a smile as she handed him back his blazer and garment bag. He looked over at Dr. Sinclair. She looked exhausted.

Immediately, Jake reached inside the bag and retrieved his BlackBerry PDA. He switched it on and waited for it to connect to the internet. He slid on his blazer, threw the strap to his garment bag over his shoulder and made his way to the front of the jet. His PDA began to vibrate, indicating unread emails, along with a voice message from Diane. He knew that none of the emails would be from Devasher because they had been in a conference call with the director during most of the flight. Just then the phone began to ring. He looked down at the caller ID and saw that it was Diane.

"Jake, I am so sorry, baby."

"I know, Di Di," he replied, as he gazed out the window at the smog hovering over the city. "Look, when this thing is over, we'll get away for a while, just the two of us. Some island with sandy beaches and palm trees."

"And no BlackBerry?"

Jake smiled. "Definitely, no BlackBerry."

Diane paused. "Jake, they're saying the death toll is over 400," she said solemnly. After another long pause, "I love you so much, Jake. I can't lose you. I mean, my father, your father...." Her voice trailed off.

"Everything is going to be fine, Di Di. I'll be home before you know it," Jake said assuredly, even though he had no idea when he'd be home.

"Okay, Jake. Call me later, please?"

Just then the cockpit door swung open. The pilot emerged carrying a small leather satchel and a metallic colored brief case. He gave Jake the thumbs-up and then signaled for the flight attendant to open the hatch. Jake nodded. "You know I will."

"And Jake, you know I have to say this: please be careful."

"Always!"

As Jake and Dr. Sinclair walked down the steps to the tarmac, they were greeted by Ken Devasher, F.B.I. Director Martin Robbins, and a third man Jake did not recognize. The group exchanged pleasantries and handshakes. Ken Devasher introduced the stranger as Captain John Danzinger of the Los Angeles Police Department who would be assisting the F.B.I. on the initial part of their investigation.

Once the formalities were concluded, the group made their way inside one of the private jet hangars and boarded a black SUV. Devasher navigated the truck back onto the tarmac and headed for the airport exit.

"Any new developments, Ken?" Jake asked, from the passenger side seat.

"I am afraid not," replied Devasher, passing over a file with the words TOP SECRET stamped across its cover.

"We got dog shit," blurted out Danzinger from the back of the SUV.

"No, that's not one hundred percent accurate," volunteered Dr. Sinclair. "We know that the terrorist, or terrorists, are extremely well funded, probably military."

"Right," agreed Devasher. "From what our forensics people have gathered so far, the device used is the same type used by Special Forces in Iraq. Very hard to get and quite expensive."

"Iraq? Special Forces? How in the fuck did an Iraq Special Forces device get to California?" demanded Danzinger, who seemed to be getting a bit edgy.

"Try to keep up, John," said Director Robbins. "As Dr. Sinclair has just pointed out, the terrorists are a heavily funded group, probably well-connected. With enough money, you can buy just about anything on the black market."

"Exactly," said Doris. "And we now know that the device was transported into the Paramount lot in one of the studio cars."

"Well, I can tell you one thing for certain. That security guard at the front gate is losing his job today. I am going to make damn sure of that," said Captain Danzinger, who was now beginning to get on everyone's nerves.

"He was killed in the explosion," said Doris.

"What if this wasn't done by terrorists at all?" interrupted Jake, momentarily looking up from the file Devasher had given him.

Danzinger let out a huff. "Of course it's terrorists! Special Forces…Iraq, remember that? It's the only reason you F.B.I. guys are here in the first place."

"What are you thinking, Jake?" asked Director Robbins, completely ignoring the ranting coming from the back seat.

"Not sure yet, just a thought," said Jake, refocusing his attention back on the notes in the file.

Devasher turned the SUV off the freeway and headed for West Hollywood. The narrow residential streets lead through quaint neighborhoods with small homes, separated by well manicured lawns. There was no shortage of palm trees or white picket fences. The entire scene could have been taken from the pages of a storybook.

"Jake, Paramount, or what's left of it, is just ahead. You and Dr. Sinclair are going to want to put these on," said Devasher, handing them each a cloth facemask.

Jake took the facemask from Devasher and placed it over his nose and mouth, securing it to his face with an elastic band that wrapped around his head. Devasher turned the SUV onto Melrose Avenue and Jake's eyes widened in disbelief. Nothing in his years at the F.B.I. had prepared him for what he was now witnessing. One minute he was driving down a beautiful street lined with palm trees, and the next he was entering a war zone. It was as bad as anything he had witnessed in the Middle East, except it wasn't the Middle East. It was Los Angeles.

Even with the masks covering their faces, the smell was unbearable, a horrific combination of burnt flesh and sulfur, so pungent Jake could taste it in the back of his throat and it made him ill.

Fire trucks and ambulances were everywhere. One side of Melrose Avenue had been turned into a triage with doctors and nurses working frantically on those lucky enough to have survived the initial blast. On the other side, various command posts had been set up by the news media, both local and worldwide. In front of each post stood a reporter and camera crew giving first hand images and detailed accounts of the unfolding devastation. Jake recognized a few faces from CNN and MSNBC.

What remained of Paramount Studios was still smoldering, and a heavy thick cloud enshrouded the entire area. It was like a scene from a bad movie.

Devasher slowly guided the SUV down Melrose, holding his F.B.I. shield out of his open window. A uniformed police officer motioned to a reserved parking spot opposite the studio's main entrance. Jake and Devasher quickly exited the vehicle and made their way across the street.

The noise level on the street was so intense that Jake had to scream to be heard. "Who's in charge here, Ken?" he yelled, as they crossed over the yellow police tape, now wearing their F.B.I. credentials around their necks.

Devasher grinned. "LAPD says it's their jurisdiction, but that won't be for long. However, I suppose for the time being it's LAPD Bureau Chief Charlie Fields who's running the show. We have a meeting set up with him in a half hour to sort out this whole mess. Jake, the Bureau wants you to sit at the head of the table on this one. Find out who in the hell is responsible, and take them down."

Ground zero was a crater almost 30 feet in diameter. There were forensic teams everywhere gathering as much undisturbed evidence as possible. Just beyond the crater was a broken aqueduct with water shooting twenty feet into the air and then raining down on what remained of the cobblestone street. There were still fires scattered everywhere, and fire companies from all parts of Los Angeles had been working together to get them under control.

Ladder 12, a unit from northern Hollywood, was battling what seemed to be the fiercest of the blazes. One of the remaining standing buildings was fully engulfed in flames and about half a dozen firemen were battling it from all sides.

Just then, Jake spotted a pierced fuel line protruding from the cracked foundation of the building, and the fire seemed to be quickly spreading in its direction. Although the firemen were merely a few feet from the fuel leak, none of them had yet noticed it. If the fire reached the line, it was going to blow.

At first, Jake began walking very quickly toward the firemen and then switched into a full sprint when the fire began closing in on the gas line.

"Get back!" he screamed, "Get the fuck back!" But with all the noise and commotion, no one could hear him. "Hey! The pipe, it's gonna blow!"

The fire was now right on top of the rapidly spreading fuel when suddenly it ignited and began burning a trail directly for the pipe.

One of the firemen looked up and noticed Jake who was charging in his direction. He couldn't have been more than 19 years old and he looked completely terrified. "Sir, I am going to have to ask you to stand back."

Not wasting a second, Jake dove on him along with two other young firefighters and knocked the whole lot of them to the ground behind a mountain of rubble.

Within seconds the pipe became engulfed in flames and exploded with a force so strong that it blew out the entire foundation and infrastructure of the building. Jake looked up, shielding his face from the intense heat with his hand. He could see the building beginning to collapse in their direction, and in the direction of two other firefighters who had been knocked down in the explosion. They were all about to be crushed to death.

"Run!" Jake screamed to the three firemen huddled next to him. As they did, Jake ran in the opposite direction, toward the two wounded men and the collapsing building.

"What in the fuck are you doing, Jake?" he yelled at the top of his lungs as he ran full speed into the oncoming avalanche. *Was this how my father went?*

As he got to the men, he noticed they were both banged up pretty bad, but one was still conscious. "Can you move?" Jake shouted over all the noise.

"Yes, I think so."

He hoisted the unconscious man over his shoulder. "Then stay close."

As he ran for safety, Jake didn't look back but could hear the avalanche quickly approaching.

Fuck! Jake, this is fucking crazy!

Suddenly, he felt something tag the back of his leg. It was the debris from the building. Then something hit his lower back. It had caught up to him! *God this is it! I'm going to die right here!*

Without a second to spare, Jake dove behind one of the abandoned fire trucks, with both men landing on top of him. The building came crashing down all around them. Suddenly, something struck Jake in the head so hard that everything started to go black. *This is it,* Jake thought. *This is how it all ends.*

CHAPTER 18

AT 2:00 PM, EAST COAST TIME, THE PRODUCER EXITED THE private jet he had boarded at LAX. Carrying his briefcase and a black garment bag, he headed across the tarmac to a waiting Lincoln Navigator.

A tall, dark, Middle Eastern man, neatly dressed in a tan blazer and khaki pants, left the driver's side door of the car with both arms fully extended in the air, emulating a V for victory. "Nuri, you fucking did it, my brother!"

Nurillo Irgashev was The Producer's real name. Of course, when you're directly responsible for something as diabolical as Paramount, one's true identity is better kept a secret. As the two men met, they embraced.

Laughing even harder now, the man gave The Producer a huge bear-hug and lifted him off the ground.

Shavka Irgashev was The Producer's brother and had helped plan the bombing of Paramount Studios from the very beginning. He was Harvard educated and was responsible for constructing the explosive device, which he had learned to do during his military training.

As they boarded the Lincoln Navigator, The Producer hung his garment bag over the hook in the rear of the truck and placed his briefcase on the floor. The two men drove out of the "Private Sky" section of Kennedy Airport and headed for New York City.

"I reserved you the Presidential Suite at the Mandarin Oriental in Manhattan," said Shavka, as he turned onto Expressway 678 and headed for the Midtown Tunnel. "There's plenty of vodka and plenty of pussy waiting for you there."

The Producer stared out the window, clenching his teeth in

frustration. Frustration at his brother's cavalier attitude; frustration at what had happened to his family and mostly, frustration at what his life had become. How did it ever come to this? He took one of the Turkish cigarettes from the pack on the dashboard, lit it and inhaled deeply. "Any word from back home?" he asked, as he exhaled a stream of smoke that loomed inside the car like a dark, heavy cloud.

Shavka smiled. "You are a hero, I told you that."

The Producer took a second drag of his cigarette, then lowered the car window and flicked the remains onto the highway. "Somehow I doubt that."

"You worry too much, brother."

The Producer shook his head. "Maybe." He loosened his shirt collar and fiddled with the controls on the car seat, adjusting it to the recline position. "Maybe," he repeated quietly, hoping for some feeling of reassurance, but felt none. He closed his eyes and recalled the events of the day, then the events of the past year. God, it seemed so long ago. "What about DD? Is he earning his share?" he asked, with his eyes still closed.

"It's all going as we planned. Didn't you receive the email he sent?"

The Producer sat up for a moment. He reached into his blazer pocket and took out his PDA. There were several unread emails. He scrolled down to the ones sent from DD. It had been sent a few hours earlier.

Gentlemen, as expected the Paramount bombing has been classified an act of terrorism. Many suspect Al Qaeda. I expect to see you all in a week as planned. DD.

The Producer shook his head in disgust. He relaxed deeper into his seat and closed his eyes again. "Wake me when we get to the hotel."

Shavka smiled and touched his brother on the shoulder. "Yes, rest up. There is much work that still needs to be done."

"Welcome to the Mandarin Oriental," announced one of the valets, awakening The Producer from a restless sleep in the passenger side seat of the SUV. "May we assist with any luggage?"

"Yes, there is a black garment bag in the back. Make sure it gets to the Presidential Suite along with a bottle of Grey Goose Vodka and a bucket of ice," replied Shavka, handing the attendant a one hundred dollar bill. "No delays, got it?"

"Yes sir, right away."

At four thousand dollars a night, The Presidential Suite in the Mandarin was a four-bedroom, three thousand square foot suite with views of Central Park and the New York City skyline from every window. The room decor was contemporary in design with all of its furnishings, wall hangings and window treatments purchased in the Far East. The walls were faux-painted a pastel yellow and were lined symmetrically with black and white Asian prints done on authentic Japanese rice paper. Under the row of windows across from the front door was a grouping of decorative gongs in various sizes and colors, and on either side of the entrance to the bedroom sat proudly two bright red ceramic elephants. No expense was spared at the Mandarin Oriental.

The Producer didn't seem to notice, as he hung his blazer in the closet and turned on the shower. "Come fetch me at ten for dinner," he called out to his brother, who was in the living room watching a CNN report about the ongoing crisis.

"They moved the terror alert from orange to red," called out Shavka, who was now making his way to the door. "I'm in the Oriental Suite down the hall. I'll be back for you at ten."

The Producer let the hot water run down the back of his neck. He twisted side to side hoping that the pressure from the water would relieve some of the unbearable tension that had built up in his shoulders. He laughed. "These fucking Americans and their terror alerts. Red, orange…what does it matter?"

He knew this would be the case, though. He was counting on it. After all, he had done his due diligence. He had been planning Paramount for more than two years.

Before the September 11th attack, the Paramount bombing may have been seen for what it really was: revenge. Now everything was an act of terrorism and the terror alerts changed color on a daily basis. *A pilot accidentally flies his Cessna into an apartment building in New York City and within seconds F-16s are scrambled,* he thought shaking his head in disbelief. The world was indeed a different place since 9/11.

The Producer finished his shower and threw on one of the complimentary terrycloth robes provided by the hotel. He cleared a small circle of condensation from the mirror and stared at his reflection. He looked tired, exhausted actually. The last two years had been hard and it was starting to show. He quickly combed the hair off his face and exited the bathroom for the study. He poured himself a tall glass of vodka, opened his briefcase and took out his laptop computer. He set it down on the mahogany desk facing the floor-to-ceiling window overlooking Central Park, and for the first time since he had arrived, he actually took notice of his surroundings. That park looked quite beautiful with all the leaves on the trees a deep shade of green. In the distance he could see the Great Lawn and the baseball fields scattered about.

He drifted off and imagined his home, his family and his life that once was. He again thought through the last two years as he had done a million times before. For a brief moment he was lost in his dream and he smiled. Then, as if coming out of a Zen-like trance, he was awakened by a female voice coming from his computer. You've got mail.

Hi Ali,

Are you back in New York? Let's meet for martinis as soon as you are in town! Miss you terribly.

Brie.

Ignoring the email for the moment, The Producer focused his attention on more important matters of business. He took a big sip from his glass of vodka and typed six words into the Google search box: Tony Awards, Radio City Music Hall.

CHAPTER 19

"JAKE, CAN YOU HEAR ME?" WERE THE FIRST WORDS JAKE could make out as he regained consciousness. He slowly opened his eyes to see Devasher waving smelling salts over his face with a group of firefighters huddled behind him.

Jake felt a sharp pain on the right side of his face and he could feel dried blood on his check and neck. "I'm fine, I'm fine," he said, making his way to his feet.

As he stood up, the firemen broke into a round of applause. "Bravest thing I ever saw, man" said one of the firefighters, shaking Jake's hand. He was followed by about ten other men, all with similar praise.

Then it was Devasher's turn. His words weren't nearly as kind. "What the fuck is wrong with you? Yesterday you jump out of an exploding helicopter and today you charge head first into a collapsing building. Do you have a death wish or something, Jake?"

Jake continued to brush himself off. "Come on, Ken, you would have done the same thing if you noticed that fuel leak before I did."

Suddenly Devasher stopped Jake in his tracks and put both hands on his shoulders. "Jake, you gotta stop living in the shadow of your old man."

By the tone of his voice Jake could tell he was serious and was probably one hundred percent correct. To Jake, Ken Devasher had become a something of a surrogate father. He looked up to him as a boss, a friend and as a mentor. Jake didn't listen to most people, but when it came to Ken Devasher, he always paid attention to what he had to say. And he was always right.

"I know, Ken, but I don't think, ya know. I just react. I mean, when I saw those boys, and you have to admit they were just boys...." Jake said, as his voice trailed off.

Devasher looked at him intently. Both hands were still firmly on Jake's shoulders as both men faced each other. "Jake, if you die out here we both die." Devasher paused for effect and then a smile came to his face. "I mean, if I have to go explain to Diane that you were killed, she's gonna have my head chopped off."

Suddenly, the two men both broke into laughter.

"Come on, Jake, let's get you some stitches."

Jake felt guilty taking up the triage nurse's time for eleven stitches when there were far more serious cases she could have been attending to. But with Devasher standing by his side, she carefully sewed the gash closed on the back of Jake's head.

"Ok, Agent Chase, good as new," she said, managing a slight smile, as she cleaned the dried blood from Jake's face. She couldn't have been more than 20 years old, and she looked completely overwhelmed. Her eyes looked tired and she had a sadness about her. A sadness that probably didn't exist yesterday.

The triage had doubled in size and had expanded off Melrose, down Bronson Avenue and onto the neighboring streets. A makeshift operating room had been set up in the lobby of a nearby building and the news media had taken over most of the area along the perimeter of the studio. There were no longer news choppers flying overhead. All air traffic had been suspended except for the military planes and helicopters.

As Jake and Devasher made their way through the throngs of military, media and medical personnel, Jake was suddenly ambushed by a reporter and camera crew from Fox News.

"That's him. That's the guy," murmured one of the camera men.

"Agent Chase, Agent Chase, a word please?"

Jake turned to find a pretty, dark-haired woman touting a microphone with a camera crew in tow.

"Agent Chase, Lisa Krycerick, Fox News. How are you feeling, Agent Chase?"

Jake smiled in her direction but kept walking.

She hurried along with him. "Agent Chase, are you aware they are calling you a hero for your efforts in the rescue of five LA fire-fighters?"

Jake thought for a moment. "No."

The reporter gave him a quizzical look, a bit taken back by his response. She quickly regained composure. "No, you weren't aware?" she asked, slightly tilting her head to the side.

Suddenly, Jake stopped walking and faced her. He was inches from her face. "Look, understand this, I'm no hero. It was just…."

She seemed to attract the attention of all the other reporters and within seconds there were dozens of microphones in Jake's face. He could hear the mumbling and excitement amongst them as they slowly realized that Jake was an F.B.I. agent and that he was the guy they had all heard about who was responsible for the daring rescue that saved the lives of five men.

"Agent Chase, who do you think is responsible for this?" shouted another reporter over the crowd.

Jake started to walk again, this time at a much faster pace. "It's way too early to speculate."

"Agent Chase, does the F.B.I. have any leads?"

"I am on my way to a meeting with Bureau Chief Charles Fields now. We will be issuing a formal press release shortly," Jake said, as Devasher pushed him through the crowd and away from the reporters.

"Agent Chase, Agent Chase, one last question. Is this definitely an act of terrorism?"

"That's a very good question," Jake said to Devasher, as they made their way under the police tape and headed back into Paramount.

He was about to elaborate when the cell phone clipped to his belt went off. Jake's shoulders dropped. It was Diane and he knew exactly what this would be about.

"Hi, Di Di," he said, as he pressed the phone to the side of his face that wasn't throbbing.

"Jake, are you okay?"

"I'm fine, no worries."

"We just saw you on Fox News. What the heck were you thinking? I told you to be careful." Then there was a long pause, "Please, Jake," came Diane's voice finally. "Do be careful."

"Always."

Jake hung up the phone and ran his hands through his hair in frustration. He accidently pressed down on the stitches and he winced in pain. He looked over at Devasher, who was now grinning ear to ear. Jake pointed a finger in his direction. "Don't even start with me, man."

Devasher shrugged his shoulders, still grinning. "I didn't say a word."

"Yeah, but you were thinking several."

"I was just thinking that you played that pretty cool for a guy who just had a building fall on him. That's all, Jake."

"Yeah, Very funny, Ken. The meeting room is up here on the right."

The meeting between the LAPD and the Feds was taking place at the far end of the Paramount grounds in the office of some studio bigwig, who had long since fled. The room was as big as a basketball court and was very masculine in its décor. The walls were adorned with expensively framed movie posters and at the far end of the room was the biggest plasma TV Jake had ever seen.

Director Robbins and Dr. Sinclair were standing beside a huge mahogany desk and were speaking with two well-dressed men at the far corner of the huge office.

Dr. Sinclair immediately spotted Jake, gave him a smile and waved him over. "Agent Jake Chase, Deputy Director Ken Devasher, I'd like you both to meet Governor Paul Kean and LAPD Bureau Chief, Charles Fields," she said.

The Governor's eyes widened. "Ah, Agent Chase, I've heard a lot about you," he said, shaking Jake's hand firmly. "I'd like to personally thank you for your heroics earlier today."

"Thank you, Governor," Jake replied, sensing the sincerity in the Governor's voice. But really, it was nothing at...."

"Nothing?" interrupted Bureau Chief Fields "You saved five of our firefighter's lives. I would hardly call that nothing," he said with a crooked smile.

Jake couldn't put his finger on it but there was just something he didn't like about Charlie Fields. It was the same feeling he got when he met Danzinger for the first time. It was this intangible hostility both men seemed to harbor. Intriguing...and weird.

"Thank you, Chief Fields," Jake replied, as he shook his hand.

"Please, Jake, call me Chuck."

Okay, Chuck, call me Agent Chase.

"Will you be in town long?" interrupted the Governor, obviously sensing some hostility between the two men.

"As long as we need to be," said Director Robbins.

"Very well," said the Governor. "Shall we start the meeting?" he asked, gesturing toward the conference table.

Once everyone was seated, Bureau Chief Fields started the meeting by reading a statement of what little they knew so far about the bombing. Seated to his right was Police Captain Danzinger, along with a few of his henchmen. Danzinger reminded Jake of that angry bull dog in the cartoon. The one that always forgets how long his chain is and winds up choking himself with his collar before he could get the bad guy.

Chief Fields slid on a pair reading glasses and cleared his throat. "There are several terrorist groups that are claiming responsibility, and we are taking the necessary steps to follow up on each one."

"Exactly what steps would that be?" Jake asked, as he scratched down some notes on a pad that had been provided to him courtesy of the LAPD.

Chief Fields looked over the top of his glasses in Jake's direction. "Please Agent Chase, save your questions for the end," he replied, sounding a bit annoyed. He cleared his throat again. "As I was saying, we are following up on all leads and we expect a full report from our forensics teams within the next few hours."

"Chief Fields, um, I mean Chuck, has anyone viewed any of the video surveillance cameras for possible photo identification?"

Danzinger huffed in exasperation. "All cameras surrounding ground zero were destroyed in the explosion."

"Any backup tapes kept off site?" asked Jake, looking from Danzinger to Fields then back to Danzinger.

"We are working on retrieving the back-up tapes, Agent Chase. We should have them shortly," replied Chief Fields.

"I'd like to see those as well as the tapes from the past few weeks, especially the ones at the gate and on Melrose Avenue. What about the flight logs and passenger lists right after the explosion? Has anyone requested those from the tower chief at LAX?"

Danzinger stood up abruptly. His face beat red. "Look, you fucking F.B.I. guys come to our jurisdiction and start telling us...."

Just then the phone rang, interrupting Danzinger mid-sentence. The sudden noise made him jerk. Jake was starting to get the feeling that Danzinger was probably used to being cut off.

One of the henchmen sitting closest to the phone began to answer it, then stopped abruptly and looked at Chief Fields for permission.

"Do you believe these fucking guys?" whispered Devasher.

"Just answer it!" barked Chief Fields angrily.

Nervously, the henchman picked up the receiver and held it to his ear. "Um, yes sir. He's right here sir," he said, passing the receiver to Director Robbins.

"This is Robbins...Hello Mr. President...Yes he is here, sir. I'll put you on speaker now."

"Jake," came the voice of the President of the United States over the speakerphone. "Are you all right, son? I heard you had a bit of a go at it this afternoon."

Jake had met the President several times before, both formally and informally. He and Devasher had served on several committees that reported directly to him, and on one occasion, Diane and Jake had been invited to a dinner at the White House.

"Yes, Mr. President, I'm fine, thank you for asking."

"And how is Diane handling all of this, Jake?"

"A bit worried, but she is fine, sir."

"Please send her my regards."

"I absolutely will, Mr. President."

"I also heard your efforts resulted in the rescue of five firemen. Is that right, Jake?"

"Yes, that's correct Mr. President."

"Top notch, Jake, top notch!"

"Thank you, Mr. President."

"Jake, is Governor Kean in the room with you? Can he hear me through the speakerphone?"

The question seemed to startle the Governor out of a trance as he suddenly sat up in his seat at attention.

"Yes, he is, Mr. President; he's here at the table with us and he can hear you loud and clear, sir."

"Hello, Paul, how are you holding up out there?"

"Hello, Mr. President, okay under the circumstances," replied Governor Kean nervously.

"Paul, I'm flying out in the morning. I need you to make sure that Agent Chase, Deputy Devasher and Dr. Sinclair get all of the assistance they need from the local authorities."

"Of course, Mr. President."

"Very well. I will see you tomorrow, Paul."

"Yes, Mr. President."

"Goodbye, Jake," said the President. "I will speak to you in a few days and you can brief me on the progress of your investigation."

"Certainly, Mr. President."

As the President hung up, Devasher stood up from his seat. "I think this meeting is over gentlemen. We'll expect those video tapes and flight logs in the morning."

"So long, Chuck," Jake said with a wink, as he and Devasher made their way out the door.

CHAPTER 20

BACK ON MELROSE AVENUE, IT SUDDENLY OCCURRED TO JAKE that it was almost eight o'clock West Coast time and he hadn't eaten all day. The lack of food was probably contributing to his already pounding head.

He wanted to head out to LAX himself because he really didn't trust that the LAPD would be very forthcoming with whatever information they gathered, regardless of what the President had just said. "I am heading out to the airport to see what I can find from the tower chief," he said to Devasher, who was busy sending an email from his PDA. "Want to get a bite first?"

"Absolutely, I'm famished," said Devasher, who apparently had forgotten to eat as well. "I think there's a place about a half mile from here. You up for a good long walk? It will give us a chance to clear our heads a bit."

Jake nodded and the two men headed away from Paramount, leaving the madness behind them. They walked along Bronson Avenue and once again passed by the well manicured lawns and the white picket fences, except this time something was different, very different. The blissful little neighborhood had been abandoned by its occupants and was now completely deserted. There wasn't a soul in sight and all of the homes were dark. The lifeless solitude was eerie and it reminded Jake of a scene from the movie *The Shining*.

The two men walked in silence, and Jake welcomed the quiet. Devasher looked as exhausted as Jake felt. Although he was in great shape, Ken Devasher was old enough to be Jake's father. He was in his mid-sixties, stood six feet two inches tall and had salt-and-pepper hair. He had been married twice. His first wife had passed away after a long bout with cancer. His second wife Martha and he had been divorced for five years now but remained friends; both live next door to one another in the same modest neighborhood just outside D.C. Oddly enough, Ken never had any children, although Jake always thought he would have made a terrific father.

He had graduated valedictorian from West Point and went on to get his law degree from Yale, where he was recruited by the Bureau. He impressed the right people early on and was quickly promoted through the ranks.

As the number two man at the F.B.I. he was on the docket to take the Director's position in a few years when Robbins retired. Jake had been working under him for the past five years and he had taught him a great deal.

After several more blocks of walking, Jake began to notice signs of life. The occasional lighted window gave Jake an odd sense of relief and the farther away they got from Paramount Studios, the more populated the streets became.

Suddenly, Devasher pointed to a small tan building with a terra-cotta roof and a large wooden door. Hanging above the door was a red neon sign that was emitting a loud buzzing sound. Although most of the letters were fighting to stay lit, Jake could make out the word *Nisos*. "It's up here on the left," announced Devasher, finally breaking the silence, as the two men entered beneath the flickering sign.

Nisos was a pub-style restaurant with a long copper-topped bar on one side and tables set up for dining on the other. The walls were a collage of autographed photos of celebrities, and each place setting came with a box of crayons for doodling on paper tablecloths. The clientele seemed to be everyone from flamboyant Hollywood types to businessmen wearing suits and ties.

Devasher and Jake were seated in the corner of the restaurant next to an autographed picture of Jack Nicholson wearing a pair of Ray-Ban sunglasses, eyebrows fully arched, flashing his trademark smile.

Seated next to them were four noticeably intoxicated men, probably in their late twenties, all wearing expensive looking suits. Judging by the number of empty Corona bottles on their table, they had probably been there since lunch. By the looks of their litigation bags and files overflowing with legal documents, Jake surmised that they were attorneys.

"Just my fucking luck," said Jake under his breath, as Devasher shot him a grin.

Suddenly, one of the men erupted. "Sloth!" he screamed out, nearly knocking his beer into his lap, as the table of drunks cheered and clinked their bottles together.

"How many sins does that make so far?" called out another, referring to The Seven Deadly Sins, which apparently had been troubling them all afternoon.

"Five," slurred the lawyer who had been nominated to make notes, as he wrote down the word "sloth" in purple crayon, adding it to the list he was keeping on the paper tablecloth.

Jake looked over at Devasher in disbelief.

"Can I bring you two gentlemen a drink?" said a cute strawberry blonde waitress who was wearing her short hair in tight little pigtails. She gave Jake an admiring stare and then set down a basket of warm bread and a small saucer of extra-virgin olive oil.

"I'll have a Sam Adams," Jake said, as he read over the list of specials from a chalkboard above the bar.

"Same," said Devasher, drowning a piece of bread in the olive oil.

"You know, Ken, you and I have been chasing bad guys together for almost five years now," Jake said, as the waitress scurried off in the direction of the bar.

"Probably close to fifty missions all over the globe," replied Devasher with a proud look.

"Yeah, and most of them for the Bureau's Anti-Terrorism Unit. With that number of cases, you kind of develop a sixth sense, you know what I mean?"

Devasher paused for a moment. "What are you getting at?"

Again, there was another outburst from the neighboring table. "Greed!" howled one of the more sober lawyers. "Greed makes six!" he boasted, as if he had just discovered the cure for cancer.

"We said Greed an hour ago, ya moron," growled the stenographer with the purple crayon.

Jake shook his head. "I don't know, Ken. Something seems different here. Different than all those other cases."

"Different how?" asked Devasher, as the waitress set the two bottles of Sam down on the table.

"You two need a little more time?" she asked.

"I'll have the steak sandwich medium rare," Jake told her, as he rolled the cold bottle of Sam Adams back and forth on his forehead, hoping for some relief from his throbbing headache.

"Make that two," said Devasher.

Suddenly, a scream came from the table of belligerents. It was so loud that it startled the poor waitress, causing her to drop her note pad. Immediately, Jake bent over, retrieved the pad from under the table, and handed it back to her. "Thank you," she said shyly, staring at him like a school girl with a crush. He gave her a smile, and then glared at the table of drunks. She giggled and scurried off.

"Read the list, douche bag! I can't remember what the fuck we said an hour ago," argued the dejected lawyer.

"Fine: Gluttony, Lust, Avarice, Envy and Sloth," replied the attorney with the purple crayon.

"Greed! It's not on the list. That's six!" shot back the embarrassed lawyer, hoping to redeem himself.

"Avarice and Greed are the same thing, ya jack off!" shouted someone, and they all broke into laughter.

Devasher raised an eyebrow. "Ya want me to cap 'em Jake? I have my Glock right here. Probably won't even catch any flack for it."

"Look, Ken, I don't think I can sit here much longer. I'm gonna head out to LAX right now and see what kind of surveillance cameras they have. Maybe somebody over there will remember seeing something."

"Pride, that's one, right? Pride, that makes six," shouted one of the lawyers, followed by a barrage of high fives and clinking beer bottles.

"Here we go," said the love-struck waitress. "Two steak sandwiches. Can I get you guys another beer?"

"I'll take another Sam Adams," said Devasher, "and bring a doggy bag for my colleague here."

"What the fuck is the seventh deadly sin?" came a frustrated plea from the table of lawyers.

"I have no clue; my brain is fried."

Jake stood from the table and Devasher tossed him the keys to the SUV. "I'll get a ride back with Robbins," he said. "We're staying at the Beverly Hills Hotel on Sunset. I'll have them leave a room key at the front desk for you, Jake."

"Okay, Ken, see if you can get your hands on the surveillance tapes from Paramount, and I'll let you know what I find out at LAX."

"Sounds like a good plan," replied Devasher. "Let's meet tomorrow morning for breakfast."

As Jake headed for the door, he stopped at the table of drunken lawyers, took a black crayon from their box and wrote down the missing sin in 2 inch high letters on their tablecloth.

WRATH.

CHAPTER 21

IT WAS A BIT SURREAL BEING ESCORTED THROUGH LAX BY TWO Marines toting M-16 assault rifles. There was still no air traffic permitted except for military aircraft, and the silence in the huge terminal was spooky. Once again thoughts of *The Shining* raced through Jake's head.

"Right this way, Agent Chase," said one of the Marines, as he led Jake down the empty corridor to the office of airport security.

On any other night, the airport would have been buzzing with travelers rushing in every direction to catch their flights or being greeted by happy family members after a weary trip. Tonight it was just Jake and the two Marines.

"Right through there, sir," he said, as he took his post beside the door and stood at attention.

"Thank you, Lieutenant," replied Jake, as he made his way into the cramped office of Airport Security Chief, Barry Conrad. The room was in complete disarray, with books and papers scattered everywhere. The void of windows cast a gloomy feeling, and the 1970s style wallpaper was peeling back in several spots.

Conrad was standing behind an old metallic desk and seemed to be in the middle of a heated phone call. He nodded to a chair. "Agent Chase, please sit down," he said, cupping the receiver with his hand. "I'll be just a minute. I have LAPD on the line."

"Thank you," Jake said, as he cleared some files from the worn-out imitation leather chair across from Conrad's desk.

Barry Conrad was in his mid 60s but looked at least ten years younger. He stood about 5'6", had a muscular build which was left over from his years in the Army; and what little hair he had left he wore shaven down military style, high and tight.

"Like I told your men earlier," said Conrad, returning to his phone call, "without a Federal Court order, the surveillance tapes remain the property of this airport, which is governed by the Federal Aviation Administration."

Jake could hear someone shouting profanities at the other end of the phone.

"Fine, you do that!" fired back Conrad, and he slammed the receiver down into the cradle. "Did any part of that seem unclear to you, Agent Chase?" he asked, as he reached over his desk to shake Jake's hand.

"Let me guess, John Danzinger," said Jake.

"Ah, I see you've had the misfortune of making the acquaintance of the infamous Captain Danzinger."

"Yes, he makes quite an impression."

Conrad smiled. "Look, Jake...can I call you Jake?"

"Why not."

"Jake, I just want to tell you that what you did today over at Paramount was nothing short of heroic."

Jake gave him a quizzical look. "How'd you hear about that?"

Conrad grinned. "Heard about it? Are you kidding, Jake? It's all over the tube," he said pointing a remote control at a television that was mounted on the wall behind where Jake was sitting.

Jake turned to face the TV and could not believe his eyes. Fox News was broadcasting the entire rescue, start to finish. Apparently some camera crew had captured the whole thing on video, and now every station was playing it over and over. "I'm not sure what to say."

"Don't say anything, Jake ol' boy. My older brother, Bob, is a fireman in Northern Hollywood. He says they're going to give you a medal."

Jake turned back toward Conrad. "Your brother, Bob, the fireman, told you that?"

"Yeah, and I think you might want to have a chat with my other brother, Barney," he said, as he picked up a microphone from what looked like an old CB radio on the corner of his desk. "Base to ground, base to ground...Come in, ground."

Jake shook his head in amazement. It was like being trapped in a time capsule that was sealed off from the rest of the world around 1975.

"Hey, Barry," came a woman's voice from the speaker on the CB.

"Hi there, Suzie-Q. Be a doll and send my brother up to the office ASAP."

"Sure will, hon."

Conrad gave Jake a wink and a crooked smile that had sexual harassment written all over it. Jake politely returned the smile.

"My brother Barney works on the ground crew for the private aviation here at the airport. Said he saw something that seemed a bit odd this morning, shortly after the terrorist attack," said Conrad, reconnecting the microphone to the clip on the side of the radio.

Jake tilted his head curiously. "Odd in what way?" he asked, as he began scratching down some notes on the pad he had taken from the LAPD meeting. Before Conrad could answer, the door burst open and in walked Barry's brother, Barney.

Barney Conrad was a lanky 6'7" tall, 145 pounds and looked like a good wind could knock him over. He was wearing faded jeans, a flannel shirt, and an LA Lakers cap turned backwards on his head like a baseball catcher. He looked like a caricature come to life.

"Barney, I'd like you to meet Agent Chase from the F.B.I."

"No friggin' way! It sure is a pleasure to meet you, Agent Chase. We've been watching you all day on the TV downstairs," he said, as he shook Jake's hand with what had to be the largest hand Jake had ever seen on a human.

Jake nodded. "Your brother tells me that you may have seen something a bit out of the ordinary this morning, just after the Paramount bombing."

"Sure did, Agent Chase, sure did," he said, nodding his head up and down.

Conrad huffed. "Well, tell him what you told me, Barney!"

Startled, Barney looked up from the spot on the floor he had been studying. "Mind if I dip? Relaxes me."

"Dip, I don't quite understand," replied Jake, looking back and forth from Barry to Barney for clarification.

Conrad looked over at his brother disapprovingly. "Oh good Lord, Barney, Agent Chase doesn't want to see that."

Still completely baffled Jake looked at the two men. "I don't understand. Did you say dip?"

Barney nodded his huge head up and down. "You know, dip," he said, pulling a pouch of Redman chewing tobacco from his back pocket.

"Oh, um sure, go right ahead," Jake said, noticing Barney was already stuffing a huge wad in his mouth, not really waiting for an answer.

Conrad sighed. "Just tell Agent Chase what you saw, Barney."

"Right-o," said Barney, with a bit of tobacco-colored saliva dripping down his chin. "This mornin' 'round 8:30, I saw this real nice private jet taxiing toward Hang 10."

Jake looked up from his notepad. "Hang 10?"

"Yeah, Hangar 10. It's where we keep all the really big private jets, mostly G fives 'n stuff," replied Barney, wiping the saliva off his chin with the sleeve of his flannel shirt. "Anyway, this towel-head," Barney paused and looked over at his brother apologetically. Jake once again stopped writing and look up at the two brothers. "Um, I mean this Middle Eastern guy, gets off the plane and just stands there on the runway talking into his cell phone. When I asked what he was doing, he told me to just refuel the plane for New York City and to mind my own business. I was about to radio security when this black Mercedes Benz comes pulling up to Hang 10...I mean, comes pulling up to Hangar 10, and this tall, dark-haired guy gets out, shakes hands with the towel-head guy and they switch places."

For the third time Jake stopped writing. This time he closed the notepad altogether and placed it on the arm to the chair, giving Barney his full attention. "Did you say they switched places?"

Barney shook his head up and down. "Yeah, that's what I said, they switched places. The dark-haired guy gets on the plane for New York, and the towel-head guy drives off in the Benz."

Jake's heart began to race. "Did you see what the guy who got on the plane looked like?"

"Not really," said Barney, who was now desperately looking for a place to spit out the chewed-up wad of tobacco in his cheek. Conrad frowned. Sensing his brother's state of panic, he handed him a half-full coffee mug. With a sigh of relief, Barney spat the wad of tobacco into the mug, splashing some of the remaining coffee onto the side of Conrad's desk.

Jake cleared his throat. "You were saying?"

"Oh, right. See, all those towel-heads look the same to me; can't tell one from the other."

"Well, maybe we could at least try with our F.B.I. sketch artist."

Waving his hand back and forth, Barney gave Jake a crooked smile. "No need. Got the whole thing on video."

Jake couldn't believe his ears. "You did what?"

"Yup, airport policy. Twenty-four-seven video surveillance on all aircraft in and out of Hang 10. You can't believe how cautious these rich guys are about their private jets."

Jake was barely able to control himself. "Any chance I could have a look at that video?"

Barry Conrad stood up and shot Jake a grin. "Already made you a copy, Jake, but um, would you mind doing us a favor first?"

"A favor? What kind of favor?" Jake asked hesitantly.

Conrad handed Jake a photo of himself, Barney and a third man Jake assumed was Bob the fireman. "Would you mind very much autographing it?"

"It's for Bob," said Barney.

CHAPTER 22

AT 10:00 PM EAST COAST TIME, THE PRODUCER WAS STILL seated at his desk in the hotel room, consumed with a file he had been studying for hours. He reached over and poured the last of the Gray Goose, then slugged it down in one gulp. He slowly stood to his feet, arching his back and twisting his neck side to side, trying to loosen the painful knots that were sending sharp pains up and down his spine.

Suddenly, there was a soft knock on the door. So faint, in fact, that he wasn't sure if the knock had been on his door, or on one of the neighboring rooms.

The Producer immediately reached for his 9mm semi-automatic and switched off the safety catch. The gun had been within arm's reach ever since the morning events.

You can never be too careful, thought The Producer. If it were Shavka, he would have just let himself in with his spare key. No one else knew to find him here. "Can I help you?" he asked, leaning up against the door, ready to fire.

There was no answer.

The Producer clenched his teeth. "I said can I help you?" he demanded, pointing the nozzle of the 9mm directly on the door about head high.

Still no answer.

"Fuck!" *Had they tracked him to NYC? Was that possible?* He thought, as his brain raced, searching for some mistake he might have made. Well, he wasn't going to go without a fight that was for sure. He stepped back from where he had been standing and turned the handle, letting the door creep open a few inches. Whoever it was on the other side didn't have much longer to live.

As he stood motionless against the wall, gun pointed at the opening in the door, he watched as whoever was on the outside slowly pushed the door open and stepped into the room.

To his surprise, the intruder wasn't an F.B.I. agent coming to blow his head off. In fact, it was quite the opposite. As the door pushed fully open, in walked a tall, beautiful Asian escort wearing very high heels, and a very short skirt. A gift from Shavka.

The moment she saw The Producer, who still had the gun pointed at her head, she let out a horrific scream, raised her hands above her head and spilled the contents of her purse to the floor.

The Producer momentarily closed his eyes, shaking his head in disbelief. "Calm down, calm down," he said, lowering the 9mm to his side and re-engaging the safety catch. "Why the fuck didn't you answer me?" he asked, amazed at how close she had just come to being executed.

"I Jung Lee. No speaky English," she said, still trembling with fear.

"No speaky? Are you fucking kidding me? I almost shot you!"

Suddenly, the beautiful escort fell to her knees and burst out crying hysterically. "No speaky, no speaky."

The Producer let out a huff, and then forced a smile. "Look, gather up your belongings," he said softly, pointing to the spilled purse on the floor. "I'm just going to put this gun away," he said gesturing toward the desk.

The gentler approach seemed to work, because the hysteria turned to light sobs as she began refilling her purse with the fallen items.

"There now, that's better, isn't it?" said The Producer, as he helped her to her feet guiding her to the door. He then reached into his pocket and counted out five one hundred dollar bills.

Suddenly, a huge smile came to the escort's face as she snatched the money from The Producer's hand. She stepped back into the room, loosening his grip on her arm, and began unbuttoning her blouse.

The Producer's shoulders dropped. "No, no, I don't want sex," he said, as he stopped her from undoing the buttons and once again guided her out into the hall. This time abruptly closing the door.

The Producer turned to make his way back to his desk but felt a sharp pain run down the length of his back. He grimaced as he slowly walked toward his computer, rubbing the back of his neck with the palm of his hand. He felt no relief. He opened his earlier email, clicked the reply icon and began to type.

Brie,

Meet for drinks at The Four Seasons Hotel. Tonight—11:00 PM.

Ali.

CHAPTER 23

BRIANNA KOE WAS ON FIRE! HER CAREER WAS OFFICIALLY AT THE next level. She had just been chosen to be the new host of the prime time tabloid show, HOLLYWOOD DIARIES. Her lawyers had negotiated a five year multi-million dollar contract, plus an extra two hundred thousand to cover the red carpet at the upcoming Tony Awards. She was only 27.

Of course, it helped that she was 5'11" with natural blonde hair, perfect teeth and even more perfect tits. Going down on the show's female producer didn't hurt either.

"Another round of shots, Ms. Koe?" shouted the bartender over the noise at the Sky Terrace Lounge in the Hudson Hotel.

To celebrate her contract signing that afternoon, Brianna Koe decided to book an entire floor of rooms at the Hudson Hotel on West 58th Street in New York City for two hundred of her closest friends. The place was rockin', filled to capacity, and everyone was well on their way to becoming sloshed. Nothing out of the ordinary for a Brianna Koe party.

Brianna leaned in over the bar so she didn't have to shout, and to make sure that the bartender got a nice view of her cleavage. "Sure, Stevie, and bring one for Stephie here, too. God knows she could use a drink."

He smiled, revealing perfectly white capped teeth. "You got it, Ms. Koe."

Stephanie Keats, or Stephie, as Brianna had nicknamed her, didn't really want a shot, but she knew better than to say no to Brianna Koe. For the past three years she had been Brianna's personal assistant, which translated to being at Brianna's beck and call 24-7.

If Brianna wanted ten bottles of Cristal and four boxes of condoms at 3:00 AM, it was Stephie who made it happen. Of course, Stephie Keats had more important duties as well, like keeping Brianna's calendar and running interference with the media; the latter was no easy task, given Brianna's fast-paced lifestyle.

"Here ya go, ladies. Two shots of Patron Tequila, two lemon wedges and a salt shaker."

"Oh, you're not having one with us, Stevie?" Brianna said with a pout.

"Love to, Ms. Koe, but they're pretty strict around here about us drinking."

Brianna pursed her lips pretending to be sad. "Oh, poor Stevie," she teased. "We'll just have to make this shot enjoyable for you anyway," she said grinning.

Without warning, she grabbed Stephie's ponytail, yanked her head back as far as it would go, and licked her neck seductively, moistening it with her saliva.

Stephanie let out a yelp. She tried to force a smile and play along but was mortified.

With her free hand, Brianna grabbed the saltshaker and sprinkled salt on the wet spot on Stephie's neck. Still holding her head in place by her hair, she then placed the lemon wedge in Stephie's mouth so that the fruit side just protruded from her lips. She gave Stevie a wink, licked the salt from Stephie's neck, drank the shot in one gulp and sucked the lemon from her mouth, hesitating for a moment to accentuate their lips pressed together.

Brianna smiled. "Did you like that, Stevie?"

Stevie was speechless. Almost catatonic.

"Ok, your turn, Stephie," she said, as she pulled her long blonde hair to one side and tilted her head, exposing her neck.

Mopping up the remains of salt and saliva from her neck with a handful of cocktail napkins, Stephie tried to think of a diplomatic way to protest her boss' request, although she knew it would be useless. Luckily, Brianna's PDA began vibrating and dancing along the bar from the spot where she had left it.

Brianna let go of her hair, allowing it to fall loosely over her shoulders. "Hold that thought," she said, as she read the email that had so rudely interrupted her fun.

Brie,

Meet for drinks at The Four Seasons Hotel. Tonight—11:00 PM.

Ali.

She looked at her watch: ten minutes to eleven. Fuck! Ten minutes to get to the Four Seasons Hotel. Not a lot of time. She tapped her finger on her lips and thought for a moment. Then she smiled. "Oh well, it's been real, but I gotta bolt. Don't wait up, Stephie-poo, and make sure everyone has a fun time at my party. Oh, and call the driver. I'll meet him out front in five, and get me a private table at Fifty Seven Fifty Seven."

Brianna took three steps towards the exit and then turned and quickly made her way back the bar. She picked up Stephanie's shot of tequila, chugged it back in one gulp, and then raced for the door.

Stephanie, who had been practically holding her breath, exhaled a sigh of relief. "Can you please bring me a Jack Daniels on the rocks, Stevie?"

"Right away, Ms. Peats."

"No, it's Keats, you know, like the poet."

Stevie's eyes widened. "Hey, you didn't tell me you were a poet."

"Never mind, Stevie."

CHAPTER 24

BAR FIFTY SEVEN FIFTY SEVEN AT THE FOUR SEASONS HOTEL was packed as always: mostly posers, with the exception of a few wealthy businessmen. At his usual table was Donald Trump. Sitting across from him was former President Bill Clinton. Secret Service agents were patrolling the area by their table, and several had taken up various command posts around the room.

Brianna entered the restaurant and was immediately greeted by a tuxedo-clad maitre d' perched behind a podium near the front door. "Ah, Ms. Koe, we've been expecting you. We have a nice table reserved for you by the window. It's a clear night and the view is spectacular."

Brianna ignored him as she scanned the room for her beautiful producer. "He's late," she mumbled to herself quietly. She waved her hand in the maitre'd's face. "No, no, that won't do. I want a private table in a secluded corner."

The maitre d' looked surprised but never lost his composure. "But, Ms. Koe, your assistant requested a view, and we interrupted a couple in the middle of their dinner, and moved them for you."

Now the maitre d' had Brianna's full attention as she looked him up and down disapprovingly. "I don't give a fuck what my dumbass assistant has requested. I am telling you I want a secluded table in the corner. Now can you accomplish that, monkey-boy?"

The maitre d' forced a smile. "Yes, Ms. Koe, of course. Right this way."

As she walked to her secluded table in the corner, Brianna continued to scan the room but all she could see were wannabes and Secret Service. She looked at her watch, 11:15. Maybe he was running late. *Just one martini and I'm outta here,* she thought to herself.

After all, she was Brianna Koe. Men waited for her, not the other way around.

"Right this way, Ms. Koe," said the maitre d', as he seated her at the most secluded table the restaurant had to offer. "A waiter will be by momentarily to take your order."

"No need," she said, still scanning the room. "Bring me a double apple martini."

"Right away, Ms. Koe."

"And make sure to use Grey Goose Vodka!"

"Of course, Ms. Koe."

Just one apple martini and I am gone, thought Brie, as she looked down at her watch.

Two hours later Brianna Koe was finishing her third apple martini, making excuses for why she had been stood up. *Stood up? Not me,* she thought. That happened to losers, not her. Something must have happened. Maybe he was killed in a car crash. Yes, that was it. He was killed in a fiery car crash racing over here to see her. *Happens all the time*, she thought, as she looked over the room one last time.

Then she saw him and her heart nearly skipped a beat. There he was, her beautiful producer from the West Coast, smiling and walking toward her with a bundle of orchids and two chocolate martinis. He was wearing a dark Armani suit and an equally dark collared shirt. His black hair was pulled off his tanned face into a small ponytail. He looked like a European movie star.

Brianna nervously bit her bottom lip with her teeth but immediately stopped once she realized what she was doing. "So, you weren't run over by a taxi," she said, as he approached her table.

The Producer smiled, kissed her on the cheek, and handed over the flowers. It made her knees tremble. "I'm so sorry, my love. You wouldn't believe the day I've had."

Brianna pouted playfully. "Well, I hope you still have some energy left for me."

The Producer leaned in close and placed his hand on Brianna's thigh. "Oh, but of course, kitten, and I have taken the liberty of reserving the penthouse suite for us. There is a bottle of Cristal chilling as we speak."

Brianna could smell his cologne and it excited her. She also found his thick Middle Eastern accent a turn on, but would never admit to it.

"What makes you think I am going to a hotel room with you?" she barked back, knowing full well she would fuck him in a second.

The Producer sat back in his chair and removed his hand from its resting spot on Brianna's leg. "Well, for one, because you adore me," he said, with a cocky grin.

Brianna fought the urge to jump across the table and rip his clothes off right there in the restaurant. Instead, she took a big sip of her chocolate martini. "Adore you? Ha, I barely know you."

The Producer smiled. "Well then, how about because I can get you interviews for your little TV program with any "A" list actor your heart desires?"

Brianna sighed in defeat. "You're lucky you're so good looking," she said, taking another big sip from her cocktail. She was starting to feel a little out of sorts, which came as no surprise considering the two shots of tequila she had at the Hudson, the three martinis she had just downed in under two hours, the 200 milligrams of Vicodin, and the four lines of coke. "How long are you in town for, Ali?"

"About a week."

Unknowingly, Brianna began to trouble her bottom lip with her teeth again. "Ali, I'm hosting the red carpet at the Tony Awards next weekend and I could use a date," she said shyly.

The Producer grinned much like the fox who had just been handed the keys to the chicken coop. "Sure, I'd love to be your date Brie, and you can be mine for the Oscars in February. A few of my projects are sure winners."

"Really, Ali?" she said, trying not to gush. "God, the Academy Awards. I would love that."

The Producer relaxed deep into his chair. "Then it's all set," he said, raising his glass. "To the Tony Awards."

Brianna smiled. "No, to the Oscars."

CHAPTER 25

IT WAS ALMOST MIDNIGHT BY THE TIME JAKE FINALLY ARRIVED at his room in the Beverly Hills Hotel. He had called ahead to request a video player be brought up and connected to the television.

The room was small but handsomely decorated. The walls were peppered with black and white prints and there was a plasma TV mounted above an oversized credenza across from the bed. As promised, a VCR had been set up and was sitting just below the plasma on a mahogany chest of drawers. The hotel had provided a complimentary basket of fruit and it suddenly occurred to Jake that he had forgotten his steak sandwich at Nisos. His stomach growled as he reached for an apple.

He was completely wired, so sleep was definitely out of the question. He considered calling Devasher, but then thought better of it. *Let the old man get some rest,* Jake thought, as he loaded the cassette into the VCR.

Sitting on the edge of the king-sized bed, he bit into the apple, and eagerly watched the TV in hopes of finding some kind of lead. Unfortunately, all he saw was a vacant tarmac with the sound of planes taking off and landing in the distance.

The security camera was mounted to the side of one of the out buildings and rotated right to left about 180 degrees. It provided a complete bird's-eye view of Hang 10, void of any activity. After about 15 minutes of staring at concrete, Jake decided to fast-forward to the good parts.

The video was time and date stamped and Jake made notes of tarmac activity in five minute intervals. 7:30 AM: airplane sounds and concrete. 7:35 AM: airplane sounds and concrete, and so on. Then, at exactly 8:00 AM West Coast time a private Gulfstream G5 was led into the blocks by two Hang 10 crewmen.

"Well, hello there," Jake said to the television, as he documented the activity. The camera angle provided a perfect view of the plane's hatch, and Jake could just barely make out the identification markers on the tail: GS540DAL. "Ok, fucker, show me your face."

Strangely, the plane just sat on the tarmac. Nothing was happening. No one got off and no one got on, *nada*. Once again, Jake began fast-forwarding in search of the action scenes. At 8:30 AM it appeared that the crewmen were growing impatient as they frantically waved lighted batons at the jet, signaling for someone to deplane.

Finally, at 8:46 AM the hatch lowered and a dark-haired man wearing khaki pants, a dark shirt and a blue blazer walked onto the runway.

Immediately, both crewmen approached him and began yelling as they pointed to the plane and the runway with their lighted batons.

The dark-haired man didn't seem fazed as he took out a pack of cigarettes from his blazer pocket and offered a cigarette to each of the crewmen. He must have said something right, because both men seemed to calm down and eventually left him alone.

At 9:07 AM a black Mercedes Benz S600 Sedan, with tinted black windows, pulled up beside the jet and a tall, well-dressed man stepped out. He was greeted with a kiss on each cheek. Jake could only see the back of his head as the two men exchanged words.

"Turn around, mother-fucker. Show me your face," Jake said, as he took another huge bite of the apple. His heart was racing as he watched the man from the Mercedes finish his conversation and walk up the stairs to board the jet.

"No, no, you fucking asshole. Turn around. Turn the fuck around!" Jake screamed at the television, as he watched him board the plane, without ever catching a partial glimpse of his face.

"Fuck! Fuck! Fuck!" Jake screamed, as he threw his notepad at the plasma and rifled the apple into the wall, exploding it to pieces. He watched angrily as the plane taxied down the runway.

Calm down, Jake, he said to himself. *You've been up almost 24 hours straight. Get it together, man.*

Taking a deep breath, Jake reached down to pick up his notepad when he noticed it: As the Mercedes Benz pulled away, he had a perfect unobstructed view of the car license plate!

He quickly hit the pause button on the VCR. Still on his knees, Jake scribbled down the plate number: VCB287.

Jake smiled and slowly stood to his feet. He walked up to the plasma television and pressed his finger on the frozen image of the Mercedes Benz. "Gotcha, asshole."

It was just about 6:30 AM as Jake chugged along on the Precor treadmill in the hotel gym. He had only gotten three hours of sleep, but was feeling pretty good. Cardio exercise always helped him think clearer. Gets the blood flowing to the brain.

Except for Jake, the gym was completely empty. Los Angeles certainly wasn't a town of early risers, especially on a Sunday morning.

He was watching CNBC on the monitor attached to the Precor. A correspondent was reporting the tumbling stock prices of the major movie studios. The worst, of course, was Paramount, which took a twenty-point dive, nearly cutting its value in half. They were comparing it to the airline stocks after 9/11.

He had to meet Devasher for breakfast in an hour for a progress update and he wanted to watch the tape again and get his input. Hopefully, Devasher would have some of the video surveillance tapes from Paramount, and maybe they could link the Mercedes Benz to the bombing.

Jake had already emailed the tag numbers from the Benz and the Gulfstream to his friend Jarvis back at Quantico. Judging by his immediate response, Jarvis had already been at his computer at 4:30 AM East Coast time...or more likely, hadn't left from the day before.

Michael Jarvis was the resident computer geek at Quantico.

Story was that he was arrested at age nine for hacking into the computers of the President of the United States, Secretary of Defense and the Treasury Department. He didn't steal any confidential information, although he very easily could have. Instead, he left animated cartoons of naked stick figures making farting sounds.

When the F.B.I. finally tracked him to his bedroom at his parent's house, they were shocked when they found out he was only a kid.

After keeping him a few months in a reformatory for boys, the government decided to put him to work on some of their more complicated military defense programs. They paid for his education, and at fifteen he graduated first in his class from MIT, their youngest graduate ever. Now he worked full time for the F.B.I.

As Jake was finishing his workout, he heard someone coming into the gym. *Another health nut up at 6:30 on a Sunday morning*, he thought. *Glad to see I'm not the only maniac*. He stepped off the Precor, threw a towel over his head and made his way in the direction of the steam room.

"Jake, do you ever sleep?" asked Ken Devasher, who was poised on a stretching matt with one leg tucked under his rear, the other extended fully in front of him. He was leaning forward grasping the ankle of his extended leg.

Jake smiled. "Morning, Ken. You must be lost. This is the health club, not the buffet line."

"Funny," replied Devasher, as he swapped legs and leaned in even closer to his left ankle, allowing the muscles in his back to stretch to their fullest capacity.

Jake was just kidding. Devasher was in great shape. He had broad shoulders, very muscular arms for a man of his age, and completely toned legs from running his regimented eight miles a day. He was wearing a blue sweatshirt and a pair of gray shorts with the letters F.B.I. on the right leg.

Devasher stood to his feet. "How did you make out at LAX last night?" he asked, getting right down to business.

"I have something that I want you to see. It's a video tape from one of the hangars at LAX, and it has some very interesting footage."

Devasher put his hand on Jake's shoulder. "Terrific work, son. Let's head up to your room right now and have a look, shall we?"

Jake gave Devasher a quizzical look. "Why not finish your workout? I can meet you there in say, an hour?"

Devasher tightened his grip on Jake's shoulder, smiled, and then let go. "No time to waste, son. Now, let's go see those tapes," he repeated, as he headed for the door.

Jake found Devasher's behavior odd. In all of the years that he had worked for him, Devasher had always been the slow and methodical type. Now he seemed a bit edgy and quite rushed. Jake figured it was just the pressure Ken must have been feeling from the Director and the President.

"Absolutely," Jake said, drying his hair with the towel, as he followed Ken to the exit. "Any luck on getting those security tapes from Paramount?" he asked, as the two men boarded the elevator.

Devasher shook his head. "Unfortunately not, Jake. That moron Danzinger is telling us that all of the tapes were destroyed in the explosion."

Jake let out a sarcastic laugh. "And the previous weeks tapes?"

Devasher was still shaking his head. "Says that there was some computer glitch and they can't be retrieved right away. Maybe never. I'll have a federal subpoena by noon. If those tapes exist, we'll have them by the end of the day."

"That stupid fuck! With the delay he is causing us, who knows what this maniac is planning next?"

The two men arrived at Jake's room. Jake went to insert the magnetic key into the lock but hesitated. He turned to face Devasher and sighed. "Look, Ken, what I found on this tape is useless unless we can tie it to the bombing. It's suspicious, not definitive. But it's all we have. We need to see what's on those Paramount surveillance tapes to tie it all together."

Devasher nodded, as they entered the room. While they watched the tape, Ken jotted down some notes, and Jake filled him in on the details from his meeting with Barry and Barney Conrad.

They watched the tape a second time and then a third. On the fourth viewing, Devasher stood and walked to the VCR. He paused the screen exactly where Jake had the night before. "You've got to get that license plate number and the ID marker on the G5 to Jarvis and the boys back at Quantico."

Jake looked up from his notes. "I emailed him both tag numbers at 1:30 this morning."

"He was still at his desk, wasn't he?" replied Devasher.

Jake laughed. "Yup. Said he'd have everything I want by 8:00 AM."

Devasher gave a big stretch and then looked down at his watch. "Fine, fine, let's get a copy of that tape to him as well. Have him run it with the face recognition software. Maybe we'll get a positive ID on whoever drove off in that Benz."

"Will do, Ken."

Just then Devasher's cell phone went off. He unclipped it from his belt and pressed the phone against his ear. "Devasher!"

It was one of the operators from the Quantico switchboard. Apparently, an F.B.I. field agent had been trying to locate Devasher all morning. Under normal circumstances the call would never have been put through, but the agent insisted he had vital information regarding Paramount.

Devasher began pacing the room as he waited for the switchboard operator to connect the call. He gave a double take as he noticed the stain on the wall where the apple had exploded. He looked back at Jake curiously and pointed to the browning core on the carpet. Jake shrugged his shoulders.

Suddenly, a voice echoed through the phone. "Deputy Director Devasher, this is Joey Grieco with the F.B.I. in Virginia."

"What can I do for you, Agent Grieco?"

"I understand that you and Agent Chase are in charge of the investigation regarding the terrorist attack on Paramount Studios."

"That's right, and we are very busy this morning, Agent Grieco. Is there something I can help you with?"

"Well, actually, I think there is something I might be able to help you with, Deputy Director. You see, my brother-in-law, Hank Peterson, is a patrolman at LAPD headquarters, and he has the most interesting videotape in his possession."

Devasher made a beeline for his note pad and wrote down the words Joe Grieco/F.B.I., Hank Peterson/Patrolman LAPD and then the word video and underlined it twice.

"Stay where you are agent Grieco," ordered Devasher. "I will have a car bring you to Langley. Agent Chase and I will meet you and Patrolman Peterson at LAX."

Devasher looked up at Jake and said, "I think we just caught a break."

CHAPTER 26

THE MEETING AT LAX TOOK PLACE BEHIND THE MASSIVE STEEL doors of Hang 10. The huge hangar was vacant of any aircraft, but was capable of housing six gulfstream G-5 jets. Barry Conrad, who was living-out some F.B.I. fantasy, had airport maintenance set up a conference table in the center of the room. He had a place setting in front of each chair consisting of a leather bound note pad, a Mont Blanc pen and a bottle of Evian water. It was all quite impressive.

As they waited, Barney Conrad gave Devasher the play-by-play from the previous day's events.

"See, I wasn't scared or nothing, but my training told me something just wasn't right about these two," said Barney Conrad, as he spat a wad of tobacco out on to the floor of the hangar.

Devasher raised his eyebrows and shot Jake a helpless look.

Then, at 12:05 PM, an F.B.I. jet taxied across the tarmac in the direction of Hang 10. The plane slowly rolled to a halt at the hanger's entrance, and two crewmen placed large wooden blocks under each of the jet wheels. There was a loud noise coming from the jet engines that echoed throughout the cavernous room, and a gust of air blew through the hangar, knocking over the Evian bottles. Barry Conrad frowned.

After a few moments, the hatch slowly opened and rested softly on the tarmac. Without delay, Agent Grieco appeared at the door to the aircraft and walked down the stairs to the runway and into Hang 10. He was a tall, good-looking black man, casually dressed, wearing a collared shirt and a tweed jacket with leather patches on the elbows. He resembled a young Denzel Washington. Jake immediately took the initiative and introduced himself, extending a hand.

Agent Grieco smiled. "Your reputation precedes you, Agent Chase."

Jake gave him a dubious look.

Grieco nodded. "Been watching you on CNN. So has everybody at Quantico, actually. Great job, Agent Chase."

"Thank you," Jake replied graciously, and then led him over to Devasher and the Conrad brothers. The four men shook hands and were about to sit down, when in walked Hank Peterson, escorted by two armed marines.

Peterson was the polar opposite of his brother-in-law. He stood only 5'5" and weighed nearly 300 pounds. His uniform was in complete disarray, wrinkled and un-tucked, and there appeared to be a large stain resembling grape jelly on his right pant leg.

The two men met and gave each other a hug. Then Grieco led his brother-in-law to the conference table and introduced him to the group. Peterson took a seat next to the Conrad brothers and grimaced as he squeezed his huge body between the chair armrests. He appeared to be sweating.

Devasher, who seemed to be growing edgier by the minute, was the first to speak. "What can you tell us about these video tapes, patrolmen?"

Jake looked at him curiously.

Peterson picked up the Mont Blanc Pen and examined it from various angles. He looked over at the Conrad brothers, arched his eyebrows, and nodded approvingly. "Well, here's the thing. My boss, John Danzinger, seems to have a problem with you Feds. Says you're stompin' on his toes with this investigation. Late yesterday, I overheard him on the phone saying he had these video tapes of this Black Mercedes Benz parked outside Paramount every morning for the past few weeks."

Jake's eyes widened.

"Then he says that no matter how crucial they were to the F.B.I.'s investigation, Agent Chase would never know they existed." Peterson looked in Jake's direction and shrugged his shoulders. "The guy's on a power trip."

"Tell them the best part, Hank," interrupted Agent Grieco.

Peterson nodded at his brother-in-law. "Right. Well here's the real kicker. As he's talkin' on the phone, he's burning a copy of the surveillance video onto a disk. Seems whoever was on the other end of that call said something that really pissed him off. Next thing you know, the guy runs out of the building in such a rage that he forgets the disk in the computer."

Jake could feel the adrenaline starting to build. "Where is that disk now?"

Peterson had a grin stretched across his face. "Right here, sweetheart," he said, pulling the disk from his pocket.

"Have you watched it?"

"Several times," Hank replied, as he reached into his other pocket and took out some wrinkled pieces of paper. They appeared to have the same curious purple stain as his trousers. He put on a pair of bifocals that looked completely lost on his huge head, and began to read from the crumpled notes. "Black Mercedes Benz Sedan S600, tinted windows, parked in executive lot on Melrose Avenue facing Paramount Studios main gate. May 11–May 25, 6:00 AM–9:00 AM. License Plate: VCB287."

Barely able to control himself, Jake jumped up from his seat, snatched the disk from Peterson and ran for the hangar door. "Gonna borrow your ride, Joey," he shouted over his shoulder, as he darted in the direction of the F.B.I. jet.

"Where are you going?" called out Devasher.

"New York City!"

CHAPTER 27

THE F.B.I. JET LANDED IN PURCHASE, NEW YORK AT 9:00 PM EAST Coast time and taxied along the narrow tarmac at the Westchester County Executive Airport. Jake pulled up the shade on his window and gazed up at the sky. It was a perfectly clear night and the atmosphere was laced with a billion bright stars. The moon was full and it cast a warm glow that illuminated the runway. Jake smiled. He was glad to be out of smoggy LA.

The jet pulled up to a small terminal building and slowly came to a halt. The flight attendant unclasped her safety belt, and walked in Jake's direction. "Is there anything else I can do for you, Agent Chase?"

Jake smiled. "Thank you, I'm fine."

He stood from his seat, arched his back, and gave a huge stretch that made crackling sounds up and down his spine. He was exhausted, mentally and physically.

He made his way through the terminal and to the front of the airport where there was a car waiting to take him home. As Jake relaxed into the back seat, he switched on his PDA and, through blood-shot eyes, read through some emails. The first of which was from Diane, who had decided to leave the Hamptons early that morning. She was home and that meant he would see her. Jake smiled and decided that the rest of the emails could wait until morning.

He made the driver stop at the local market and he bought a large bunch of sunflowers, neatly bound in clear cellophane, and a six pack of Becks beer, both Diane's favorites. But, as the car drove up the winding driveway and approached the house, Jake immediately knew that something was wrong.

The Rover was parked by the entrance, but all of the lights were off. The place was completely dark. Jake exited the car and slowly approached the house. He quietly placed his garment bag on the front steps and peered through one of the windows. He could see that the home security system had been turned off. Something was definitely not right!

He quietly unzipped his garment bag and removed the Glock from its leather case. Switching off the safety, Jake guardedly made his way through the front door. He could feel his pulse rising as he squinted to see through the darkness. "Diane, are you here?"

No answer. This was bad.

With his Glock clenched tightly between his fists, Jake made his way through the kitchen into the den. He called out once more. "Diane, are you all right?"

Just then, something caught his eye. It was movement outside in the garden. Through the moonlight, Jake could just about recognize what appeared to be a person kneeling or hunched over. Jake couldn't tell if it was Diane or not. Terrified, he raced into the backyard with his Glock pointing directly at the object in the garden.

"Diane, is that you?"

As he got closer, Jake could hear the sound of faint sobbing. He squinted harder, but was still too far to make out the object. His brain was tired and he was completely confused. He approached cautiously, clenching his gun so tightly the veins in his arms began to protrude. "Diane, is that you?"

Then finally, he could see through the darkness. It was Diane and she was slouched over in the rose garden. She was on her knees crying and she was holding a piece of paper. It took a minute for Jake to process what he was seeing. He let out a deep breath and immediately lowered the weapon.

Diane looked up startled. "Oh Jake, thank God," she said, as she jumped to her feet and ran to him. She wrapped her arms around his body and fell into his chest. "Thank God you're home."

Jake was still baffled. "What is it Diane? What on earth is going on?"

Diane picked her head up from Jake's shoulder and looked into his eyes. "It's my father, Jake," she whispered.

Jake took a step back and placed the palms of his hands on either side of Diane's face. "Your father? What are you talking about?"

Diane struggled to catch her breath with short gasps of air. "They've discontinued the search for his killer. This came in the mail today."

Jake took the crumpled piece of paper she had been holding and began to read it. It was from the Malibu Police Department.

Dear Dr. Chase:

We regret to inform you that due to the amount of time that has passed and the lack of evidence obtained, we have officially shelved the case regarding the death of your father Jack Shepard and have placed it among our cold-case files.

Should any new evidence arise, we will be in immediate contact with you.

Sincerely,

Officer Daniels, Malibu Police

Jake's shoulders dropped. "Oh, Diane, I am so sorry," he said, as he held her close and gently guided her head to his chest.

Diane closed her eyes. "It's not fair, Jake. It's just not fair!"

Jake was speechless and for a long while they stood in the moonlit garden holding each other in silence. Finally, Jake pulled away and took her by the hand. "Come on, let's get you inside."

As they made their way through the rose vines Diane suddenly stopped walking. "Wait, the rest of the mail, it's on the potting table."

Jake gave her a smile. "I'll get it," he said, as he made his way around the rose covered pergola to the small potting shed. He grabbed a stack of envelopes which were bound together by a large rubber band and an antique letter opener. He remembered it was made of pure ivory and had been given to Jack by Michael Eisner, the CEO of the Disney Corporation. It seemed somewhat ironic that it was used to open a letter concerning his murder.

As Jake approached Diane she let out a yelp. "Oh Jake, your head," she cried out.

Jake gently placed his hand on his head and rubbed his fingers along the line of stitches. He chuckled. "It's nothing, Di Di, I'm fine," he said, as he took her by the hand and led her in the direction of the house. Suddenly he remembered the beer and flowers. "Oh, and by the way. There's a surprise waiting for you on the front porch."

Once inside, Jake went to the den and put the letter opener back on the leather writing table where old Jack had kept it. It was prominently displayed in Jack's office, along with a collection of other Hollywood business mementos.

Among the many items on Captain Jack's desk were a framed copy of a check for sixty million dollars made payable to Jack from MGM (his first movie deal), and a picture of Jack, Hugh Hefner and two other men Jake didn't recognize. Then, Jake's personal favorite, the actual hat worn by Robert Redford in the movie *Butch Cassidy and the Sundance Kid.* It was autographed, "To my poker buddy Jack, Royal Flush Shepard. Robert Redford."

"Are you hungry?" called Diane, who was much calmer now and was filling a vase in the kitchen.

Jake thought for a moment and looked at his watch. 11:00 PM. "Not really, Di Di. Kind of exhausted, actually."

The adrenaline rush was quickly starting to fade, and Jake could barely keep his eyes open. They were red and they burned. He reached into his pocket and pulled out his PDA. For a moment he considered turning it on but then came to his senses. He flung it onto the writing table and began to massage the back of his neck. He let out a deep sigh.

Just then, Diane came into the room carrying a vase filled with sunflowers. "Me too," she said, as she carefully set the vase on a small wooden table and fell backwards onto the couch. She smiled. "Come sit with me, Jake."

Lying down next to her on the couch, Jake realized just how tired he actually was. He started to drift off as she gently ran her fingers through his hair. It was heaven. "Oh yeah, Jake, I forgot to tell you.... I'm pregnant."

CHAPTER 28

AT 4:30 AM JAKE WAS STARTLED FROM A PEACEFUL SLEEP ON the couch by a loud buzzing sound coming from his PDA. He attempted to get up without waking Diane, but the position they were in made that impossible.

"Don't answer it, Jake. It's 4:30 in the morning," she mumbled, still half asleep.

Jake grabbed the PDA and made his way into the kitchen. It was Jarvis. "I swear this guy has no social life," Jake said to himself.

To: Jake Chase
From: Michael Jarvis
Date: Sunday, May 27, 2007
Re.: Gulfstream G5—GS540DAL/Mercedes S600-VCB287

Jake,

The Gulfstream G5, tag number GS540DAL, is part of a fleet of fractional ownership jets owned by a company out of Dallas, Texas called Brigade Aviation.

FYI. Individuals and companies that don't want the expense of owning their own jet can pay a yearly fee to have a fractional ownership of one.

This specific jet was owned by several companies but the flights in question were chartered by a Swiss company called Zurich Holding, LLC.

Interestingly, the S600 was a rental to guess who? Zurich Holding, LLC.

It is virtually impossible to get any information on specific officers of these Swiss corporations, but I may be onto something.

I'll let you know in a day or two.

Jarvis

Jake peered back into the den and watched as Diane struggled to find a comfortable position on the couch. He smiled, and then quietly closed the door behind him. There was no going back to sleep now. He made his way to the sink and turned on the faucet. He reached for a glass coffeepot and held it under the water until it was full. He counted out eight scoops and set the machine to brew. As the pleasant aroma of fresh brewed coffee began to fill the kitchen, Jake emailed some thoughts to Devasher who was still in LA. He also looked up the number for Brigade Aviation in hopes of locating the pilot who had been on that flight.

When the coffee was done, Jake poured himself a cup and made his way upstairs to the bathroom. He set the coffee down on the counter and turned on the shower. The room immediately filled with steam. He wanted to get out to Kennedy Airport. Possibly someone had noticed something out of the ordinary. Jake took a sip from the mug, opened the glass door to the shower and stepped in. The hot water felt good. He lowered his head and allowed it to run over his neck and shoulders. He closed his eyes and began to process the last 48 hours. Suddenly, Jake heard the bathroom door creak as it slowly swung open.

"Knock, knock," said Diane smiling, as she entered the bathroom carrying her own steaming cup of coffee. She placed it on the counter next to Jake's, took off the oversized tee-shirt she had slept in the night before, and stepped into the shower. "Want some company?"

Jake raised an eyebrow and grinned. "Absolutely," he said, as he began massaging shampoo into her long brown hair.

"So, I suppose you're working today, huh?"

Jake continued to rub the shampoo into Diane's hair and it began to form a thick lather. "I'm just going to snoop around Kennedy Airport for a while and see what I can dig up. I'll be home for dinner, I promise."

Diane stepped back and let the warm water rinse the shampoo from her hair. She tilted her head and pulled her hair off her face with her hands. She opened her eyes and smiled. She pressed her body tightly against Jake's and kissed him softy on the lips. "We can get Chinese and rent some movies."

Jake ran his hands up and down her back. He could feel himself starting to get excited. "That sounds wonderful."

Diane raised an eyebrow. "You think that's wonderful, here is a sample of dessert," she said, as she dropped down onto her knees.

She looked up at him and grinned. "Now promise me you'll be home for dinner, Jake."

Jake laughed. "Oh, I promise, Di Di. I promise!"

CHAPTER 29

KENNEDY AIRPORT WAS JAM PACKED WITH TRAVELERS. THE HOLiday weekend made it even busier than usual, and for some reason, the place was swarming with NYPD. For a brief moment Jake missed the solitude of LAX, then remembered *The Shining* and quickly reconsidered.

He had phoned from the car and set a meeting with Airport Security, and was greeted in the parking lot by Sergeant Raymond Powers. "Agent Chase, Ray Powers," said Sergeant Powers, extending a hand. "I imagine you are here regarding the murders?" he asked, gesturing toward the terminal building as he began to walk in that direction.

Jake narrowed his eyes and gave confused look. "Murders? You mean the Paramount bombing, don't you, Sergeant?"

Powers shook his head. "I thought you heard." Then he paused. "On Friday afternoon?" He paused again, but continued when he realized that Jake had no idea what he was talking about. "Three days ago a pilot and co-pilot were shot to death and then torched, along with their plane."

Jake closed his eyes. "Let me guess: a Gulfstream G5, ID number GS 540DAL, point of origin, LA."

Powers stopped walking. "Yeah," he said slowly, allowing the word to linger in the air. "That's right. How did you know that? That information hasn't been released yet."

Jake grinned and started dialing Devasher's number. "Lucky guess," he replied, placing the cell phone against the side of his face. "Look, Sergeant, the F.B.I. is gonna need a complete report from your forensics team."

Powers let out a loud cackle. "Forensics team, are you kidding?

There's nothing left except a charred frame of what used to be a jet plane, and some dental work."

Suddenly, Ken's voice was echoing through the speaker on Jake's PDA. "Devasher."

"Ken, our man is in New York City. He's murdered the pilot and co-pilot and torched the plane to cover his tracks."

There was a long silence. "Those bastards," whispered Devasher so softly that it sounded almost unintentional. He was silent again, longer this time. So long that for a moment Jake thought he had been disconnected. Then Devasher spoke. "Okay, listen to me, son. Find out what you can. See if anyone out there saw anything. I'll be back in town tomorrow."

"I'm on it!"

Jake re-attached the PDA to his belt. "Sergeant, have you reviewed the surveillance videos?"

Powers shook his head. "Unfortunately not, Agent Chase. Our video surveillance doesn't extend to the private aviation hangars. We only have wide-angle footage of the jet as it landed and taxied toward the hangar."

"I'd like a copy of that tape anyway, Sergeant Powers."

Powers nodded. "We can dupe one for you. Should take about an hour."

"Fine. I'm gonna have a look at the crime scene. I'll be back for that tape."

"Very well, Agent Chase. I'll have one of my men take you down."

The jet had been parked in front of a large steel building with the words Private Sky painted across its rooftop. The entire area was cordoned off by yellow police tape, and two armed guards were checking identification. Jake pulled out his F.B.I. shield and hung it around his neck from a thin metal chain. There were still some local guys milling about, taking notes and photographs.

Powers was right. There was nothing left of the jet except a charred frame and broken glass. Whoever was on that plane certainly wanted to remain anonymous. Jake jotted down some notes and snapped a few pictures on a small cardboard camera he had purchased from the airport gift shop.

Just then, a man walked up to Jake and tapped him on the shoulder. "Agent Chase, right? I recognize you from CNN. Detective Sandy O'Malley," said the man.

Jake smiled. "Nice to meet you, Detective O'Malley." Then he started snapping pictures again.

"Please, call me Sandy," he replied, as he followed Jake to the far side of the charred plane.

Jake paused momentarily. "Ok, Sandy, I'm a little busy here. Is there something I can help you with?"

O'Malley shot Jake a huge grin which revealed a large gap between his two front teeth. "Agent Chase, I just wanted to tell you that I come from a family of firefighters. My dad, his dad, both my uncles, and all three of my brothers. We all owe you a debt of gratitude for what you did for those firemen."

Detective Sandy O'Malley was as Irish as they come. He stood a towering 6'3" and was 260 pounds of pure muscle. His red face matched his even redder hair which at the moment was covered by a gray tweed cap. O'Malley sighed and shook his head as he looked over the rubble. "I've been on this crime scene for the past 48 hours."

Jake looked down at his cardboard camera. He had already snapped off twenty-four pictures. Then he looked back up at O'Malley. "Any leads?"

"Zilch," replied the big man, as he reached into his blazer pocket and pulled out a silver-colored flask. "Little toot?" he asked, angling the canister in Jake's direction.

Jake shook his head. "No thanks." Then he smiled. "I usually stay away from the hard stuff before 10:00 AM."

O'Malley shrugged his shoulders. "Suit yourself." He then put the flask to his mouth and took a huge gulp. When he was done, he screwed the cap onto the flask, and placed it back in his jacket pocket. Then he grinned. "Zilch, unless of course you consider an eyewitness a lead."

Jake, who had been fighting desperately to un-jam a small plastic wheel on the top of the camera, froze. Slowly, he looked up at O'Malley and grinned. "Are you saying you have somebody who witnessed this thing, Sandy?"

O'Malley nodded.

"Who is it? Where is he now?"

"He works for airport sanitation and he's back at the precinct with my lieutenant and a sketch artist. I can take you there if you like."

Jake grinned. "You know, Sandy, I think I will take a toot from that flask after all."

The 43rd Precinct in Astoria, Queens looked like something you'd see on a late night movie. It was located in an old pre-war building on Astoria Boulevard, and at 11:30 in the morning, it was sheer pandemonium. Uniformed officers ran in every direction, telephones rang off the hook, and the desk sergeant was cursing out some rookie cop about a "fucked up arrest warrant." At the far end of the room, three prostitutes, wearing very little clothing, were being fingerprinted, and one of the ladies was screaming about her damaged manicure.

The large room was lined with rows of old, metal desks and the worn out wooden floor seemed to slope to the right. "Hey Sandy boy, hey Sando," was heard from every direction as the two men made their way across the crowded room and into the lieutenant's office.

O'Malley placed his hand on Jake's shoulder. "Lieutenant, I'd like you to meet...."

"Agent Jake Chase," interrupted Lieutenant Mike Spinelli. "Good to meet you, Agent Chase. Great job out in Tinsel Town!"

Jake nodded and the two men shook hands

Spinelli fell back into his chair. "So, how can we help you today, Agent Chase?" he said, gesturing to a seat across from his desk.

Jake sat down and leaned forward with his elbows on his knees. "It's about the double homicide over at Kennedy. I understand that you may have an eyewitness, Lieutenant."

Spinelli leaned back in his chair and put his feet on top of his desk. "Sure do. He's giving a full description of the men he saw to our sketch artist as we speak."

Jake gave Spinelli a sideways look. "Excuse me, Lieutenant, did you say men?"

Spinelli nodded. "Yeah, apparently two guys from the Middle East. No fucking surprise there, huh, Agent Chase?"

Jake took out a small notepad and opened it to a clean page. "No, I suppose not," he replied, as he began making notes. "So, let me get this straight: There were two men on that plane."

Spinelli shook his head and waved a pencil back and forth in disagreement. "No, one man was on the plane. The other guy was waiting for him on the tarmac in a black Lincoln Navigator. They drove off together and within seconds the plane exploded."

Jake continued to write down what Spinelli was saying when suddenly the door to the office swung open and in walked the sketch artist holding a composite. He was accompanied by an older gentleman who looked to be in his late seventies. It appeared that the older man had been snatched from his job as he was still wearing his work uniform; blue trousers and a matching blue shirt with a patch that read Airport Sanitation. On his head he wore a faded blue and orange New York Mets cap.

Spinelli leaned further back in his chair and pointed the pencil in Jake's direction. "Gentlemen, this is F.B.I. Agent, Jake Chase. He would like to ask you a few questions, if that's okay," said Lieutenant Spinelli, directing his attention to the elderly man.

The old-timer looked up from under the brim of his cap and nodded.

Jake stood and extended a hand. "Hello, my name is Jake Chase and I'm an agent with the Federal Bureau of Investigations."

The old man smiled. "Hello, Agent Chase. My name is Giuseppe Rina and I work sanitation at Kennedy Airport."

Jake motioned toward two empty seats in front of Spinelli's desk and waited for Giuseppe to sit before doing so himself.

"OK, Jake, like I was telling these fellas, I work the 11-6 shift over at the airport. I was doin' my rounds emptying dumpsters when I heard what sounded like two gunshots from the inside of one of the private jets."

Jake momentarily looked up from his pad. "How close were you to the sound of the shots?"

Giuseppe shrugged. "Five, maybe ten feet. See, the dumpster is just around the corner from the hangar and the plane was pulled right up close."

Jake leaned in. "Then what happened?"

Giuseppe paused and looked down at his shoes. "Well, I am embarrassed to say, but I hid behind the dumpster. Didn't want to get hit by a stray bullet."

Jake leaned in closer. "Did you still have a clear view of the plane?"

Giuseppe nodded. "Oh yes, I could see it perfectly. And when the door opened, I saw this tall fella walk to the runway."

"Did you get a look at him?"

Giuseppe frowned. "No, he was looking down the whole time."

Jake began writing again. "Did you notice if he was carrying anything, Mr. Rina?"

"Yeah, he had a briefcase and one of those big suit bags. Then this other fella comes running up to him. Seems real happy, waving his arms in the air. Him, I got a good look at," said Giuseppe, nodding in the direction of the sketch artist.

"And?"

"Both men got into this Lincoln Navigator and drove off. I know it was a Lincoln Navigator cause my son has one," Giuseppe said proudly.

"Did you happen to see a plate number?"

"No. I started to get close enough to make out the numbers, when I saw smoke pouring from the plane, and seconds later there was this huge explosion. Musta knocked me back 20 feet."

Jake raised an eyebrow. "Were you injured?"

Giuseppe let out a huff. "Course not! I was a Marine in the

Korean War, ya know. We dealt with stuff like that all the time!" he said, drawing a smile from everyone in the room.

"Well, Mr. Rina, what did the man you were able to see look like?"

Giuseppe stood from his chair and took the composite from the sketch artist and turned it to face Jake. "He looked exactly like that."

CHAPTER 30

IT WAS NEARLY DUSK BY THE TIME JAKE WAS FINALLY BACK IN the car and heading in the direction of his house. He and O'Malley had planned to meet later in the week for a progress update. He had phoned Diane, who had declared that she was in charge of movie rentals, and that Jake was in charge of providing the Chinese feast.

God, that sounds good, Jake thought, as he drove the Range Rover through the toll booth and onto the Throgs Neck. Cruising over the bridge, Jake looked out over the Long Island Sound and could see the Manhattan skyline, with its lights twinkling in the darkening sky. He frowned as his eyes settled upon the void where The World Trade Center once stood. He thought of his father and felt sad. He sighed, and decided to think happier thoughts.

He turned his thoughts to movie night and Diane. *A stress free night at home, what could be better than that.* This made him smile. Plus, the Paramount case had just taken a positive turn. By now, every cop in the city was on the lookout for the black Lincoln Navigator and its driver, thanks to the sketch provided by Giuseppe Rina.

When he finally arrived home, Diane had already set two place settings in the TV room. She had opened a bottle of Shiraz, lit some aromatic candles and had Michael Buble's new CD playing softly in the background. It was wonderful.

The feast consisted of egg rolls, spare ribs, Moo Shu Pork and steamed dumplings. They ate and laughed and Jake almost finished the entire bottle of wine himself. Diane stuck with sparkling water and lime. Jake was completely relaxed, and for the first time in two days, he hadn't been totally consumed by the Paramount bombing.

Jake leaned forward and stabbed the last steamed dumpling with the business end of a chopstick and brought it to his mouth. "So what movie did you rent us?"

Diane smiled. "Well, you have a choice. Our old favorite, *Die Hard* with a young Bruce Willis."

Jake let out a groan. *"Die Hard?* Where they blow up that building in LA? That's all I need, Di Di."

Diane raised her eyebrows. "You're right, baby, I am so sorry. It didn't occur to me. Luckily, I also rented *How Stella Got Her Groove Back."*

As Jake loaded *Die Hard* into the DVD player, he switched his PDA to vibrate and set it on the table next to the couch where Diane was eagerly waiting. She had brought down two large pillows from their bed and a huge down comforter.

Diane sighed in exasperation. "What's that doing here?" she protested, gesturing to the PDA.

"It's just in case, baby."

"Just in case what, Jake? It's 10:30 at night and this is our time."

Jake's shoulders dropped. "I know, Di Di, but until this case is solved, I have to," he said, although he completely understood her frustration.

Diane fell back onto the pillows. "Fine, but as soon as this case is over...."

She didn't have to finish the sentence. Jake knew exactly what she meant and he knew she was one hundred percent right. He put his arms around her and gave her a big hug as they lay on the couch watching John McClain shoot up the bad guys. Things were near perfect, and then it happened: Jake's PDA began to dance around on the table, indicating an incoming call.

"Grrrrr! Don't answer it, Jake, please don't answer it!"

Jake looked down at the caller ID. It was Devasher. "I have to, baby, it's Ken. It will just be a second," he said, as he grabbed the phone and made his way to the kitchen.

"Hey, Ken, what's up?"

Devasher sounded tired. "Jake, I just heard from Jarvis. We got a positive match on the guy who drove off in the Benz. His name is Dante Irgashev."

Jake gave a Tiger Woods style fist pump. "That's awesome, Ken! Do you need me back in LA?"

"No, Jake, stay in New York and follow up on that composite."

"OK, I already sent it to Jarvis. Maybe we'll get lucky twice."

Devasher's voice was more deliberate now. "Here's the interesting part, Jake. This guy Dante comes from a very wealthy oil family in Dubai."

Jake furled his brow. "Dubai, you say?"

"Yeah, that's right, why?"

Jake thought for a moment. "Nothing really. Just that there are not a lot of terrorists coming out of Dubai these days, that's all."

"Yeah, I agree. But Danzinger has every cop in the city looking for this guy. If he's still here, we should have him in custody shortly. Now go back to Diane. I've kept you long enough."

Jake nodded. "Right, Ken. I'll speak to you in the morning."

As he returned to his spot on the couch, Diane gave him a kiss on the cheek and said, "Just in time for our favorite part."

Jake looked up at the screen to see John McClain reach behind his back and pull a gun from where he had stuck it with Christmas tape.

"Holly…duck," he screamed, as he blew away three bad guys and saved Holly Genero's life.

"Yippee Kayay, motherfucker!"

At 6:00 AM on Tuesday morning Jake was almost done with his daily workout. The stress of Paramount was starting to get to him and he had a strange feeling that he was running out of time. But for what he didn't know. In hopes of some relief, Jake decided to spend his hour in the gym bobbing and weaving around the heavy bag. After about fifteen minutes he was in perfect rhythm as he danced around the bag, striking it with great force. He felt strong, very strong, and he had great stamina. He could hear the chains rattle as he jabbed and punched the big black bag knocking it further back with every blow: right-right left, right-right left. "Keep your guard up!" he shouted through faded breath, as he struck the Everlast so hard that it nearly came off its hook. Jake smiled as he continued to spar with the bag, and block out all thoughts Paramount.

But now it was back to reality.... Back to the real world.... And back to the stress. As he sat at Jack's writing table, staring hopelessly at pages of notes, Jake searched for a way to put the pieces of the puzzle together.

What the fuck was a guy from a wealthy Dubai oil family doing bombing a Hollywood studio? It just made no sense. Maybe he had nothing to do with it at all. But what was he doing on the jet? And why would he drive off in the Benz that had been parked outside of the studio?

Jake closed his eyes and rubbed his temples with his fingers. When he opened them, he found himself staring down at a framed picture of old Jack and a few business associates in front of the fountains outside the Bellagio hotel in Las Vegas. The man next to Jack was Hugh Hefner and he had his arm around Jack's shoulder and they were laughing. The other two men seemed somewhat distant. Jake smiled. "I'm in the wrong business, that's for sure."

Just then his PDA went off. He slid it out of its leather case and looked down at the screen. It was an email from Devasher.

Jake, the LAPD has just arrested Dante Irgashev. Get on the next flight out here.

This was incredible news. Maybe now Jake would be able to put some of the pieces of the puzzle together. Although he was pretty sure that Dante Irgashev was merely a foot soldier, he might be able to lead them along the right path to the general.

Jake quickly gathered up the papers and stuffed them into a folder. He made his way up the stairs and quietly entered the bedroom. He didn't want to wake Diane until he absolutely had to. He needed to take a quick shower, pack a bag and get to the airport ASAP.

Jake set the folder down on the credenza in the corner of the bedroom. But, as he hurried to the bathroom, the file fell to the ground. With a thud the papers scattered all over the floor.

Jake could see the covers on the bed rustle. "Where are you going, Jake?" asked a groggy Diane.

Jake sighed. "I have to get back to LA. They have a suspect in custody and Devasher wants me to be there for the interrogation."

Diane abruptly pulled the covers over her head. "Grrrr!"

Jake approached the bed and put his hand on the lump. "I'll call you from LA, baby," he said, and then he kissed her through the comforter.

Diane's voice was low and muffled. "Be careful, Jake."

"Always!"

CHAPTER 31

IT WAS 9:00 AM AND FOR THE SECOND DAY IN A ROW JAKE WAS back at Kennedy airport. The next flight to the West Coast wasn't until noon, but it was still faster than waiting for the F.B.I. to send a jet. He considered taking old Jack's Gulfstream, but figured he could use the time to get his thoughts together.

Jake situated himself at a small table in one of the airport lounges. It was a sports bar called the Crooked Knife located between gates 61 and 62 in the Virgin America terminal. Although there was a host of empty tables, most of the patrons at The Crooked Knife were huddled around the bar.

The Paramount file was poised on a chair next to Jake and papers were scattered out on the table in front of him. He ran his fingers through his hair as he stared down at his notes. Still, he couldn't connect the pieces of the puzzle.

He sighed, and then looked up at a TV mounted on the wall behind the bar. The volume was low and completely overpowered by the noises from the customers. Jake squinted, and then smiled when he recognized the Fox News reporter. It s was Lisa Krycerick, the pretty little brunet, who had attempted to interview him in front of Paramount. His smile widened as he made his way to the bar. "Hey, can we get a little volume on this thing."

"In a dramatic raid that took place in the wee hours of the morning, a special forces team from the LAPD led by Captain John Danzinger captured the leader of the terrorist group believed to be responsible for the Paramount bombing."

The photo of Dante Irgashev Jake had sent to Jarvis from the Hang 10 video was now on the TV screen.

"With just this photo, LAPD technicians were able to use sophisti-

cated face recognition software to determine the terrorist's name: Dante Irgashev, believed to be from somewhere in the Middle East."

Jake let out a huff in exasperation. "Yeah, Dubai, ya moron!" Jake yelled at the TV, to the alarming dismay of the other customers.

"Captain Danzinger will be holding a press conference shortly and Fox will be there to report all of the details."

"A press conference? Are they fucking kidding me? To say what? After intense investigation into the details of this case and the sophisticated software of the LAPD technicians, we have captured the wheel man, who may or may not have had anything to do with the Paramount Bombing. Bravo, Danzinger, Bravo. Ya fucking jerk!" Jake said, as he began clapping his hands and looking around the bar. "Hey, can I get a Bloody Mary?"

Just then, Jake's PDA went off. It was Devasher.

Jake put the phone to his ear but Devasher was first to speak. "Are you watching this, Jake?"

Jake laughed in jest. "Yeah, what the fuck is Danzinger doing holding a press conference? He's only gonna drive the real bad guys further into hiding."

Jake could hear frustration in Devasher's voice. "I know, Jake. Dr. Sinclair and I have been trying to convince him of that all morning."

Jake shook his head. "Has anyone had a chance to question this guy Irgashev yet?"

"No one. LAPD just finished processing him. Now Danzinger is making this his own publicity stunt."

"Amazing," Jake said. He took a big sip of his Bloody Mary, but nearly choked at what he saw next on the TV. "Ken, am I seeing what I think I am seeing?"

There was silence from Devasher. The two men both watched in shock as Captain John Danzinger approached the podium to give his press conference, except he wasn't alone. For dramatic effect, he decided to bring along the suspect.

Jake stood abruptly and nearly knocked over his chair. "Why in the fuck is Dante Irgashev at that podium?" he shouted into the phone. A few customers in Jake's proximity quickly reached for their drinks, and relocated to the other side of the bar.

"Jake, that's not the only thing," said Devasher. "He's not cuffed."

Jake's eyes widened. "You have got to be kidding me."

Danzinger walked to the podium, smoothed the wrinkles from his blazer, cleared his throat and began to speak.

Through the diligent efforts of the Los Angeles Police Department, we have apprehended the chief suspect in the Paramount terrorist attacks. I know that most of you have many questions, but I ask that you hold them until the end.

I would like to start by sharing with you all of the tactics I used to track down….

Suddenly, Dante Irgashev reached inside Danzinger's blazer, freed his revolver from its holster, put the nozzle in his mouth and blew his brains out all over Danzinger and anyone within a 10-foot radius.

"Oh my God, oh my God!" screamed the lovely Lisa Krycerick, who was now covered in blood, as sheer mayhem broke out all around her. People were running in every direction and screams of absolute horror echoed over the airwaves. Someone quickly threw a coat over what remained of Irgashev's head as Danzinger stood motionless, covered in brains and blood, and paralyzed with fear.

"No need to come to LA, Jake. I'll be on the next flight east," said Devasher, and then hung up the phone.

Jake calmly reclaimed his seat, placed his PDA on the counter and slid his drink in the direction of the bartender.

"Can I get a little more vodka in this?"

CHAPTER 32

THE SOUND OF BREAKING GLASS ECHOED THROUGH THE PRESidential Suite of the Mandarin Hotel as The Producer threw an antique vase, just missing Shavka's head. It smashed into what seemed like a million jagged pieces. He then flung a remote control at the plasma television, which now displayed graphic pictures of the blood-drenched coat covering their brother's lifeless body. "How could this have happened?"

Shavka knelt down and began to pick up the shards of glass from the broken vase. "We must leave, Nuri," he said. "We must go back home while we still can."

Abruptly, The Producer stopped and turned to face his brother. "What did you just say?" Shavka shrank back at the rage in The Producer's eyes. "Did I just hear you say we should go back home?"

Shavka swallowed deeply. "It's just that I was talking to our friends in Switzerland. The one hundred and seventy-five million...."

The Producer cut him off. "Don't talk to me about money, you little pissant. This was never about the money to me," he said, and then he picked up a remnant of the vase and walked deliberately toward his brother.

Shavka backed up. "But, Nuri, I thought...."

The Producer grabbed his brother by the shirt collar and put the jagged edge of the vase to his throat.

With his mouth inches from his Shavka's face The Producer whispered intently. "You thought? You thought? You don't have the right to think, you little fuck. You nearly bankrupt our family and you have the nerve to tell me you thought! You are lucky I let you breathe! I should cut your throat right now," said The Producer, as drops of blood began trickling down the ceramic shard and onto the carpet.

Shavka could feel his brother's breath on his skin. He was terrified. "Nuri, I'm sorry," whimpered Shavka, with a tear in his eye.

The Producer pushed his brother, face to the ground, and then threw a handkerchief from his pocket. "Get out of here! You make me sick," he said, as he poured himself a glass of vodka from the bar. "I will come for you if and when I need you," he shouted, as he drank the vodka in one gulp and immediately poured another.

Shavka stood to his feet and collected himself. "Yes, Nuri," he said, wiping the blood from his neck with handkerchief. He then silently walked to the door and exited the room.

The Producer slugged down the second glass of vodka and approached the television. He placed his hand on the image of the bloody coat covering his dead brother. "No, this is not about money. This is about revenge!"

CHAPTER 33

"HOW WAS LA?" QUIPPED DIANE, AS JAKE HUNG HIS GARMENT bag on the door and fell backwards onto the leather couch in the den.

He closed his eyes and began massaging his temples with his fingers. "Uneventful."

"Poor baby," she said, as she came into the den with an ice-cold Becks beer. "Here, you look like you could use this."

Jake looked at her and smiled. He sat up on the couch and took a big swig from the frosty bottle. He closed his eyes and rubbed the icy glass along his brow and then exhaled through closed lips. "I can't seem to put the pieces together on this one."

Diane tapped her finger on her lips and thought for a moment. "Well, tell me what you have so far. Maybe I can help."

Jake removed the bottle from his forehead and took another big sip. "Not much more than you've seen on the news, unfortunately. Three men, one of whom is now dead, thanks to the incompetence of the LAPD. We are pretty sure he came from money. Somewhere in Dubai."

Diane tilted her head. "That's odd. I was in Dubai with my father a few months before he was murdered. He had some business deal he was finalizing. Hardly seemed like terrorists to me."

Jake nodded. "The dead guy's name is Dante Irgashev. Just after the bombing, Dante Irgashev got off a private jet at LAX and met up with a second man we haven't been able to identify."

"The guy from the black Mercedes?"

"Yeah, he's our chief suspect. That Benz was parked in front of Paramount Studios for the two weeks straight, including the morning of the bombing."

"Probably casing the joint!"

Jake gave her a sideways look. "Casing the joint?"

Diane smiled shyly. "Yeah, casing the joint. You know, evaluating the security and all."

Jake grinned. "Cute. Anyway, he boarded the jet Irgashev was on and flew to New York City. When he landed, he murdered the pilot and co-pilot, torched the plane and met up with a third man. We believe they are still here."

"Why New York City, Jake? What are they doing here?"

Jake shrugged his shoulders. "Dunno. I have been racking my brains to come up with that answer for days, baby."

"Maybe another attack on a local movie production."

Jake raised an eyebrow. "Well, that would be their MO if they are planning another attack."

Just then, Jake's BlackBerry began vibrating. Diane gave him a look and let out a sigh. He checked the caller ID and saw that it was Mike. He hit the connect button and placed the phone against his ear. "Hey."

"Hey, Jake."

Jake placed his hand over the speaker and looked at Diane. "It's Mike," he said with a smile, as if that was any consolation, and then returned to the call. "Mike."

"How's the noggin, buddy?" Mike asked, referring to the stitches on Jake's head.

Jake gingerly traced the line of stitches with his fingers. "Wonderful."

Mike laughed. "Well, you looked great on TV, Jakey. Like a superhero. Anita and I are going to start calling you Captain Courageous."

Jake shot Diane a grin. "How does it feel to be married to Captain Courageous?"

Diane folded her arms and stuck out her tongue.

"Oh, and congratulations! I hear Diane's pregnant," said Mike.

Jake's shoulders fell. "Yes, yes, it really is awesome," he replied, suddenly realizing that he and Diane hadn't actually discussed the impending baby. He had been so involved in the Paramount bombing that it almost slipped his mind. Jake suddenly felt horrible.

"Mike says congratulations, Di Di," Jake said to Diane, who was now pretending to ignore him by filing her nails.

"Thank you, Mike," she shouted at the PDA, and then mumbled, "at least someone remembered."

"Listen, Jake, there is someone I'd like you to meet. He may have some interesting information for you on your Paramount Studios investigation."

Jake eyes narrowed. "Oh yeah, who's that?"

"Harvey Wallace."

"You mean Harvey Wallace, Chairman of the Securities and Exchange Commission? That Harvey Wallace?"

"Yes, that Harvey Wallace. He and old man Reif are friends and they have their weekly poker game at the Grand Havana Room tonight. Reif knows you and I keep in touch. Says he saw you on CNN. Thinks what Wallace has to say might tie into the bombing somehow."

Jake rubbed his chin. "Sure," he said. "Any idea what it's all about?"

"A little bit, Jake. I'll fill you in tonight when I see you, say sevenish. Ask Diane along. I'll bring Anita and we'll celebrate over dinner."

Jake nodded. "Ok, Mike. We'll see you guys tonight at 7:00."

CHAPTER 34

THE GRAND HAVANA ROOM TOOK UP THE ENTIRE THIRTY-NINTH floor of the Orrick building on Fifth Avenue in New York City. At one time, the space was home to a restaurant called Top of the Sixes, which derived its name from the building's street address, 666 Fifth Avenue. Now it was a members-only cigar lounge that attracted wealthy businessmen, politicians and movie stars.

A thirty foot-long bar in the center of the lounge faced floor to ceiling windows with spectacular views of the northern skyline. On a clear night in the summer, you could see the lights from Yankee Stadium. In front of every window, were two deep back leather chairs, perfect for relaxing with a cigar and a cocktail, while taking in the breathtaking views of the city skyline. There was also a separate five star dining room, with one of the city's best wine lists, a walk-in humidor, and a billiards room.

Jake and Diane met Mike and Anita in the lobby of the building and took the private elevator to the club together. Both women looked incredible. Anita was wearing a short black dress, four-inch stiletto heels, her hair teased over half of her lacquered face; very Victoria Beckham. Diane went with perfectly tailored, form-fitting, black wide-leg trousers that showed off her perfect little bum, and a burgundy blouse buttoned seductively low.

As they exited the elevator, the four were greeted by the club manager, Randall Coughlin. As always, Randall was impeccably dressed in a black Armani suit. He stood about 6'2" tall with dark hair and green eyes. He looked like he just stepped out of the pages of GQ magazine.

"Mr. Dumont, very nice to see you again," he said, as he shook Mike's hand. "Will you be joining Mr. Reif in the card game tonight?"

Mike laughed. "Actually, Randall, we are here for dinner."

"Very good, Mr. Dumont. I believe the special tonight is the duck a l'orange."

Mike then introduced Randall to Anita, Jake and Diane.

"Very nice to meet you all," said Randall, shaking Jake's hand. "First time to the Grand Havana Room, ladies?"

"Yes it is," said Diane. "It's absolutely lovely."

"Thank you, Dr. Chase," he replied graciously. "Would anyone care for a tour of our club?"

Anita raised her hand. "Oh, I would."

"Me too," said Diane.

Randall smiled. "Wonderful," he said. "Your usual table is ready, Mr. Dumont. I'll have the hostess take you there."

"Thank you," said Mike. "We'll find our own way."

"Certainly, Mr. Dumont. It was very nice to meet you, Mr. Chase," said Randall, and then he turned to face Diane and Anita. "Ladies, right this way."

As the three left for their tour, Mike and Jake made their way to the club's humidor room at the far end of the bar. The room was about forty square feet, completely enclosed in glass, and the subtle smell of cedar completely filled the area. The walls were lined with hundreds of small boxes, each containing the private stock of cigars belonging to the member whose name appeared on a gold plate affixed to the front.

As they made their way to Mike's box, Jake noticed some very well-known names on some of the gold plates. Mostly Hollywood stars, sports figures and politicians.

"Don't most of these guys live in California?" Jake asked, as Mike opened the door to his humidor.

"Yeah, The Grand Havana Room has a West Coast location similar to this one. I think it's in Beverly Hills. Bi-coastal members have boxes in both clubs so they can enjoy their stogies when they are in town."

Mike pulled out two wooden boxes from his humidor, each with a red "Habana" stamp.

Jake's eyes widened. "Are those what I think they are?"

Mike grinned and handed Jake a cigar. "Yup, contraband. They're the real deal all right. Cohibas, straight from Cuba."

Jake nodded. "I'm impressed," he said, as he inhaled the aroma from the tobacco.

Mike relocked his humidor. "Let's bring a box out to our table. You never know who you might run into at this place."

Jake laughed. "Always thinking business, huh Mike?"

Mike bit down hard on his stogie. "You know me."

By the time they arrived at the table, Diane and Anita were already seated. Anita had ordered a Cosmopolitan and Diane was sipping from a tall glass of sparkling water with lime. In the center of the table was a silver tray holding a scissor-type cigar cutter, a small candle and some thin strips of cedar.

"Hello ladies. How was the tour?" asked Jake, as he sat down next to Diane, and reached for the cigar cutter.

Diane smiled. "Jake, this place is beautiful."

"Yeah, and tell him the best part," murmured Anita, who was sipping her pink concoction from a hand painted martini glass.

Diane's eyes widened. "Oh yeah, guess who's shooting pool in the billiards room?"

"Bill Clinton and Monica Lewinsky," Jake said with a laugh, as he lit a piece of the cedar in the candle and brought the flame to the tip of his cigar.

Diane frowned. "Very funny, Jake. No, it's Donny Osmond."

Just then, Mike burst into hysterical laughter. Jake fought to stay serious, but began cracking up as well. Even Diane and Anita gave a chuckle under protest.

Suddenly, a dark shadow fell over the table. "Hope I'm not interrupting," came the somber voice of Clifford Reif.

Immediately, Mike slid his chair back and stood at attention. "No, not at all, Cliff, please join us," he said, gesturing at an empty seat.

Jake nodded but didn't bother to stand. "Hello, Cliff. Nice to see you again," he said. "This is my wife, Diane. I think you two may have met at a firm function some years ago."

Reif flashed a charming smile. The kind of smile only a man of his age and accomplishment could pull off. "Hello, Dr. Chase. My, time has certainly stood still for you," he said, as he shook Diane's hand. "Oh, and hello, Anita, you look ravishing as usual," he said, kissing her on the cheek.

Mike took his seat and slowly repositioned himself at the table. "Can I order you a drink, Cliff?"

Reif shook his head. "No thank you, Mike. I like to keep my wits about me during these little poker games."

Reif then walked around the table to where Jake was sitting and put his hand firmly on Jake's shoulder. "I'd like to commend you on a job well done this past weekend."

Jake nodded and laid his cigar down on the ashtray. "Thank you, Cliff. It really means a lot coming from you."

Reif smiled and removed his hand from Jake's shoulder. "There is someone I'd like you to meet. I think what he has to say may be quite helpful in your efforts to capture whoever is responsible for this travesty."

There was a look in Reif's eye which gave Jake pause. He looked at his former boss suspiciously. "Sure, Cliff, I'll take any help I can get."

"Well, Jake, his name is Harvey Wallace. He is the Chairman of the Securities and Exchange Commission and he's in the back room right now, trying to figure out a way to win back the money he lost to me last week."

Now Jake was curious. He wondered how the head of the SEC could have any information that would be useful to him.

Reif stepped back to address the entire table. "If you can spare a moment, Jake, I can introduce you to him now."

Jake nodded, and stood. "Certainly."

Reif flashed a final smile. "Sorry to interrupt your evening, ladies. I promise to keep him only for a moment. Wonderful to see you all again."

CHAPTER 35

SEC CHAIRMAN HARVEY WALLACE WAS AS IMPRESSIVE LOOKING as his title might suggest. Upon inspection, one would immediately conclude that he was a man of power and high stature. A company CEO or perhaps a successful Wall Street executive. He was slight in build but stood nearly six feet tall. He had salt and pepper colored hair which was combed back off his face, and wore round metal-framed eyeglasses like Harry Potter's, only smaller. He was sitting at an octagonal shaped poker table, wearing a well tailored pinstripe suit and a dark red tie with small white polka dots; a "power tie."

Reif wrapped his arm around Jake's shoulder, and led him to the card table. "Harvey Wallace, I'd like you to meet F.B.I. Agent Jake Chase."

Wallace looked up at the two men, smiled and stood from his chair. "Very nice to meet you, Agent Chase," he said, extending his hand. "May I call you Jake?"

Jake was taken back by the question. Here was one of the most powerful men in the world shaking his hand and asking for permission to call him by his first name. *Diane's gonna love this one.*

Jake smiled. "Of course."

Wallace sat and gestured to a seat across the table. "Care to sit in on a few rounds, Jake? Watch me win all of Cliff's money," he said, smiling at Reif.

Jake shook his head and politely declined the offer. "I'd love to, Commissioner Wallace, but I'm having dinner with my wife and some friends in the next room."

Wallace chuckled. "Yes, of course…family. Family is very important. Remember that Jake." He paused. "Oh, and please, call me Harvey."

Jake nodded.

Wallace cleared his throat, picked up a deck of cards and began to shuffle. "Let me get to the point then. You understand, son, that what I am about to tell you is completely confidential. Only a few top men at the SEC are privy to this information."

Jake glanced over at Reif who had taken a seat at the poker table. "Yes, I completely understand and thank you for your confidence."

Wallace placed the shuffled deck back on the table and looked up at Jake with great intensity. "A few days before the September 11th attack on the World Trade Center, the SEC noticed a handful of individuals and investment companies shorting airline stock, betting that the stock prices would fall. We thought nothing of it until the planes hit the towers. On September 12th the airline stocks fell greatly and every one of those individuals and companies made money off the tragedy, Jake."

Jake looked over at Reif who was listening to Wallace as well. But he appeared more interested in watching Jake's reaction…trying to sum up his body language…forever the lawyer.

"Needless to say, everyone who made money on shorting airline stock was investigated for a possible tie to Al Qaeda."

Jake lifted a curious eyebrow. "How much money are we talking?"

Wallace nodded. "Good question. We narrowed the investigation to net gains of over one hundred thousand dollars. The biggest gain was a Wall Street investment bank that made nearly two million dollars."

"And?"

Wallace went back to the deck of cards. "Pure coincidence on every last one of them." He looked over at Reif and started to shuffle again. "Now, a few days before the Paramount bombing, we notice this Swiss company shorting Paramount stock."

Jake's pulse began to quicken. "Let me guess, Zurich Holding, LLC?"

"Ah, I see you've done your homework, Jake," Harvey said, smiling at Reif. "We are doing our best to locate anyone associated with Zurich Holding but haven't had much luck. We do know, however, that the money didn't stay in Zurich Holding for more than a few minutes. It was wired dozens of times to banks all over the world to throw us off the scent. Our latest data tells us it may be in a bank in the Cayman Islands."

Jake looked back and forth between Wallace and Reif. "How much, exactly, did Zurich Holding make shorting Paramount stock?"

Wallace began to deal out the cards. "One hundred seventy-five million dollars."

Jake returned to the table, barely able to contain himself and sat down next to Diane. He was totally pumped, wired with adrenaline. The pieces of the puzzle were finally starting to come together. He leaned over and gave Diane a kiss full on the lips. She smiled. Then she rubbed her nose against Jake's like an Eskimo and nodded in the direction of Anita. "We've decided to finish up our drinks and move the party to our apartment in Trump Tower."

Jake leaned back in his chair and reached for his stogie. He took a drag and exhaled a row of delicate smoke rings that sailed across the table and then disappeared into the room. "Sounds great," he replied, looking over at Anita, who was on her third Cosmo and appeared to be having an argument with Mike. He placed the cigar back on the ceramic ashtray and leaned in close to Diane. "I may have just figured out a motive for the Paramount bombing," he whispered into her ear excitedly.

She turned to face him and once again began rubbing her nose against his. "And I may have figured out what they're doing in New York City."

This sounded interesting. Jake pulled back and narrowed his eyes curiously. "Care to share your findings, detective?"

Diane smiled and gestured in the direction of the bar. "See Donny Osmond over there?"

Jake looked up at the bar. There were a group of men drinking espresso and laughing amongst themselves. One of whom was Donny Osmond. "Yeah, I see him."

Diane looked back at Jake. "Well, Donny Osmond and his son are in town because they are presenting at the Tony Awards at Radio City Music Hall next weekend."

"So?"

Diane huffed. "The Tony awards." She paused. "Here in New York City."

Just then, Jake's eyes widened and the smile vanished from his face. "Oh my God, you're right. That's what they're doing in New York. They're planning another attack. They are going to bomb the Music Hall!"

Jake stood from his chair and quickly crushed out his cigar in the ashtray. He looked up in the direction of Mike and Anita, who were still deep in conversation. "I'm so sorry guys, but I've got some pressing business that has just come up which can't wait till morning. You'll have to excuse me."

Mike gave an abbreviated salute and then went back to Anita.

Jake then turned to Diane and with his palms raised to the ceiling, gave her a pleading smile. "Di, I have to meet with Ken immediately and tell him what we've found. He's staying at the...."

Diane raised a hand and cut him off. "I know, Jake. But when you do finally catch the bad guys, you owe me big."

Jake smiled and kissed her on the cheek. "I promise," he said, and then ran for the elevator.

CHAPTER 36

DEVASHER WAS STAYING AT THE GRAND HYATT HOTEL ON 42ND Street in mid-town Manhattan. Jake had sent a detailed email regarding his conversation with Harvey Wallace. Devasher had suggested an immediate in person briefing. Jake had known this would be the case, and was already at the Hyatt when Devasher called, and suggested the Sky Lounge on the second floor.

Jake entered through the revolving doors on 42nd Street and took the escalator to the second floor balcony. Ken was already seated at a table. Behind him a tall row of windows curved into the ceiling like a glass atrium. He was leafing through a thick file and was working on his third Glenfiddich when Jake approached. "Hey," Jake said, as he gave Devasher's shoulder a squeeze before sitting. He spent a moment gazing out at the headlights from the traffic on 42nd street. It seemed peaceful.

Devasher looked up from the file and caught Jake staring off into the distance. He grinned. "Looks a lot different without Momar firing a semi-automatic weapon at you, doesn't it, son?"

Jake looked at Devasher and smiled. "I'd like to get Jarvis on the phone. I copied him on the email I sent you, and he has some interesting thoughts."

Devasher shook his head and went back to flipping pages. Jake looked at him curiously. Then Devasher looked up and flung the file on a nearby chair. "Fine, Fine. Make the call," he said, gesturing toward Jake's PDA.

Jake gave him a sideways stare. He reached down and undid his PDA from his belt and dialed Michael Jarvis' direct line. Within moments, Jarvis' voice was echoing through Jake's phone. "Hey Jarvis, it's Jake Chase. I'm here with Ken Devasher and we'd like to put you on speaker."

Jake then placed the PDA on the table between him and Devasher and pressed a small button. A red light illuminated indicating the phone was set to hands-free mode. "Hey, Jarvis ol' boy, I hope we're not keeping you up."

Jarvis' voice boomed through the PDA loud enough for both men to hear him clearly. "Not at all, Jake. I was still here in my cubicle at Quantico when I got your email."

Jake looked across the table and silently mouthed the word, "cubicle."

Devasher shrugged his shoulders.

Jake laughed. "You need to get yourself a girlfriend, you know that, Jarvis?"

The banter seemed lost on Jarvis. He was silent for a long moment. "Maybe, Jake. But, if I had a girlfriend, I might not have had the time to create a computer virus so kick-ass, that it could bypass all Swiss Bank Security."

Jake raised an eyebrow and looked at Devasher. "What are you saying?"

"I am saying that fifteen minutes ago I gained access to all corporate and bank records regarding one Zurich Holding, LLC."

Jake reached into his blazer pocket and took out a small note pad and a pen. "That's incredible," he said nodding at Devasher. "What have you found out?"

Jake began to make notes as Jarvis continued. "Well, Zurich Holding, LLC is now a completely defunct corporation. Zurich's board of directors consisted of three brothers from Dubai, all independently wealthy." Jarvis paused. "Family money. Their names are Dante, Shavka and Nurillo Irgashev. Dante is that guy who blew his brains out on Fox News. Awesome!"

Jake shook his head in amazement. "This is great work, Jarvis!"

"Thanks, Jake. Unfortunately we didn't get as lucky with a match on the sketch of that guy from Kennedy Airport. The computers are not coming up with a name. Very difficult with a sketch.

Now if you had a photo, like the one you sent me of that Dante guy, the chances of a hit would be much better."

Jake closed his note pad and slid it back into his blazer pocket. "I don't think that's gonna be necessary. I'm certain the man in the sketch is either Shavka or Nurillo, and if it is Shavka, then Nurillo Irgashev is the man who is responsible for the Paramount bombing."

"Oh yeah, guys, one more thing," said Jarvis excitedly. "For about fifteen seconds Zurich Holding had one hundred seventy-five million dollars transferred into their Swiss Bank Account. That makes them almost as rich as you, huh, Jake?"

"Very funny. Any idea where the money is now?"

"Well, I'm working on it. Seems they bounced it in and out of banks all over the world. It's gonna take some time, but I'll track it down!"

Jake nodded and glanced at Devasher who was finishing the last of his Glenfiddich. "Okay, thanks for your help. Call me as soon as you find something out."

"Will do."

Jake picked up his PDA from the center of the table. He powered it down and reconnected it to his belt. He looked over at Devasher. "What do you think?"

Devasher nodded solemnly. His eyes were shadowed and he looked tired. "Well, I guess you were right, buddy boy. This was nothing more than a heist."

Jake narrowed his eyes and cocked his head sideways. "Yeah, but here's what I don't get. If you're from Dubai, and you're rich, what are you doing dropping a bomb on LA and shorting Paramount stock? You already have more money than you know what to do with."

Devasher looked up from his glass of melting ice. "Greed, Jake. You remember. It's one of the deadly sins."

Jake nodded. "I suppose. But why come to New York then? Why not get as far away as possible?"

Devasher shrugged.

Jake leaned into the table. "Hear me out for a moment. What if it goes beyond money? What if there is something else?"

Devasher looked confused. "I am not following you."

Jake was quiet for a moment as he desperately searched for a way to piece together the puzzle. Then he spoke. "Nurillo chose to come to New York where we now believe his brother Shavka had been waiting for him when he landed at Kennedy Airport. He could have gone anywhere in the world to avoid capture, but he chose New York City, where the likelihood of getting caught is increased considerably."

"So?"

Jake grinned. "Ken, are you a Donny Osmond fan?"

CHAPTER 37

AT 11:00 PM THE PRODUCER WAS SITTING AT HIS DESK, MAKING notes on a set of detailed blueprints. Earlier that day he had made a trip to the New York Public Library on Fifth Avenue. The young librarian had been eager to help him search the library archives, and in less than an hour, he had copies of everything he needed to take down the entire Radio City building.

Suddenly, there was a loud banging on the door. So loud in fact that it startled The Producer and made him jump. *Not again.*

He closed his eyes and let out a deep sigh. Carefully, he folded the blueprints and placed them inside the desk. He reached for his 9mm and switched off the safety catch. As he stood, he felt a sharp pain at the base of his neck, causing him to wince.

Once again, there was banging at the door. This time even louder. "Nuri, its Shavka. Open up."

The Producer exhaled and re-engaged the safety on his gun. He placed his hand on the back of his neck and attempted to squeeze away some of the tension. But it was useless. He looked through the small viewfinder and saw Shavka standing in the hall, growing impatient. He had a black garment bag over his shoulder and was holding a small package. The Producer undid the lock and opened the door. "Why didn't you use your key?"

Shavka shook his head in frustration. "You are so consumed with your revenge that you didn't notice that I left it on the table when you threw me out this morning."

The Producer glanced at the table and frowned. "So you did."

"Nuri, I am leaving tonight for the Cayman Islands. I will meet you there next week. I don't share the same hatred you do, my brother."

The Producer placed his hands on his brother's shoulders. "But it is you who they took advantage of, Shavka, not me. How can you not want your revenge?"

Shavka brushed his brother's arms away. "Maybe I was naïve, Nuri or, maybe just drawn in by the allure of Hollywood. Either way, you recaptured our money. All of it. There is one hundred seventy-five million waiting for us on Grand Cayman Island."

The Producer let out a sound of disgust. "I told you, Shavka, it's not about the money. They must pay for the shame they have caused our family, and now they must pay for the death of our brother."

Shavka's shoulders dropped. "They have paid, Nuri. Hundreds of lives were lost at Paramount. How many more have to die for you to feel vindicated? You told me it was over when you killed Jack Shepard two years ago."

The Producers eyes narrowed as he became enraged. "That fuck, Shepard, deserved to die. It was Shepard who set up that deal in the first place. He makes sixty million dollars and you lose our entire fortune. My only regret is that I didn't make him suffer longer before I shot him in the head."

Shavka shook his head in defeat. "Well, it's over for me, brother," he said, handing over the package he had been holding. "We just received another email from DD; it is not safe for us in New York anymore. He wants to meet us in the Caymans immediately. I came here with the hopes that you would choose not to use this and join me there tonight, but I can see that is not the case."

The Producer set the package on the desk and turned to face his brother one last time. "You will never understand, Shavka."

"Well, I truly hope that once you're done with Radio City, you will have satisfied your thirst for vengeance," he said, as he turned and walked into the hall. "The device is in that package, along with ID and passport. Goodbye, brother."

The Producer closed the door, engaged the dead bolt and attached the chain lock. With his eyes closed he rested his head against the wall. He then took a deep breath and exhaled. As he made his way back to the desk, he looked at the package and smiled. He thought about what his brother had said. He reached into his brief case and pulled out a manila folder. To truly satisfy his thirst for revenge, there was still one more person that had to die. He opened the folder and pulled out a photograph. It was a picture of Diane Shepard Chase.

CHAPTER 38

AT 1:30 AM JAKE WAS WALKING ALONG FIFTH AVENUE IN THE direction of Trump Tower. He was still several blocks away but could see the enormous skyscraper ahead in the distance. The night air was crisp and it made him feel alive. Finally, the case was starting to make sense to him. The puzzle was beginning to come together, to take form. And, as Devasher had put it, that form was greed. Jake smiled. Life was good.

After walking a few more blocks, Jake finally arrived at the Trump Tower residence entrance on Fifty-Sixth Street. Trump is an eighty story luxury high-rise, located in one of the most exclusive neighborhoods in New York City. It's a place where the very rich live and shop. There are five levels in the grand atrium where there are some of the world's most exclusive stores. There are marble floors, mirrored walls and a two-story high cascading waterfall. Pure opulence.

Jack had bought the place in the mid-eighties when he was still working on Wall Street. He and Donald Trump were good friends and had been involved in a few real estate deals together. In fact, "The Donald" had actually said a few words at Jack's funeral.

Jake approached the entrance and was greeted by a short, well-dressed doorman. His uniform resembled those worn by the guards at Buckingham Palace. "Good evening, Mr. Chase."

Jake smiled. "Good morning, actually."

The man looked down at his watch and frowned. "Dr. Chase and her guests are already upstairs," he said, as he held open the door.

Jake nodded and made his way to the elevator.

The 8700 square foot apartment took up one half of the sixty-third floor. At one time, the other half had been owned by, Doug Flutie while he played football for the USFL's New Jersey Generals, which Trump also owned.

Jake put his key in the lock, quietly opened the door, and stepped inside the apartment. "Hello, anyone home?" he whispered, as he made his way through the entrance.

"We're in here, Jake," came Diane's voice from the kitchen.

Jake set his keys down on a brass table beside the front door and hung his blazer in the foyer closet. He gave a huge stretch and walked into the kitchen. Mike and Diane were leaning over the snack bar feasting on a bowl of trail mix. Jake nodded at Diane. "Where's Anita?"

Just then he heard an awful moan coming from the powder room.

Mike looked up bleary-eyed. "Dry heaves," he said, and then took a gulp from an almost empty bottle of Heineken.

Jake looked at Diane, who just shrugged. "I held her hair for a half hour."

Jake looked back at Mike and then headed in the direction of the powder room. "How long has she been in here?" he shouted from the hallway.

"She's fine, Jake," replied Diane. "We check on her every fifteen minutes."

Jake opened the door to the powder room cautiously, afraid of what he might find. He looked down at the floor and shook his head. Instinctively he made a tisk tisk sound with the tip of his tongue. Anita was hunched over the commode, gripping it tightly with both hands. Every few seconds she would lunge forward and make a loud heaving sound. He was amazed that such a pretty little thing could make such an awful noise.

Jake ran some cool water over a washcloth. "Here you go, baby," he said, as he brushed the cool cloth across her face.

Her makeup was smudged, and her hair a tangled mess. But, Anita Dumont was still an attractive woman. She slowly opened her eyes and gave Jake a distant stare. "Oh, Jakey, I missed you so much," she slurred, and then lunged forward headfirst into the toilet and made that horrible noise again.

Jake shook his head. "Yes, Anita, and I missed you too, darling."

Anita placed her elbows on either side of the seat and slowly pried her head from the bowl. "You know what, Jake? You and Diane are so perfect together. You look so much in love all the time."

Jake continued to rub the cloth across Anita's forehead. "Yes Anita, and so do you and Mike."

Suddenly the distant look vanished. She looked more deliberate now, more focused. She tried to lift herself up, but fell backwards onto her butt. She paused momentarily, then pushed her hair back off her face and propped herself up with her back resting against the door.

Jake fought not to laugh.

She swallowed hard and pointed an unsteady finger in his direction. "He's fucking someone at work. Someone from that damn law firm."

Jake couldn't believe what he was hearing. All thoughts of laughter had quickly fled his conscience. "Come on, Anita. Not Mike. I've known him for years. He wouldn't do that."

Anita let out a sarcastic laugh. "Don't be so sure, Jake. You don't know him as well as you think you do. He's a liar. Don't they teach you guys that in law school? How to lie."

Jake shook his head in disagreement. "Okay Anita, let's get you to bed."

Anita slowly closed her eyes and a smile came to her face. "Mmm, you're so sweet, Jake," she said, and then she leaned forward and kissed him on the cheek. "Jake Chase, everyone's hero. No, I like it here," she said, as she lowered her head and rested it on the marble floor. "It's so nice and cool," she muttered, as she began to fade.

Jake stood up and rested the wash cloth on the sink. "Okay, Anita, but I am coming back in a little bit to bring you to bed."

"Oh, I would like that," she whispered, her lips poised in a smile as she drifted off to dreamland.

"No, that's not what I meant," Jake quickly retorted, but she was already sound asleep.

He looked down at her and smiled. She was beautiful. Even passed out on our bathroom floor, Anita looked beautiful. Jake shook his head. Who would cheat on her? Not Mike, that was for sure. Just the insecure babble of a girl who's had too many cosmopolitans.

Jake shut the lights and closed the door. "Sleep well," he said. "Things will be better in the morning. They always are."

When Jake returned to the kitchen Mike appeared to be knocking back his fourth Heineken and Diane, who'd finished the bowl of trail mix, was searching for another bag. "How's she doing?" asked Mike.

"Passed out," Jake replied, as he walked up to Diane and gave her a huge hug.

Diane smiled. "What was that for?"

Jake shrugged. "Just felt like it, that's all."

Diane opened a cabinet over the stove and took out a small cardboard box. "Hey, I'm making some chamomile tea. Any takers?"

Jake nodded. "I'd love some," he said, as he fell back onto one of the stools at the snack bar.

"Not me," said Mike, as he polished off the last of his beer. "I'd better get sleeping beauty to bed."

Diane gave him a mournful look. "I left fresh towels and soap in the green bedroom for you and Anita," she replied, as she set two ceramic mugs down on the snack bar in front of Jake.

Mike stood up and had to steady himself against the bar. He carefully picked up his empty beer bottles, and gently placed them in a recycling bin by the sink. "Thanks. Goodnight," he said, as he tentatively made his way down the hall.

The moment Mike was out of site, Jake grabbed Diane by her hips, swung her around and kissed her full on the lips.

"Jake, what's gotten into you?"

Jake grinned and held her close. "You know what I want to do right now, Diane?"

Diane laughed. "Oh, I can imagine."

Jake shook his head. "No, it's not that at all. I mean, its 2:30 in the morning and Devasher and the rest of the F.B.I. are out tracking down the bad guys, and all I want to do is sit here with you, drink chamomile tea, and pick out a name for our baby."

"Oh my, Jake, I do love you."

CHAPTER 39

IT WAS NEARLY 5:00 AM AND THE PRODUCER LAY AWAKE IN BED listening to the rain as it beat down against the window of his hotel room. The room was dark and he hadn't slept. A brutal combination of remorse for his brother's death and the revenge he would reap forced his brain to stay occupied and kept him awake. He slowly stood and braced himself for the familiar pain. It felt like a sharp knife relentlessly stabbing his neck and spine. He grimaced and made his way to his desk.

"Come back to bed, baby," cooed the tired voice of Brianna Koe. "It's only five in the morning."

The Producer clenched his teeth tightly, and then forced a smile. "Princess, I have work to do. Go back to sleep."

Brianna buried her head deep into the goosedown pillow and let out a big yawn. "Okay, wake me at eleven. I have a noon rehearsal over at Radio City that I can't be late for."

The Producer didn't reply. He closed the door to the bedroom and made his way to his desk. Suddenly, there was a bright flash of light that momentarily illuminated the dark room. It was immediately followed by a loud clap of thunder that echoed in the distance, off the tall New York City buildings. The Producer could hear the pulse of the rain quicken as a howling wind swept through the streets below. He turned on a small desk lamp and reached for the package his brother had given him. With a letter opener, he sliced open the top and carefully folded back the flaps. He smiled. "Oh, Shavka, you have outdone yourself, brother."

He reached into the box and took out what appeared to be a woman's necklace. He held it to the light and meticulously inspected it from all sides. It was made of turquoise-colored stones, all strung together by a thin silver wire. It was large and meant to be worn loosely looped around the neck. Although the necklace looked like it was purchased from a gift shop on a tropical island, the stones were hollow and filled with enough C-4 to take down a small building.

The Producer carefully set the necklace down on the desk. He reached back into the box and took out a small radio transmitter very similar to the one he had used days earlier. Suddenly, The Producer heard a voice and it startled him.

"Whatcha got there?" asked Brianna, who was standing in the darkness wearing only a pair of g-string panties.

The Producer quickly slid the necklace and the remote back into the box and covered the top. Slowly, he turned to face her. "It is a gift for you, my love."

Brianna gushed. "Oh Ali, really?"

The Producer nodded. "Yes, Brianna, it's a surprise. It's for your big night on the red carpet."

Brianne raised a curious eyebrow. "Can I see it?"

The Producer smiled and shook his head. "It wouldn't be a surprise then, now would it?"

"Oh Ali," she said, pouting.

The Producer leaned back against the desk and folded his arms in front of him. "That look may get you what you want on that little TV show of yours, but it won't work with me."

Brianna smiled seductively. "Well, maybe this will," she said, as she pulled off her panties, tossed them at his feet and ran back to the bedroom.

The Producer grinned. "Yes, a little snack before my drive to the country would be perfect," he said to himself, as he locked the box in the hotel safe and made his way to the bedroom.

CHAPTER 40

FOR THE THIRD TIME IN AS MANY MINUTES STEPHANIE KEATS looked down at her wrist and checked the time. That motion had become routine, practically a habit. It would always start about twenty minutes before any meeting Brianna needed to be at, and ended whenever she finally arrived, if she arrived at all. Stephanie found herself doing it compulsively, even on days when she wasn't wearing a watch. Ten past one, this isn't good, she thought, as she nervously gazed up and down 6th Avenue for some sign of Brianna. Well at least the rain had stopped.

"Where the fuck is she?" raved a manic Travis Cole, the executive producer of this years Tony Awards. "I've been waiting on this goddamn sidewalk for almost a bloody hour now!"

Travis Cole was Hollywood elite. He produced and/or directed everything from television commercials to sitcoms to motion picture blockbusters. Everything he touched made hundreds of millions of dollars, and everyone in Hollywood wanted to work with him. He was tinseltown's soup du jour.

He currently had three commercials slated for next years Super Bowl, two major sitcoms being released in the fall, and a major motion picture with an unlimited budget from MGM.

Although he stood only 5'4", had a rather high-pitched voice and a pronounced English accent, he only dated models and starlets. In fact, according to the tabloids, his latest conquest was supermodel Gisele Bundchen, whom he had been seen clubbing with all week.

"She'll be here any minute. There was a family emergency," retorted Stephanie, as she nervously sipped from her Starbucks coffee.

Travis pointed a deliberate finger. "That's bullshit and you know it Stephanie," he screamed, as he turned and walked head-on into some poor intern, spilling a tray of Venti Vanilla iced coffees all over her.

Travis threw his hands in the air. "Fuck! That's twice today. Someone get a goddamn mop!" he yelled, ignoring the stunned intern who stood motionless, drenched in coffee.

"I'm so sorry, Mr. Cole," she said tearfully, but Travis Cole was already marching in the direction of the building. "I'm such a klutz," mumbled the intern, as she dropped to her knees and began picking up the coffee cups from the sidewalk.

Stephanie knelt beside the stunned intern and placed a hand gently on her shoulder. "You don't have to apologize to him. That was completely his fault."

The intern didn't bother to look up. "Yes, but that's Travis Cole. He's a legend at New York University Film School."

"N.Y.U Film? Are you a student there?" asked Stephanie, as she helped gather the coffee cups from the floor.

The intern nodded. "Just finished my first year. They gave me this internship. Now they probably won't let me back."

"Don't be silly, of course they will." Stephanie laughed as both women stood to their feet.

The intern's eyes widened as she quickly brought her hand to her open mouth. "Oh my God, you're Stephanie Keats."

Stephanie smiled warmly. "Yes, and you're drenched. Let's get you some dry clothes," she said, motioning in the direction of Brianna's trailer.

Nervously, the intern repeated, "You're Stephanie Keats. You're Brianna Koe's personal assistant."

"And you are?"

The intern froze. She took a moment to gather herself, took a deep breath and exhaled. "Sydney. Sydney Banks."

"Well, nice to meet you, Sydney Banks," replied Stephanie, as she reached out her hand.

"Oh, yes of course," said Sydney, as she fumbled with the empty coffee cups, shifting them all into her left hand. "It's an honor to meet you Ms. Keats," she said, as she reached out her wet hand. "I am a huge Brianna Koe fan. Have been since the Mickey Mouse Club actually."

Stephanie shook her head. "Wow, the Mickey Mouse Club, huh? Brie will love to hear that. Now come on, let's get you cleaned up. And please stop calling me Ms. Keats. My name is Stephanie."

The intern shrugged her shoulders. "Oh, okay…Stephanie. It's just that Keats has such a nice sound to it. Reminds me of the poet, John Keats."

Stephanie looked at the intern and smiled. "You know, Sydney, I'm starting to like you."

Just then, both women were startled by the sound of screeching brakes as a dark blue Mercedes SL65 AMG convertible halted within inches from where they were standing. Although the top was up on the Mercedes, Stephanie could see that the passenger was Brianna, and she was passionately kissing the dark-haired driver.

The intern squinted against the glare from the car window but could not make out who was inside. "Is that her?" she asked nervously.

Stephanie shook her head disapprovingly. "Yes, that's her all right," she said, as she tapped on the window of the Mercedes.

Undeterred by the tapping, Brianna continuing to force her tongue into the mouth of the driver. She then raised her hand behind her and pressed her index finger against the glass, suggesting she needed another minute.

Stephanie backed away from the car. "Yup, that's our little Mouseketeer."

Somehow, Stephanie's job had become making one excuse after another for Brianna and her antics. It wasn't what she signed up for and it was beginning to get on her nerves. After all, she didn't graduate second in her class from The Wharton School of Business to go on midnight tequila runs for a spoiled little brat. Even if that brat was on the fast track to Hollywood superstardom.

Suddenly, Brianna jumped out of the car and watched as it sped off along 6th Avenue. She then turned and faced her assistant. "Hey, Stephie-poo."

"My God, Brie, did you get any sleep at all last night?"

Brianna grinned. "Sleep? Who needs sleep when you have these," she replied, as she put two pills into her mouth and reached for Stephanie's coffee.

Stephanie sighed. "Look Brie, you're over an hour late for rehearsal. Travis is pissed."

Brianna's eyes narrowed. "Travis. Are you joking? I know how to calm Travis down."

"Yes, well I am sure his wife and...."

"What the fuck smells like vanilla?" demanded Brianna.

"Oh yes, I almost forgot. Brie, I'd like you to meet a big fan of yours," said Stephanie, as she put her arm around Sydney. "Brie, this is...."

"Travis!" shouted Brianna with a smile, as she pushed past the two women, knocking the empty coffee cups back to the sidewalk. "I haven't seen you since Cannes."

Travis frowned. "Yes, and if I remember correctly, you were late there too," he replied, as he crushed out a cigarette beneath his boot.

"Oh, Travis, don't be such a monkey," she said, as she kissed him softly on the lips.

Travis laughed sarcastically. "A monkey? We have less than four days to get ready for the red carpet ceremonies and Hollywood Diaries wants you to be spot on."

Brianna smiled. "Oh you're such a worrier, Travis."

Travis shook his head. He looked serious. "No, you're the one that should be worried. After all, you're the one going on national television, baby doll, not me."

Brianna's smiled was suddenly replaced by a look of concern that she couldn't hide. "Okay, I'm all yours Travis. Where do we start?"

Travis reached over and grabbed a clump of Brianna's hair, looked at it disapprovingly and let it fall to her shoulders. "We start by working with a stylist to get some of those knots out of your hair. Then we'll practice interview techniques. The way I like them done! You'll be interviewing over fifty celebrities from right outside these doors."

Brianna sighed in defeat. "Ok, Travis. You're the boss."

CHAPTER 41

WITH THE SATELLITE NAVIGATION SYSTEM GUIDING THE CAR, THE Producer raced the SL65 along the winding streets of Bedford, New York. *"Next left turn, onto Penwood Avenue,"* came the female voice, through the car speakers, leading him to the home of Dr. Diane Chase.

As The Producer turned onto Penwood, he opened the glove box and pulled out his 9mm semiautomatic. He knew he had a full clip of ammunition, but checking the clip had become a habit since Paramount.

"Second right turn."

The Producer turned onto Farmhouse Lane, leaving behind the paved roads for the more "charming" dirt covered horse-trails for which Bedford was famous.

What a joke, thought The Producer, as the car bounced along the narrow uneven terrain of the horse trail. The trees that lined the trail were still wet from the rain, and their heavy leaves caused the branches to sag. It created a glistening green tunnel to drive through. The effect was beautiful but was lost on The Producer.

"Next right turn and destination is ahead, on the left."

Suddenly, The Producer's PDA began to vibrate. He reached over and picked it up. It was an email from Shavka.

Nuri,

I'm at the Hyatt on Grand Cayman Island. Everything went according to plan. One hundred seventy-five million dollars is here waiting for us in an offshore account—Number: 001-7589-484-6 at Deutsche Bank (Cayman) Limited. *It is under the name: Saudi Investments, LLC. I hope you will reconsider and join me here without any more bloodshed. We have our victory! Any more killing is pure madness.*

In a rage, The Producer flung his PDA to the floor of the Mercedes. "Madness!" he screamed, as the back of the car fishtailed around a tight curve. He was driving erratically now, speeding down the narrow roads. "The madness has only just begun!" he swore, as the car screeched to a halt.

"Destination."

The Producer left the SL65 parked on the side of the road about a hundred yards from the driveway gates. He knew the car wouldn't cause suspicion, even in Bedford. After all, a two hundred thousand dollar car was not out of the ordinary for the neighborhood.

It didn't take long for him to bypass the security panel on the wrought iron gates and make his way up the long driveway. As he cautiously approached the house, he turned off the safety on the 9mm and placed it in the inside pocket of his blazer. He was pretty sure that he had gone undetected as he made his way to the back of the home.

The Producer nodded in approval. "Ah Jack, I see you've spent my money well," he said, as he peered through the French doors and into the kitchen. The house appeared to be empty but he didn't mind. It would give him an opportunity to look around and get the lay of the land. Killing Diane and her F.B.I. agent husband was not something he wanted to do quickly. He wanted to take his time, make them suffer, as he wished he had done with Jack. He wanted to savor the moment and indeed he was doing just that.

The Producer reached for his cell phone and saw his own reflection in the glass screen. The effect was weird. His mind drifted off to two years earlier when he had broken into Jack's Malibu beach house.

"Nuri, what brings you to Malibu, old boy?" Jack had said, smug as usual, apparently not the least bit concerned about the gun pointed at his head.

"Shut the fuck up! How dare you mock me?" The Producer had screamed.

"It's just business, baby. You need to learn how to lose, Nuri." He pointed to the empty glass he was holding, and said, "Now be a sport and go fetch us some scotch."

"You cheated my family out of over a hundred and fifty million dollars. You are the one who is going to lose now, Jack," said The Producer as he turned off the safety catch on his 9mm.

"Come on, Nuri, you don't have the balls to use that thing. God knows if you had any balls you might not have lost your entire family fortune to me and Evans over at Paramount."

"In my country, business is conducted with honor!"

"Spare me the honor speech, Nuri. Your brother Shavka tried to fuck every starlet and model in LA. Heard he gave a few of them a venereal disease, too. Maybe he should have paid a little more attention to business and a little less attention to his cock. That would have been honorable. Now put that gun away before you hurt yourself, Nuri, and for Christ's sake, take a shower. You smell like a fucking cab driver."

As Jack turned to walk to the balcony, The Producer pulled the trigger and put a bullet in the back of his head, splattering blood and brains all over the sliding glass doors.

Yes indeed. The Producer remembered every word and every detail as if it were yesterday and now it was time to finish the job!

He dialed the number to the Bedford house and listened as the answering machine picked up the call. *You have reached (914) 555-3738, the home of Jake and Diane Chase. At the sound of the tone, please leave your name and a return number and we will call you back as soon as possible. Thank you.*

The Producer grinned. Just as he thought, no one was home. He placed his phone inside his blazer pocket and took out a pair of bifocals and small leather pouch. He placed the glasses on his face so that they rested on the tip of his nose. Next, he unzipped the pouch and took two elongated picks. They looked like something you'd find in a dentist's office. He inserted both picks into the lock and smiled. This was going to be easier than he thought. After a few seconds he heard a click and the lock was opened. *Piece of cake.*

He returned the tools to the pouch but left it unzipped. Cautiously, he turned the handle on the French door and entered. Suddenly, a loud, high-pitched, beeping sound echoed throughout the home. The security system had been engaged, and was now counting down the seconds before the alarm would sound.

The Producer wasn't concerned. He calmly walked to the main panel by the front door, and set the pouch down on the floor in front of him. He removed the panels plastic faceplate and unhooked four internal wires: red, green, yellow and black. He then reached down into the pouch and removed a small black box. It was no bigger than a cell phone, with an LCD screen on the front, and four red clips on the side. He adjusted his bifocals and went to work.

He turned the device on and the LCD screen illuminated with four digits: 0 0 0 0. He then pulled back one of the red clips, exposing a pin-sized hole. Next, he inserted the black wire from the alarm panel into the hole and pushed the clip back into position, thus locking the wire into the device. He repeated this procedure with the remaining three wires.

Once the final wire was secured into the device, the first 0 displayed on the LCD screen began quickly scrambling through random numbers between 1 and 9. After a few seconds, it settled on the number 9, the first number of the security code. The Producer smiled.

With the number 9 set on the LCD screen in the first position, the second 0 began scrambling until it locked in on the number 4 as the loud beeping continued echoing throughout the home.

Within seconds of the alarm sounding and alerting the Bedford Police of a break-in, the last digit locked into position on the device. Instantly the house became quiet. The indicator screen on the alarm panel now read: Alarm disengaged. The Producer grinned.

He then disconnected the device and placed it back in the pouch, but not before making a mental note of the four digit security code. So as not to leave behind traces of his visit, he carefully reconnected the wires and closed the face plate. "Now let's get a look at this place, shall we?"

As he made his way between rooms, The Producer kept a log on his PDA. He detailed floor plans, room sizes, contents and anything else that struck him as noteworthy. Carefully and meticulously he wandered throughout the large home imagining how he would torture and eventually murder Jack Sheppard's only daughter. When he entered the den, he was immediately drawn to the leather-topped writing table and Jack's collection of Hollywood memorabilia. "What have we here?" he asked, as he picked up the picture in front of the Bellagio fountains. Suddenly, he heard a door open in the direction of the kitchen. "Maybe I won't have to make a second trip after all," he said, as he replaced the photograph and pulled out his 9mm.

The voice was growing nearer. "Hola, Senora Chase?" came a female voice from the next room.

The Producer quietly made his way to the adjoining door and peered into the kitchen. He released the safety on his gun and watched from behind the door as an elderly couple made their way through the kitchen towards the den. The Producer frowned. *Goddamn servants.*

The man and woman appeared to be very confused and were pointing to the unlocked door. "Senora Chase? Estas aqui?"

The Producer's eyes narrowed as he watched the two quickly approaching the door and quickly approaching their untimely demise.

"Vamos, Maria," said the man. "You are hearing things again."

The woman nodded but still seemed unconvinced. "Maybe you are right, Carlos. But while we are here, let me get the laundry," Maria said, continuing in the direction of the den. "Come, Carlos. I could use your muscles carrying the heavy basket."

Maria noticed The Producer first. She gasped and threw her hands in the air.

"Por favor, NO!"

CHAPTER 42

TOMMY IF IT'S A BOY AND CYNTHIA IF IT'S A GIRL WERE THE names Jake and Diane had finally settled on as they drank chamomile tea and watched the sun rise over midtown Manhattan.

Diane yawned and gave a big stretch from under a goosedown comforter on the living room couch. The two had set up their baby-naming command post there hours earlier, and at one point had almost settled on Bray for a boy and Tuesday for a girl. Jake immediately thought of that spooky little girl from the Addams Family, but Diane insisted that her name was Wednesday. Either way, they finally agreed on Tommy and Cynthia and spared the child a lifetime of teasing. "Do you have time for breakfast, Jake?" called Diane.

Jake emerged from the bedroom. He was wearing a pair of shorts, a tee shirt and running sneakers. "I'm going to head down to the health club and work out a bit."

Diane smiled seductively. "You know, Jake, having sex burns as many calories as a cardio workout at the gym. And it's a lot more fun."

Jake grinned and knelt down beside the couch. He began brushing Diane's tangled hair off her face. "Is that right?"

"Oh yes, it's a fact," she replied, looking ever so serious. "Well documented, actually." She then lifted the comforter, looked at Jake and raised an eyebrow. She was completely naked. "It's in all the medical journals."

Jake eyes widened. "Sounds like a win/win to me," he replied and then kicked off his sneakers and climbed under the comforter.

As the yellow taxi pulled in front of Radio City Music Hall, Jake knew immediately that securing the Tony Awards against another possible bombing was going to be no easy task. The paparazzi were already running wild and it was only Friday morning.

There were reporters and camera crews everywhere. The entire corner of 50th Street and 6th Avenue was lined with news vans from every entertainment show imaginable. Antennas and satellite dishes were jutting into the sky like flagpoles.

Just then, a hand slammed down hard on the car's windshield and the loud noise startled both Jake and the driver. "Hey, asshole! Ya can't park here," shouted a small angry man.

The driver didn't seem affected one way or the other. He just shrugged his shoulders and turned to face Jake. "Six bucks."

Jake handed over the money and exited the cab. He watched as the car peeled out and sped down the avenue. Jake laughed and began walking in the direction of the Radio City building, only to be accosted by the same little man who'd punched the taxi. "Look, dickhead, all reporters and camera crews behind the yellow tape. Or can't you read?"

Jake looked down at the little man and then in the direction he was pointing. He scanned the area just outside the music hall, but found nothing. "I'm sorry, I don't see...."

The man threw his arms in the air and let out a huff. "The bloody pole. On the bloody pole."

Jake squinted at the pole and noticed a hand-written sign. It was done in red marker and had been attached to the pole near the entrance to the building. It was completely surrounded by reporters and camera crews milling about aimlessly.

ALL REPORTERS AND CAMRA CREWS
MUST STAY BEHIND THE YELLOW TAPE!

Jake returned his attention to the little man. "Yes, well, I see that, but my name is Jake...."

Suddenly, the man exploded. "I don't give a rat's ass what your name is. I'm Travis Cole and I'm in charge of this production. All reporters behind the yellow tape," he screamed, as he turned a bright shade of red.

"No," Jake said with a slight laugh. "I don't think you understand. I'm with the...."

"No, you don't understand dickhead." Travis Cole said, as he lunged forward and shoved his hands against Jake's chest. However, the effort fell short as the man's arms buckled and he fell to the floor. Immediately, Jake grabbed the man's hand, twisted it behind his back and pushed him down to the sidewalk face first.

With Travis Cole's head pressed hard against the pavement, and his arm firmly behind his back, Jake said, "Now, let's try this again. My name is Jake Chase. I'm with the F.B.I. and I have a two o'clock meeting with Chairman Daryl Spencer."

"Second floor, third office on the left," Cole replied as best he could, with his mouth pushed against the ground.

"And, another thing. You spelled camera wrong...dickhead."

"Agent Chase, please come in," announced Chairman Spencer from behind the blizzard of papers that were scattered on his large mahogany desk. He peered over the top of his glasses, and gestured in the direction of a small leather couch and two matching chairs. They were set neatly under a row of windows, and were arranged to form a handsomely decorated sitting area in the corner of the room. One of the windows was open and a light breeze caused the curtains to flutter.

Daryl Spencer was dressed in a dark blue blazer, tan slacks and a bright yellow tie. His hair was combed back off his forehead and he wore a neatly trimmed goatee. As chairman of Madison Square Garden, he was in charge of all MSGs many subsidiaries, which included, among other ventures, Radio City Music Hall.

Jake smiled. "Thank you, Chairman Spencer," he said, as he took a seat in one of the wingbacked chairs.

Spencer let out a long drawn-out sigh. Appearing frustrated, he scooped together the papers, shuffled them together and shoved them into a thick file. "Please, call me Spence," he said, walking in Jake's direction with his hand extended.

Jake stood and the two men shook hands. Spencer motioned to Jake's chair and waited for him to sit before falling back into the leather couch. He let out another sigh, and then leaned forward to the glass table separating the couch from the chairs. He opened the lid of a decorative humidor and then smiled. It seemed that all of the grief caused by the paperwork had been magically erased by whatever was on the inside of that box. "Cigar?" he asked, tilting the humidor in Jake's direction.

Jake shook his head. "No, thank you, Spence."

Spencer nodded, and then gazed inside the open box rubbing his chin with a look of concern. "So Jake, Mayor Bloomberg tells me you have reason to believe that the terrorists responsible for the Paramount bombing may be planning to strike again here in New York City."

Jake leaned forward in his seat. "Yes, well, more than that, actually."

Suddenly, the smile returned to Spencer's face. "Ah, here we go," he said, appearing relieved. "Opus X. Forty-five bucks apiece. Sure I can't tempt you, Jake, old boy?"

"No really, that's quite all right," Jake replied and then paused. "As I was saying, I have credible evidence to suggest that during the Tony Awards, the person or persons responsible for the Paramount bombing are going to strike again."

Spencer cackled. "Nonsense, Jake," he said, as he slowly twirled the tip of the cigar in front of a flame from an expensive-looking lighter. "They caught that guy in LA. Blew his brains out on national TV."

Jake leaned in closer. "Yes, but he wasn't acting alone. Our theory is that there are three men responsible for the Paramount bombing, possibly more. All from Dubai."

Spencer coughed out a mouthful of smoke. "Did I hear you right, Jake? All from Dubai?"

Jake nodded. "Yes. We believe one of the men may be in the Cayman Islands and the other is here in New York, planning another attack. An attack on Radio City, the night of the Tony Awards."

Spencer cocked his head. "Come on, Jake, how can you know that?"

"It's just a hunch."

Spencer grinned as he relaxed into the leather couch. "Do you know who I am, Jake? I didn't get to the position I'm in by acting impulsively on speculations." Then he clenched the stogie between his teeth and gazed out the window. He laughed and repeated Jake's words. "A hunch."

Jake shook his head in amazement. Somehow he had expected more from a man like Daryl Spencer. It's what he and Diane refer to as "The Britney Spears Syndrome."

Officer, do you know who I am?

Oh gosh, you're Britney Spears. I'm so sorry, Ms. Spears. Please forgive me for pulling you over for driving your Mercedes 110 miles per hour with your infant son on your lap. Um, and Ms. Spears, can you autograph this? It's for my daughter.

As much as Jake hated people with "Britney Spears Syndrome," he knew how to play their game. Appeal to their ego.

"Of course I know who you are. You're Daryl Spencer, CEO of Megavision. You run Madison Square Garden, the Hartford Civic Center and Radio City Music Hall."

Spencer looked at Jake and smiled. "That's right. I see you've done your homework," he said, as he exhaled a series of small smoke rings that floated gracefully in Jake's direction. Then he grinned and clenched down on the cigar. "I like that, a man who comes prepared."

Jake knew he had Spencer right where he wanted him, but decided to put on the finishing touch for good measure. "I also know that you are a humanitarian, Spence. You've spearheaded numerous charitable events that raised millions, and I know you've donated your own money to September 11th victims."

Spencer shook his head solemnly. "Yes, we really couldn't do enough for the September 11th victims."

Jake leaned back into his chair. "I also know that in 1999 you spent a small fortune on a restoration project of this very building."

Jake paused for effect. "Sure would be a shame to have all that effort blown to pieces, wouldn't it, Chairman?"

A smile began to form around his tightly clenched cigar. "Let me take you on a little tour of the building and we can talk about this hunch of yours, Jake, old boy."

CHAPTER 43

JAKE SPENT THE FOLLOWING THREE HOURS TOURING RADIO City Music Hall and the surrounding area. After much debate, he was finally able to convince Chairman Spencer to allow the Feds to step in. The two men agreed that the F.B.I. now had complete authority to secure the site in any way they deemed appropriate.

It was now almost 5:00 o'clock and Jake still had to meet with the mayor's office to coordinate efforts with the NYPD. He needed to call Diane and see how she had made out with Mike and Anita that morning and to make sure she got back to Westchester okay. He also wanted to touch base with Ken Devasher, who had caught the first flight to Dubai.

As he crossed over 6th Avenue, Jake reached for his PDA. He stared down at the phone for a long moment trying to decide who to call first. He closed his eyes and attempted to switch from F.B.I. Agent to loving husband. Once the transformation was complete he dialed Diane's cell.

After three rings she picked up. "Hey, Jake."

Jake hurried across 49th and slowed down to a fast walk when he reached the sidewalk. "Hi, baby, how was your day?"

Diane huffed. "Oh my God, Jake, you don't even want to know."

"Why, what happened?"

"Mike and Anita had a huge fight that lasted all morning."

Jake shook his head. "About what?" he asked, although he already knew the answer.

"Well, I think she was still a bit drunk from last night, but she accused Mike of sleeping with one of the other lawyers at the firm. Rebecca someone."

Jake waited patiently for the light to change at 45th Street. "Becky North. Not a chance. Mike wouldn't do that."

Diane's voice was more deliberate now. "No, Jake, you're wrong. They've been having problems for over a year now."

Jake thought for a moment. He and Mike really had lost touch. Even though they would get together once in a while for a beer or two, their conversations had become very superficial, and were constantly interrupted by phone calls and BlackBerry emails. Jake frowned as he watched a yellow cab screech to a halt, as it nearly collided with a bike messenger. "I don't know Diane, Becky North is like two hundred pounds. I just can't imagine...."

"Nope," interrupted Diane. "Had the staple thing done to her tummy. Lost 85 pounds and had her boobs done too."

Jake laughed. "Wow! I wonder if she has a friend for me," he joked, but was met with silence. Jake paused and cleared his throat. "Look Diane, DR&R has a very strict policy against that sort of thing. Even if Mike was going to cheat on Anita, there is no way he would jeopardize his career over it."

Diane was silent for a moment and wondered if Anita was just being paranoid. "Maybe you're right, Jake, but she's really upset. I drove her back to the house on Long Island, and Mike is staying at the Marriott in Times Square. Maybe you should go see him if you have time."

Jake looked down at his watch. "I have a 6:00 o'clock meeting at the mayor's office. If it doesn't take too long, I might be able to go see Mike tonight."

Diane sighed apologetically. "Jake, I'm so sorry. Here I am babbling on about Anita's marital problems. How did it go at Radio City today?"

Jake raised his free hand and began the arduous task of hailing a cab at rush hour in New York City. "It went pretty good. I have to meet with the NYPD, but we're in charge of the all security at the Tonys." Jake paused as a taxi halted abruptly in front of him. He hopped into the back seat and directed the driver to head downtown. "I'm pretty sure the police will be on board."

Diane smiled. "You know I don't say it often enough, but I'm so proud of you, Jake."

Jake was silent. He was already planning his meeting with the mayor's office in his head.

"And Jake...please be careful."

"Always."

Jake was about to hang-up when he heard Diane speak. "Wait. Jake, are you still there?"

"Still here."

She hesitated. "Jake, did Maria or Carlos say anything to you about going away for a few days"

"No...why?"

"Well, it is kinda strange." She paused. "When I got home today the house alarm was turned off and there were two full baskets of laundry on the floor in the den."

Jake stared out the window and watched as the rows of buildings sped by, briefly interrupted by the passing streets. "You know Maria. She's losing her mind. Probably going through menopause or something."

Diane sighed. "Very funny, Jake. Except I tried calling and they're not picking up. I even knocked on the door to their cottage. They're nowhere to be found."

Jake chuckled. "Okay, I'll tell ya what. If they don't surface by tomorrow morning, I'll go into their cottage and have a look around. But personally, you know what I think?"

Diane hesitated. "I'm afraid to ask."

"I think you've been reading too many James Patterson novels. That's what I think."

CHAPTER 44

AT 5:40 PM JAKE WAS STILL SITTING IN THE BACK OF THE TAXI. Except, now the rows of buildings were no longer speeding by. In fact, everything was at a complete standstill. Jake frowned and looked out the window. It was starting to drizzle and the sidewalk had become a sea of umbrellas bustling in every direction. Jake looked at his PDA and decided that calling Mike would be the next item to remove from his to do list. After four rings, voice mail picked up. Jake left a cryptic message about going for a beer, although he assumed Mike would immediately know the real reason for the call.

Next, he decided to phone Devasher who probably had just landed in Dubai. As he was dialing, his phone started vibrating. He looked down at the caller ID, but didn't recognize the number. "What now," he said, as he placed the phone to his ear. "Jake Chase."

"Jake, Ken Devasher here."

Jake glanced back down at the caller ID. "Ken, I didn't recognize the number."

Devasher huffed. "Right. I was in such a rush this morning that I seem to have lost my PDA. I'm using my personal cell phone."

Jake smiled. "Well, I seem to have gained the full support from the powers that be over at Radio City. They'll let us call the shots so long as we play nice with the NYPD."

Jake looked out the window of the cab. The rain was coming down harder now and the number of umbrellas had tripled. On the bright side, traffic had picked up and he was only a few blocks from City Hall.

"What kind of security is currently in place?"

Jake laughed sarcastically. "There's an obnoxious little man with a clipboard, a misspelled sign and some yellow police tape."

Devasher was silent for a long moment. Jake looked down at his phone to see if they had been disconnected. Then Devasher finally spoke. "Well, get things under control, son. I have a meeting with some Sheik at his palace just outside Dubai. He and our three men apparently had some pretty lucrative business deals together. If he has any information on this thing, I'll get it out of him."

Jake laughed. "I'm sure you will, Ken."

"Listen, Jake. Keep your eyes open. If these guys are going to pull another stunt like Paramount, it's not going to be that easy to detect. They're very crafty."

"I'm on it, Ken."

Just then, Jake's PDA began to vibrate again. He looked down at the caller ID and saw that this time it was Mike. He thought for a moment and decided he'd better answer. He put the phone back against his ear. "Ken, I should take this call."

"That's fine," replied Devasher. "We're just pulling up to the hotel anyway. I'll ring you back tomorrow."

Jake took a deep breath and then exhaled. He closed his eyes and allowed his brain a moment to switch gears. "Hey, buddy-boy."

Mike's voice sounded tired. "Yeah, well I guess you've heard."

"Heard what?"

"Don't bullshit me, man. I'm sure Diane told you about the blow-out at the apartment this morning."

"Yeah, well she might have mentioned something." Jake paused as the car came to a stop in front of City Hall. "I'm in the city now. I'll be free in a few hours. Maybe we can meet for a beer or two," he said, as he handed the cab driver a twenty dollar bill and made his way to the sidewalk.

Mike hesitated. "That's really not necessary, Jake. I'm fine."

Jake nodded, and began walking in the direction of the building. "I'm sure you are, but I just love that spinning bar at the top of the Marriott."

Mike was silent.

"Look, man, I'll call you in a few hours. Truth is, I have a couple of things I'd like to bounce off you regarding this case."

After a long moment Mike let out a laugh. "Fine, just as long as I'm not getting marriage counseling from the F.B.I."

Jake hung up with Mike and slid his PDA into his blazer pocket. The rain had momentarily stopped and the umbrellas had vanished. He paused and looked up at the massive stone building. He shut his eyes and began massaging his temples in a slow circular motion, recounting his conversation with Chairman Spencer. He hoped he would have the same luck with the NYPD. If things went according to plan, he might even have time for a little one-on-one with Mike. Jake then remembered what Mike had said about not wanting to get marital advice from the F.B.I. *God, I've got a lot on my plate,* he thought, as he opened his eyes and made his way into City Hall.

CHAPTER 45

AT 5:50 PM JAKE ENTERED A LARGE CONFERENCE ROOM ON THE first floor of City Hall. Despite the long journey from midtown, he was ten minutes early and immediately greeted by James Erlanger, the mayor's top aid, and Bureau Chief Joanie Spota.

Spota stood only 5'4" but was as tough a police officer as any man on the force. She had graduated top of her class at Annapolis and had been part of D.C.s finest until reaching the rank of deputy inspector. For personal reasons she had relocated to New York City in 2000, and had been placed in charge of the mayor's special anti-terrorism unit since the World Trade Center attack.

"Hello, Agent Chase," said Chief Spota, extending her hand to Jake.

Jake smiled as the two shook hands. He then followed her to an oval shaped conference table where James Erlanger was eagerly waiting.

James Erlanger, or "Jimmy" to his friends and the media, had been with the Mayor's office for many years. He was a company man. Before Bloomberg came to power, he had been in charge of Mayor Giuliani's organized crime task force, and although the press didn't give him enough credit, he was responsible for the arrest and conviction of the one-time mob boss, John Gotti. "We've heard a lot about you and your work concerning the Paramount bombing," he said, as he stood from his seat and extended his hand.

Jake nodded. "Well, I think this meeting should shed a lot more light on what you've already heard, Mr. Erlanger."

Erlanger smiled and motioned to a seat next to where Jake was standing. "Please, call me Jimmy."

Jake sat down and placed his leather briefcase on the floor

beside him. He leaned over and unzipped the top. He pulled out a large file and a legal pad, and set them down on the table in front of him.

Erlanger shot Spota a look, then cleared his throat. "Jake, let me start by saying that New York City cannot afford another September 11th type situation. Even the threat of another possible attack could send the city into a tailspin."

"I get that completely, Jimmy, and the F.B.I. will do everything in its power to prevent that from happening."

"I don't understand," said Chief Spota, shaking her head. "The memo we received said that you believe the terrorists are planning an attack on Radio City Music Hall?"

"Yes, and why is it that Homeland Security doesn't share your theory, Jake?" interrupted Erlanger, nodding in Chief Spota's direction.

"It's true," agreed Spota. "I've spoken with our people at Homeland Security, and they have no reason to believe that there will be another terrorist attack so close in time to the one on Paramount. Especially, not here in New York City."

Jake let out a huff. "I respect that," he said. "But you have to understand that Homeland Security deals primarily with issues of potential acts of terrorism against the United States."

"Yeah, so?"

Jake looked from Erlanger to Spota, trying to detect if he was making any progress. "I do not believe that terrorists are responsible for the Paramount Studios bombing." He paused. "At least not by what we've come to classify as terrorism anyway." Jake opened the file in front of him and took out a stack of documents that Jarvis had sent him. "If you take a moment and look at these, I believe things may become a little clearer." Jake then handed a set to each of them. "These are the corporate bank records of the now defunct Zurich Holding, LLC."

Spota's eyes widened. "My God, are these numbers accurate?" she asked, shaking her head in disbelief. She then looked up at Jake. "One hundred seventy-five million dollars?"

Jake nodded. "Yes, I am afraid so. The company was merely a shell set up to short Paramount Stock. It made a fortune for its officers. Our man at Quantico tells us that the company was owned by three brothers from the United Arab Emirate of Dubai: Dante, Shavka, and the man who we believe is directly responsible for the Paramount bombing, Nurillo Irgashev."

"I still don't see how this has anything to do with Radio City Music Hall," said Erlanger, as he slid the documents back across the table to Jake.

"Let me take a guess," volunteered Chief Spota. "You've tracked the three brothers to New York City."

Jake picked up the papers Erlanger had just handed over and put them back in his leather case. He looked up at Spota and smiled. "Precisely," he said. "Except, of course, for Dante, who took his own life in LA two days ago."

Erlanger sighed in exasperation. "So what? They're here in New York City. Maybe they want to see the Empire State Building," he muttered.

"I don't think so," replied Jake. "We've tracked the money to an offshore account on Grand Cayman Island."

"So, the money is on Grand Cayman Island. I still don't see how that ties into the Tony Awards"

Spota put down her set of papers and leaned into the table. "Look, Jim, if you just blew up Paramount Studios and had one hundred seventy-five million dollars waiting for you in an offshore account in the Caymans, would you come to New York City, or would you get away as fast as possible?"

Jake's head was bobbing up and down, agreeing with every word Spota was saying. "You'd run as far as possible unless of course you had another compelling reason to be here."

Erlanger rubbed his chin. "Right," he said, letting the word linger as he uttered it.

"How can we help?" asked Chief Spota.

Jake stood from his seat, reached down for his case and flung the leather strap over his shoulder. "We'll meet tomorrow in front of Radio City at 8:00 AM," he said. "We can go over the security detail and strategy then."

Erlanger smiled as he made his way to his feet. He shot Spota a look and then extended his hand to Jake. "Well, Agent Chase, you have the full support of the Mayor's office."

CHAPTER 46

IT WAS ALMOST 8:00 PM BY THE TIME JAKE FINALLY ARRIVED AT the Marriott Marquis in Times Square. He looked down at his watch and shook his head. It was getting late and he still had a million things he needed to get done before morning. He took the elevator to the top floor and made his way down a long corridor to the hotel lounge. It was appropriately named "The View" because of the spectacular views of the New York City skyline and because the entire room slowly revolved in a complete circle.

"Hey, Jake, over here," slurred Mike, who was sitting alone at a table in front of an enormous window.

Jake gave a smile and made his way across the crowded room. "Hey, Mike," he said, and then fell back into a chair across from his friend. "Been here long?"

Mike scanned the room for a waitress, spotted one and waved her over. He reached for his beer and gulped down the last sip. Then he grinned. "About three revolutions." he said making a spinning motion with his index finger.

Jake gave him a sideways look. "Did you say three revolutions?"

Mike pointed out the window. "When I got here we were just passing the Chrysler Building. That was four Heinekens ago." Mike's grin widened. Now we're passing it for the third time," he paused, let his hand drop to his side and turned to face Jake. "Three revolutions."

Jake looked out the window. "I see what you mean."

Just then a waitress appeared. She knew Mike by name. He gave her a wink, handed over the empty bottle and ordered two more. "Dos mas," she said, and then left for the bar. Mike sighed and then leaned forward. He looked serious. "I know why you're here, Jake, and it's cool, but really not necessary."

Jake shrugged. "What do you mean? I'm here for the wonderful views," he said sarcastically, then nodded at the Hudson River that was slowly passing by.

Mike sighed again. This time much deeper and longer. "I had sex with Rebecca North."

"Here ya go guys, two ice-cold Heines."

Jake took the bottle from the waitress and gave her an abbreviated smile. Although he struggled to control his facial expression, it was no use. He looked shocked. Mike took his beer, tilted it to his mouth, and nearly polished it off in one gulp.

Jake leaned into the table. "What do you mean you had sex with Rebecca North?" he demanded in a low voice.

Mike shrugged his shoulders. "I don't know what to say, Jake. It was just once, and we are both very embarrassed and very sorry it happened."

Jake leaned in even closer. His voice was still low but deliberate. "But why? How?"

Mike frowned. "It's a long story, Jake."

"Yeah, well, I have all night," Jake said, and then took a sip from the bottle of Heineken.

Mike leaned back in his chair. He ran his hands through his hair and exhaled through closed lips. Jake looked at him and noticed that his friend looked tired. His eyes were shadowed and his expression was sad. "Not to sound too cliché but it just happened. I mean, it's not like we planned it or went to a motel or anything like that."

Jake was silent.

Mike took another sip from his bottle. "Devon assigned us to the Myers file."

"Myers, as in *United States v. Myers,"* Jake asked, recognizing the case from what he had been reading in the *New York Times.*

"Yup, *U.S. v. Myers,*" Mike replied, in a very low voice.

Jake raised his eyebrows. "That's a big case."

Mike scanned the room for the waitress but then gave up.

"Yeah, well, it was my file and Rebecca was picked by Devon himself to second chair at the trial. We put in eighty hour weeks for over a month and then one night it just happened." Mike paused and gave a defeated look. "It was a huge mistake. Monumental. It's extremely awkward around the office and we still have to work together on the file. If I could take it back I would." His voice trailed off. "We both would."

"Who else knows about this?" Jake asked.

"No one. Well, no one for sure. Except you."

"What about Anita? She knows," Jake said.

Mike shook his head. "Not really."

Jake let out a laugh. "What do you mean not really? She told Diane you were having an affair with someone at work. Time for a reality check, buddy. She knows."

Mike closed his eyes and began to rub his temples. The look of sadness had suddenly turned into frustration. "Jake, Anita has suspected me of cheating on her since I started with Devon, Reif & Reed. You remember the hours they make us work. Not to mention the weekends. She's very insecure and a bit paranoid. Why do you think she had all that plastic surgery done? That wasn't my idea. She has this fucked up idea in her head that I'm going to run off with some twenty-one year old or something."

"So why now? If Anita really doesn't know about Rebecca, then why tell Diane all this stuff?"

Mike's eyes narrowed. Hesitantly, he said, "because of the lipstick and smell of perfume on my shirt last week."

"You've got to be kidding me."

"Nope," he said, shaking his head as if he still couldn't believe it himself. "Just like ya see in the movies, Jake, old boy. The quintessential tell-tale signs of a man who has cheated on his wife: lipstick on the collar."

"My God," Jake mumbled to himself as he took a big sip from his bottle.

"Yeah, well, I blamed it on a stripper."

Jake coughed out a mouthful of beer. "You did what?"

"Craig Roffman is a second year associate at the firm. He and his fiancée Joanne are getting married next month. I told Anita that a bunch of the attorneys in his section threw him a bachelor party and hired a stripper."

"I suppose that works better than the truth."

"It was that or lose her forever. I've never lied to her before and I certainly have never cheated on her before. I just don't know what else to do."

Jake leaned in close and put his hand on Mile's shoulder. "Ok, buddy, we'll figure this thing out together."

Mike looked up at Jake. The sadness had returned to his face. "I can't lose her, man."

"No one's going to lose anybody," Jake said. "Even if we have to sit here all night, we'll figure…."

Just then, Jake's PDA went off. He removed it from his belt and looked down at the caller ID. "It's Diane. Should I let it go to voice mail?"

"No, man, don't be silly. Answer it." He paused. "But, Jake, what I told you is just between two friends, right?"

Jake smiled. "Absolutely." He then took a deep breath and put the PDA to his ear. "Hey, we were just talking about you." Immediately Jake could tell something was horribly wrong. Diane was hysterically crying and gasping for air. "Diane, what's happened?"

"Some…some…something terrible, Jake."

"What's wrong?" Mike asked, sensing the urgency in his friend's voice.

"Diane, you have to calm down. Are you all right?"

Diane's voice was shaky and she was still short of breath, but she managed to speak. "Jake, they're dead. It's so horrible. I think they were murdered."

Jake could feel his pulse quicken as he clenched his PDA tightly between his fingers. "Who Diane? Who was murdered?"

Mike jumped up from his seat. "Murdered? Did you say murdered?"

"Diane, baby, who was murdered?"

There was a long silence that seemed like an eternity. Then Diane finally spoke. "Ca…Carlos and Maria. Oh my God, Jake! There…there's blood everywhere!"

Jake stood up and began walking toward the exit. "Okay baby, I need you to take a deep breath, can you do that for me Diane?"

"Yes," she replied tearfully. Then she inhaled deeply.

"Okay honey, now listen to me closely. I need you to hang up the phone and run, Diane. No hesitations. Get out of the house immediately and run next door to the Carlin's. Can you do that for me?"

"I…I think so."

"Okay Diane, do it now. I'm on my way home!"

As Jake hung up the phone, he and Mike were already at the elevator bank. He immediately dialed 911and was assured that the Bedford Police were being notified, and would be at the house within minutes. He next phoned the Carlin's who informed him that Diane had just arrived and that besides being shook up, everything was under control. He felt relieved, but his mind was racing, searching for some kind of an explanation. But he could come up with none.

CHAPTER 47

JAKE CONTINUED TO STAY ON THE PHONE WITH DIANE AS MIKE raced his BMW along Interstate 684. She was much calmer now. The Bedford Police were at the house and a female detective had been assigned to stay with her at all times. Nevertheless, Jake felt better keeping her on the phone until he was home.

"Jake, who could have done this?" she asked.

Jake shrugged. "I have no idea. They were very quiet people. I don't really even remember them having any friends besides one another."

Diane thought again of how she had found the two of them lying side by side behind the potting shed. The gory image of their blood drenched clothes and lifeless bodies made her shiver. She closed her eyes for a moment and tried to rid her brain of the horrible memory, but it was no use. "Oh God, Jake, it's just so sad," she said, as a tear trickled down her cheek. She quickly reached into her sweater pocket, pulled out a clump of tissues and dried her eyes.

Jake rubbed his forehead. "I know, baby, we're at the exit now. We should be home in five minutes. We'll figure this out together. I promise."

Diane let out a sigh. She put the crumpled tissues back into her pocket and made her way up the steps to the front door of the house. "Ok, Jake, I'm going to go splash some cold water on my face. I'll see you in a little while. I love you."

"Love you too," Jake said, as he hung up the PDA and flung it onto the dash.

"How's she holding up?" asked Mike, as he veered off the highway at the Bedford Hills exit.

Jake put his hands in his pockets and shrugged his shoulders.

"I don't know, man. She's pretty thick-skinned, but something like this. . . ." His voice trailed off and then he was silent.

Mike turned the Beamer onto Jake's street, and from the bottom of his driveway Jake could see the red and blue lights from the multitude of police cars swirling through the trees. The gates had been left open to allow the police access to the property. As the two men pulled up the long driveway, Jake's eyes widened in disbelief.

"Wow!" said Mike. "Think there are any cops in Westchester that aren't here?"

There must have been at least fifteen emergency vehicles scattered about the front of the house: police, fire, ambulance, and coroner. The scene was completely surreal. Then suddenly, the front door to the house burst open, and Diane came running out toward the car. Jake immediately jumped out of the BMW and ran in her direction.

"Jake, thank God you're home," she said, as the two embraced. She held him tightly for a long moment and then gently rested her head against his chest. Jake gazed over her head. Everywhere he looked, police, firemen and EMT's were hurrying in one direction or another. It reminded him of Paramount and it made him angry. Just then, a man approached. He was holding a leather billfold with a gold detective's shield pinned inside.

"Excuse me," said the man. "I'm sorry to interrupt this little reunion, but are you Agent Chase?"

Jake momentarily pulled away from Diane. "Yes, I'm Jake Chase."

The man smiled and extended his hand. "My name is Joseph Leary. I'm a detective with the Bedford Police Department."

"Hello, Detective," Jake said, as the two men shook hands.

"I understand you're with the F.B.I."

Jake nodded.

"Well, it will be nice to work with a professional for a change," Leary said, as he reached into his back pocket, took out a small notepad and opened it to a fresh page. "May I have a word with you in private, Agent Chase?"

Jake looked back at Diane who was still visibly upset. "I don't think so, Detective. Anything you have to ask me, you can ask us both," Jake said, as he held Diane's hand.

Leary gazed up from his notepad, looked at Diane and raised an eyebrow. "Fair enough," he said. He then gestured to the throngs of emergency personnel. "But is there a place where we can speak with a little more privacy?"

Jake looked around and shook his head. "Of course, Detective. Right this way," he said, motioning to the front door.

Just then Mike approached. "Everything okay, Jake?"

Jake shrugged his shoulders and turned to face Leary. "Detective, this is Mike Dumont. He's a friend of the family."

Mike extended his hand. "Nice to meet you, Detective," he said with a grin as he shook Leary's hand firmly. "I'm also the family's attorney and I'd like to be present during any questioning of my clients."

Jake put his hand on Mike's shoulder and smiled. "I really don't think that's necessary."

"No, no, Agent Chase. It's perfectly all right," interrupted Leary who was still gripping Mike's hand tightly. Then he grinned. "Might not be a bad idea to have your lawyer present," he said, as he released Mike's hand and turned to face Jake. "Shall we?" he said, gesturing toward the door.

The four made their way into the house and proceeded down the hallway to Jack's office. Jake held Diane close by his side. It was almost 3:00 AM and she looked absolutely exhausted. The area under her eyes was shadowed and it made her look old. Jake gave her an affectionate squeeze and kissed the top of her head.

"Nice pile of bricks ya got here, Agent Chase," said Detective Leary. "Must have cost ya a small fortune."

"Wise investments," interrupted Mike. "Find out who committed these murders and we'll give you some stock tips, Detective."

"Right in here," Jake said, as they entered the study. "Can I offer anybody something to drink? Bottled water maybe?"

Diane made her way to the leather couch. She turned on a decorative table lamp and fell backwards into the sofa. She sighed and folded the sides of her button-down sweater in front of her. Jake watched and gave her a smile. She caught his eye and smiled back at him sadly.

"Pellegrino and lime would be nice," said Detective Leary, with a smirk.

Jake rubbed the back of his neck and turned to face Leary. "Right. Pellegrino." He paused and then dropped his hand to his side. "Look, Detective, we are all a bit tired here, as you can imagine. You have some questions?"

Leary motioned to a chair in front of Jack's writing table. "May I?"

Jake sighed in frustration and then smiled. He looked over at Mike who was growing impatient. "Of course, Detective."

Leary took a seat and then reached forward and picked up a framed picture from the top of the desk. He turned it to face him and his eyes widened. He looked up at Jake and for a moment seemed a bit awestruck. "You knew DiMaggio?"

Mike let out a huff. "Detective please, can we move this along."

Leary set the picture of Jack and the Joltin' Joe back down on the desk and turned to face Mike. "Look counselor, I'm not trying to bust balls here, but I got two dead Mexicans in a potting shed in one of the wealthiest neighborhoods in the United States."

"They were Ecuadorian," said Diane, from the couch as she blotted her eyes with the crumpled tissues.

Leary spun to face her. "Pardon me?"

"Ecuadorian. They were Ecuadorian. Not Mexican," said Diane softly.

"Yes, of course," he replied, as he placed a pair of bifocals on his face. He looked up at her and smiled. "Ecuadorian."

Mike made his way across the room and stood directly in front of Leary. He looked intimidating. "Listen, Detective, the sooner you get to the point here, the sooner you and the Bedford Police can begin to track down the killer," he demanded.

Leary didn't seem fazed. "Ok, Counselor, as you wish. I was just wondering where your clients were the day before yesterday."

Mike looked at Jake and Diane and then back down at Leary. "Why the fuck do you need to know that?"

Leary glared up at Mike from over the top of his glasses. "Because forensics tells us that your two Ecuadorians have been rotting away in that potting shed for at least forty-eight, that's why."

"Oh God, Jake, I think I'm going to be sick," said Diane as she jumped up from the couch and ran for the door. "You're an ass, you know that, Detective!"

Jake let out a long drawn-out sigh. "Excuse me for a moment, Detective," he said, as hurried into the kitchen. "Carolyn, a little help here!" he shouted to his neighbor who was sitting at the table sipping a mug of hot tea.

Immediately, Carolyn jumped up from her seat and ran to Diane. "Oh you poor thing," she said, as she put her arm around Diane and led her to the powder room.

Jake took a deep breath and made his way back into the study. He shot Mike a look as he walked to the couch and paused at the spot where Diane had been sitting. He turned and let his body fall backwards into the cushions. He looked up at Leary. "Hell hath no fury, eh Detective?"

Leary raised an eyebrow. "You like Shakespeare, Agent Chase?"

Mike let out a sarcastic laugh. "Congreve!"

Leary looked over at him and narrowed his eyes. "Excuse me?"

"It's from a play by William Congreve, not Shakespeare, genius."

Jake cleared his throat and slowly stood to his feet. "I think we've all had a trying day. Maybe we could finish up another time, Detective?"

"No need, Jake," interrupted Mike. "If the good detective needs anything, he will call my office."

"Fine," said Jake.

Leary stood from the chair. "No, on the contrary, Agent Chase, nothing is fine here. I'm leaving two business cards; one is for your wife." He reached forward and placed two small white cards on the desk beside the autographed photo of Joe D. "Call me if you remember anything. My cell number is on the back." Then he made his way to the door. "I can show myself out," he said, as he left Mike and Jake standing in Jack's office.

Jake looked over at Mike and gave him a smile. "Congreve?"

"Are you kidding, Jake? "The Morning Bride" is my favorite play," he said, and then he started cracking up.

Jake fell back into the couch again. "Bullshit. Now I know you're just fucking with me."

Mike smiled. "Heav'n has no Rage, like love to Hatred turn'd, Nor Hell a Fury, like a Woman scorn'd."

CHAPTER 48

BRIANNA WAS CAREFUL NOT TO COME TOO CLOSE TO THE GASH on The Producer's cheek as she kissed his face and gently ran her fingers through his long black hair. *Probably could have used a few stitches* she thought, as she carefully traced the line with her finger. *It would be such a shame to mess up that pretty face.* He told her he'd cut himself shaving, but it looked more like he got punched to her. *Why do guys have to be so macho?* she thought, as she continued to pepper his face and neck with baby kisses.

"Wake up, sleepyhead," she whispered in his ear, but it was no use. He was dead…dead to the world. She grinned and began kissing her way down his chest in the direction of his cock. If anyone knew how to wake the dead, Brianna Koe did; that was for sure.

"Well I see someone's awake," she said, and then she took him in her mouth.

Just then she felt The Producer put his hand on the back of her head and force himself down her throat. *How fucking predictable*, she thought, trying not to gag. She closed her eyes and allowed him to pleasure himself for what seemed like an eternity. Maybe she could entice him to give her the present he bought her. After all, he said it was for the red carpet, and that was less than eight hours away.

When he finally finished, Brianna resurfaced from under the sheets and nestled her head against his chest. "Good morning," she said, with a naughty little giggle.

The Producer grinned. "Yes, it certainly has started out to be a good morning, hasn't it?" He looked down at the top of her head. "Are you getting nervous yet?"

Brianna laughed sarcastically. "Are you kidding? I have been in front of the camera since I was four."

"Ah, I see, a seasoned pro," joked The Producer. He then moved Brianna's head off his chest and swung himself out from under the covers and placed his feet on the floor. He arched his back and gave a huge stretch. Brianna smiled and rubbed her hand up and down his spine affectionately. He put his hand on the back of his neck and tried to squeeze out some of the sharp pangs. He frowned and stood to his feet letting Brianna's hand drop to the mattress. "You've been a good girl. Perhaps, I will give you your gift."

Brianna smiled and flipped over onto her stomach. She rested her elbows on the bed, propped up her head with two fists under her chin, and watched as he exited the room still completely naked. Then she began to trouble her bottom lip between her teeth as she thought about what he had just said. The truth was Brianna Koe was completely terrified. What if she flopped? What if no one liked her? God, how could she be so insecure? After all, she was Brianna Koe, star of "Hollywood Diaries." Either way, she would never admit to being scared, especially not to her beautiful producer, who was going to put her in his next movie.

The Producer came back into the room and Brianna smiled. He was carrying a small box neatly gift-wrapped.

Brianna raised a curious eyebrow. "Is that for me?"

The Producer nodded and sat beside her on the bed. "Yes, my love, it is a very special gift. It was once owned by a very wealthy man. It had been in his family for many generations. He told me it was the reason his family had so much good fortune. It was their talisman."

Brianna turned her head sideways. "Their what?"

The Producer laughed. "A good luck charm," he said handing over the box.

Brianna sat up and crossed her legs Indian style. She pushed her hair off her face and examined the package from all sides. She lifted the top off the box, took out the necklace and smiled. "Oh, Ali, it's so beautiful."

The Producer grinned. "I'm glad you like it," he said, as he took the necklace from her hands. "Now remember, you must not take this off so it can bring you all the luck and fortune you desire." He then unhooked the clasp and placed the necklace around Brianna's neck. She held up her hair and tilted her head forward. He reconnected the clasp and let the stones fall over her bare breasts.

She leaned over and gave him a kiss on the cheek. "Oh Ali, I love it!" She then hopped off the bed and made her way to the full length mirror. She looked at her reflection and smiled. "It's perfect."

CHAPTER 49

IT WAS ALREADY NEARLY ONE HUNDRED DEGREES AS KEN Devasher drove the Rolls Royce Phantom toward the palatial estate of Sheik Abdul Roheem. He glanced down at the screen from the navigation system which was handsomely set in the cherry wood dashboard. He was close.

Located in the heart of the Arabian Gulf, Dubai had become a world-renowned tourist attraction, especially for the rich and famous. In addition to a seven star hotel, shaped like a huge sailboat on the Persian Gulf, there was an indoor ski mountain built under a giant dome with slopes ranging from beginner to black diamond. The entire Emirate oozed money, from its local population to the very wealthy tourists who vacationed there. The Sheik's palace was no exception.

The main building was forty thousand square feet with numerous guest cottages, out houses, swimming pools and tennis courts...a city unto itself. It was completely surrounded by a ten-foot high cast-iron fence with laser-beam motion sensors and infrared security cameras, all camouflaged by sprawling rows of beautiful royal palms. It was *Soldier of Fortune* meets *Architectural Digest.*

Devasher slowly brought the Rolls to a stop in front of a massive stone pillar. There was a camera mounted to the top pointing in the direction of the car. Attached to one of the stones was a small grey intercom. A green light turned on as a voice came through the speaker. "May I help you?"

Devasher could not actually see the house from where he was sitting, just a long winding road lined with endless palm trees. He pressed a button on the dash and his window lowered into the door. "Yes, it's Dr. William Monaco," replied Devasher, "I have a 10:00 AM meeting scheduled with Sheik Abdul and Fuad Irgashev. He leaned over to the passenger seat and snapped open his briefcase.

"One moment," replied the voice, "I am checking my computer now." A brief pause. "Right, here you are. Dr. William Monaco with Exxon Mobil."

"Yes," said Devasher, "We have a 10:00 AM meeting," he repeated in the direction of the intercom, as he screwed a black metal silencer into his 9mm and placed it into a hidden compartment in his bag.

"Certainly, drive right in, Dr. Monaco. I will meet you in front of the main building," replied the voice, as the gates at the bottom of the driveway slowly began to open. *That was easy.*

Devasher closed the case and scrambled the wheels on the two combination locks. He then drove through the gates and began the long journey up the private road leading to the main house.

At the top of the driveway stood an enormous circular stone fountain with a massive sailboat its center. Laminar jets were shooting water at the boat from all sides and would cascade off the stone sails and ripple the water beneath it. It gave the illusion that the boat was actually in forward motion. The driveway circled completely around the fountain with the main house just beyond it.

Devasher pulled the Rolls to the entrance and turned off the ignition. A man appeared at the top of the steps and slowly made his way in the direction of the car. He was tall and dark-skinned. He must have stood 6'3" and weighed nearly three hundred pounds. He looked like a walking mountain wearing a turban.

When he finally arrived at the car he smiled politely. "Hello, Dr. Monaco. My name is Omen. I work for the Sheik."

Devasher nodded and reached into the car for his briefcase.

Omen's eyes immediately fixed on the case. "I am sorry, Doctor, but I am going to have to pat you down and search your bag."

Devasher smiled. "Of course," he said, raising his arms as the giant man frisked him.

The mountain's eyes narrowed. "What's this?"

Devasher frowned. "It's a Walther PPK semiautomatic. I carry a great deal of cash." He paused for effect. "Just makes me feel safer."

Omen gave Devasher a stern look. "Well, you'll have to leave it with me, Doctor," he said, as he removed the gun from the leather shoulder strap and shoved the muzzle down the front of his trousers so that the butt of the gun hung over his belt. "You can have it back on your way out."

"Of course," said Devasher calmly, as he lowered his arms. He then glanced down at the gun and shook his head. "You might want to switch on the safety catch though."

"Now the case, Doctor."

Devasher placed the briefcase on the edge of the fountain, turned two small wheels to the correct combination, and the latches sprung open. He then angled the bag toward the man-mountain, "Here you go," he said, completely confident that the giant would pay little attention to the case, having already confiscated the Walther PPK. "You guys are really thorough."

"Can never be too careful," said Omen, as he shuffled around some papers and closed the case. He slid it back to Devasher and then began walking in the direction of the house. "Follow me."

Devasher relocked the case and followed Omen around the fountain. "No, you really can't," he replied, as the two men made their way up the large stone steps and into the grand palace. Devasher looked around. "It seems very quiet around here this morning."

Omen nodded. "Yes, the Sheik has sent the entire staff on holiday for the weekend."

Devasher grinned.

"It's right this way," said Omen, as he led Devasher down a long corridor to the Sheik's private office. Although the hallway was quite large, it had a restive feel to it. The floors were a light colored Italian marble and the walls were lined with colorful tapestries. Everywhere you looked there were potted palm trees in decorative ceramic vases, and a gentle breeze was blowing from the rattan fans that lined the ceiling.

When they arrived, Omen knocked but did not wait for an

answer. He pushed open the door and the two men entered the large study. "Sheik, Dr. William Monaco has arrived for a 10:00 AM meeting," announced Omen.

The Sheik was sitting behind a large desk that could have passed for a small dining room table. It was completely barren but for a plasma screen computer monitor, a keyboard and some old leather-bound books. He was short in stature with a thin frame and an olive complexion. He looked good for a man approaching seventy. He was wearing the traditional dark suit with large pinstripes and a white turban. "Yes, yes, come right in. Hello, Doctor," said the Sheik, as he stood from his desk and made his way across the room.

"He was carrying this," interrupted the mountain, pointing to the gun tucked into his trousers.

The Sheik frowned. "Oh yes, I see," he said. "I'm sorry, Doctor, but we have to be very cautious in our business. I hope you understand."

Devasher nodded and the two men shook hands.

"Doctor, I think you know Fuad Irgashev," said the Sheik, motioning to an elderly man also wearing a suit and turban. He was seated on the couch and looked nervous.

Devasher turned to face the man and approached the couch in a threatening fashion. Fuad's hands began to tremble. "Yes, I know Fuad well," replied Devasher, as he loomed over him.

The Sheik swallowed hard and then looked over at Omen. "That will be all," he said.

"As you wish, Sheik," he replied, as he walked to the door and exited the room.

Once Omen was gone, Devasher's face hardened. His Doctor William Monaco persona was quickly replaced by that of an enraged psychopath. His eyes narrowed as he quickly turned to face the two men who were now both visibly frightened. His voice was low but deliberate. "I have no time for this fucking bullshit. Do you understand that? You think I want to fly half way around the fucking world to deal with this shit?"

Fuad slowly stood to his feet. He was trembling harder now

and his voice was shaky. "I know, Ken," he said, now referring to Devasher by his real name.

Devasher pointed an angry finger in the old man's face. "Your sons are completely out of control, Fuad!" he exploded. "They have fucked up this whole thing!"

Fuad sighed and looked to the ground. "You don't think that I know that, Deputy Director. I had to bury one of my sons yesterday and I have been forced to hide out here at my friend's home. Don't you think I know this has gotten way out of control?"

Devasher threw his in hands into the air and then grabbed the timid man by the lapel from his suit. He was completely out of control. "Deputy Director. Did you just call me Deputy Director?" He then brought his mouth inches from Fuad's ear. "Is that some kind of a fucking threat, you little prick?" he whispered, through clenched teeth.

"Gentlemen," interrupted the Sheik. "Please, let me pour us a drink and we can sort things out."

Slowly Devasher loosened his grip on Fuad's suit jacket and took a step back. He smiled and then smoothed the wrinkles he had just caused. "Fine," he said as he turned to face the Sheik. "Who is in the palace today?"

The Sheik shrugged his shoulders. "Just Omen," he replied nervously, as he glanced over at Fuad.

Devasher nodded. "And the video surveillance?"

"All powered down last night, Ken. Just like you requested."

Apparently pleased by what he had heard, Devasher turned his attention back to Fuad. "We agreed no one would get hurt! The explosion at Paramount was supposed to be in an abandoned studio set. What the fuck happened to that?"

Fuad turned his palms upward. "I don't know," he replied. "I have been unable to communicate with Nurillo since the bombing. He refuses to speak to me. I can only talk to him through his brother Shavka."

"He is planning another attack. Did you know that?"

Fuad's shoulders dropped. "Yes, I know," he replied sadly, "But

I have been assured by Shavka that the explosive device is a fake. There will be no more bloodshed, I can assure you of that."

"Yeah well, I think I am going to take out a little insurance policy of my own," said Devasher, as he made his way to the Sheik's computer.

Fuad looked panicked. "What are you going to do?"

"I'm afraid you are wrong about one thing, Fuad. There is going to be more bloodshed. Nurillo's blood," replied Devasher, as he set his briefcase down on the desk and began to type an email on the Sheik's computer.

Jake,

Your hunch was correct. Nurillo Irgashev AKA Alisher (Ali) Nurmatov is planning another attack. It's tonight at the Radio City Awards show. Attached are several recent photos of Nurillo.

Do not take any chances. We have a direct order from Robbins. All agents have shoot-on-site authorization!

D.D. Ken Devasher

"Now then, gentlemen, I was promised a drink," said Devasher, as he hit the send button and stood from the computer.

The Sheik forced a smile. "Yes, of course," he said as he opened a small cabinet from behind the bar and pulled out a bottle of Cognac.

Devasher cackled. "Cognac? Come on, Sheik, we just made one hundred seventy-five million dollars. Recouped the family fortune that Fuad's idiot sons squandered away. I think this calls for champagne."

The Sheik sighed. "Yes, champagne," he repeated unenthusiastically, as he placed the bottle of cognac back in the cabinet. He knelt down and opened a small wine refrigerator and took out a bottle of Cristal.

Fuad made his way to the bar and took a seat. "Ken, we have been waiting for wiring instructions for your share of the money," he said cautiously.

"Don't you worry about my share of the money," replied

Devasher. "I'm meeting Shavka tomorrow in the Caymans. I'll go over the account numbers and my share of the money with him then."

The Sheik carefully poured out three flutes and handed one to each man. Devasher took his glass and made his way back to the desk. Fuad gave him a curious look. Devasher sat down and rested his glass on the desk. He then clicked the two latches on either side of his briefcase and slowly opened the top.

"What should we drink to?" asked the Sheik.

Devasher grinned. "How 'bout we drink to not sharing the money?" he replied, as he pulled out his 9mm from its hidden compartment and put two rounds into the Sheik's chest. There was no sound from the 9mm as the silencer muffled the noise of the gunfire. No bang, no explosion, just a slight wisp of air with each shot. *Chooot, Chooot.*

Devasher then walked up to the Sheik's lifeless body, now on the ground, drenched in blood. His expression was stern. He slowly pointed the gun at the man's head and fired a third shot. *Chooot.*

In a complete state of shock, Fuad dropped his champagne flute. He jumped up from the bar stool and began backing up in the direction of the door.

Calmly, Devasher raised his 9mm and pointed it at Fuad's head. Fuad raised his hands in front of his face. Devasher smiled. He then fired two shots hitting the old man both times. Fuad's eyes rolled into the back of his head, as he collapsed and hit the floor with a loud thud. Devasher then approached the body and fired a third shot point blank into Fuad's head. He lowered his weapon, turned and walked back to the desk. He then relaxed into the leather desk chair, pulled a handkerchief from his pocket and wiped off the keyboard from the Sheik's computer. With the same handkerchief he picked up the champagne flute, tilted the glass in the direction of the two dead bodies, and took a sip. "Not bad," he said, as he stood from the desk and pointed the gun directly at the door.

"Omen, come quickly. Something terrible has happened!"

Within seconds the door burst open and Omen came charging

into the room. Devasher immediately squeezed off two rounds. Both direct hits. Omen's eyes widened in shock as he grasped his chest and fell to the ground. Devasher walked to Omen's dead body. He knelt down beside him and reclaimed his Walther PPK. He then put the 9mm inches from Omen's head and squeezed the trigger. *Chooot.*

CHAPTER 50

JAKE PULLED HIS ASTON MARTIN INTO ONE OF THE UNDERground parking garages along 6th Avenue, and brought the car to a halt in front of the security booth. He looked at his watch: 8:20, right on time, and he was only two blocks from Radio City. Luckily, it was a Saturday morning and traffic had been light on the Hutchinson River Parkway.

Jake raised his arms over his head and took a big stretch which eventually turned into a long drawn-out yawn. Needless to say, no one had slept much the night before, and he felt awful leaving Diane at the house. Mike had volunteered to spend the day with her and run interference with the media, who were now camped out at the bottom of the driveway. Jake felt guilty not finishing their conversation about Anita, but it was on his to do list.

Once the yawn had subsided, Jake reached into the back seat, grabbed his briefcase and swung the leather strap over his shoulder. He exited the car and a pimply faced parking attendant, who looked as tired as Jake felt, handed him a small white voucher. He gave the kid a smile and made a beeline for the street.

As Jake surfaced to the street, he immediately felt the warm sun. He took a deep breath and filled his lungs with fresh air. He slapped himself in the face a few times to chase away the tired. Today, of all days, he needed to have his A-game.

He looked ahead and could see the myriad of media vans lined up in front of the building. It was a clear spring morning and the streets were already crowded with tourists and lookie-loos. Jake frowned. He then crossed over 6th and made his way to Radio City.

Chief Spota was already on the sidewalk in front of the building. She looked frustrated, and as Jake got closer he could see why.

"I don't give a rat's ass who you are. We're not letting the NYPD search the celebrities as they arrive on the red carpet," barked Travis Cole who was still toting his clipboard.

Spota let out a huff. "Mr. Cole, you are not listening to me. I didn't say that we have to…."

"Maybe I can explain," interrupted Jake, as he stepped in between Chief Spota and the clipboard guy.

Suddenly a look of fear came over Travis' face. "Oh no…not you! You stay away," he whimpered, and then nearly tripped over himself as he ran for the building.

Chief Spota laughed as she watched Travis scurry off. She looked back at Jake and smiled. "Good morning, Agent Chase."

Jake returned the smile. "Good morning, Chief Spota."

She then gave Jake a curious look. "What the heck was that all about?"

Jake shrugged. "What that? Oh that's nothing. Maybe he had to use the bathroom or something."

Spota grinned. "Yeah, right," she said. But then the grin disappeared and her face turned serious. She scanned the area and shook her head disapprovingly. "It's as bad as you said, Jake. Completely disorganized."

Jake nodded in agreement. "So here's what I was thinking. The F.B.I. will have ten teams of undercover men." He pointed to a series of buildings across 6th Avenue. "We'll have sharp shooters there, there, there and there."

Spota held her hand in front of her face and squinted against the sun as she noted the four buildings Jake was pointing to. "That's fine, Jake, but my fear is that he will have an explosive device in one of the cars or media vans. That's how he did Paramount, right?"

Jake looked at Spota and considered what she had just said. She was very smart and Jake liked that. "Good thinking! I'll have another team search every news and media van and we'll set a 'no vehicle' perimeter of one hundred yards from the building."

Spota shook her head. "That's practically impossible, Jake. The celebrities are not going to get out of their limos and walk down 51st Street in their Gucci shoes and Vera Wang gowns."

Jake put his hand on his forehead and thought for a moment. He tried desperately to fight off the sleep deprivation. Then it came to him. "Okay, then we set up a check point."

"A what?"

"Yes, that's it," Jake said, with a look of enlightenment on his face. "A checkpoint!"

Spota cocked her head and turned her palms upwards. "I'm not following you, Jake."

Jake smiled. The adrenaline was kicking in and it was bringing with it his A-game! "Look, you hit the nail on the head, Chief. The problem with Paramount was that the security detail didn't properly search the cars entering the studios." Jake paused for a moment and thought. "He knew they weren't going to search the studio limos. That's how he knew he could get the bomb in."

Right," said Chief Spota, "and he figures they're not gonna search the limos as they pull up to the red carpet either."

Jake exhaled and clasped his hands on top of his head. "That's how you're gonna do it, isn't it, you son of a bitch."

"Two checkpoints," shouted Spota, and startled Jake out of his own thought process.

"What?"

Spota nodded. "Yes. Two checkpoints. One on 49th Street between 5th and 6th and one on 47th Street between 5th and 6th."

Jake agreed. "And every car must pass through one of the checkpoints before gaining access to the red carpet."

Just then, Jake's PDA went off. He reached down and removed it from his belt. It was an email from Devasher. He read the message and a huge smile came across his face.

Spota's eyes narrowed. "What is it?"

Jake clicked on the attachment icon and there it was: a full color close-up of the man who bombed Paramount Studios. But suddenly, the smile disappeared from Jake's face. He felt his pulse spike as he studied the picture more closely. "Where have I seen that face before?" he mumbled. He could feel his whole body tighten as stared down at the picture, but could not figure it out. He took a deep breath. "Now we know what the bastard looks like," he said, as he turned the PDA to face Chief Spota.

CHAPTER 51

IT WAS ALMOST TWELVE NOON AND JAKE WAS BUSY REVIEWING a set of blueprints in one of the private rooms on the first floor of Radio City Music Hall. He had already scouted out the four buildings across 6th Avenue, and had strategically positioned four, two-man sharpshooter teams in top floor apartments. And, he had made sure that every man had an eight-by-ten glossy of Nurillo Irgashev.

Chief Spota had spent the morning setting up the two limo checkpoint sites and had successfully moved the media vans off the Avenue. *Things were going as planned.*

Just then, Jake's PDA began to vibrate and dance around on the corner of the large table he was working at. He looked up from the blueprints, arched his back and twisted his neck from side to side. His muscles were tight and he could hear crackling noises coming from his spine. He frowned and reached for the PDA.

"Jake, I just got some interesting news from Detective Leary!" boomed Mike's voice excitedly through the tiny speaker.

Jake put his hand on the back of his neck and tried to squeeze out some of the soreness. "How's Diane?" he replied.

"Oh Jesus, I'm sorry buddy. She's doing fine." He paused. "Considering the circumstances, that is. She's in the garden with your neighbors, Carolyn and Danny. They're planting a tree in memory of Carlos and Maria."

Jake sighed and went back to the blueprints. "So, what's the news?"

Mike continued. "Well, seems like old Carlos must have gotten a punch or two in before he and Maria were murdered. They found blood on his knuckles, and it wasn't his or Maria's."

"Good for him."

"No, good for you and Diane actually," Mike replied. "They checked the blood type with the F.B.I. and the records at Blythedale Children's Hospital and it's a negative match on both of you."

Jake leaned back in his chair. "Yeah, well, no fucking kidding."

Mike chuckled. "I know, I know, but on the bright side, you and Diane are no longer persons of interest to the Bedford Police. Maybe now Leary can start looking for the real murderers."

Just then, Chief Spota poked her head through the door. "Agent Chase, got a second?"

Jake gave Spota a nod and waved her into the room. She entered, but was closely tailed by Chairman Spencer and Travis Cole and they both looked upset. Jake's shoulders dropped. "Look Mike, I gotta go."

"Agent Chase, are you actually suggesting we frisk the celebrities as they walk down the red carpet?" demanded Chairman Spencer, with clipboard-man cowering behind him.

Jake stood from his seat and walked in the direction of the angry mob. He looked at Chief Spota, who just shrugged her shoulders and gave him an apologetic look. He smiled and put his hand on the chairman's shoulder. "Look, Spence, what we're suggesting is two checkpoints, completely off camera. It will be perfectly...."

"You know what you can do with your checkpoints?" shouted Travis, but then froze when Jake shot him a look.

Jake laughed. "Spence, is there a place we can speak in private?"

Spencer nodded. "Travis, why don't you go check on the swag bags?" he said, and motioned toward the door.

Travis threw his hands in the air and headed for the door. "Fine, you can just forget winning any awards with this production," he shouted, as he stormed out of the room.

Spencer turned back to face Jake. "You'll have to excuse him, Agent Chase. He's under a lot of pressure."

Jake began rubbing the back of his neck again. "Like I was saying, we'd like two check points, both completely off camera."

"Yeah," interrupted Spota. "We'll be in and out of those cars before you can say Go Rangers."

Spencer laughed. "So you think he's gonna try to pull another stunt like Paramount, huh?"

Jake smiled. "It's just a hunch."

CHAPTER 52

AT 3:00 PM BRIANNA KOE ARRIVED AT RADIO CITY MUSIC HALL an hour late. She was still pissed off that her date had suddenly been called back to Hollywood, but she understood that in this business timing was everything. Plus, if things went well for him, he promised her a role in his new film.

She walked in the direction of her trailer and noticed something wasn't right. Something was missing. People. People were missing. "Where the heck is everyone?" she said, as she picked up the pace and quickly approached the steps to her trailer. Suddenly, she heard a loud voice and it startled her.

"Where the fuck have you been! I've been calling your cell for over an hour," screamed Travis Cole, who was lurking at the bottom of the steps.

"Travis, you scared the shit out of me," she replied, as she walked passed him and entered the trailer. She smiled and began to relax as she saw her closest friends: her stylist, her make-up artist, her voice coach, her massage therapist and of course, Stephanie.

She let out a deep sigh as she fell back into her styling chair and summoned her assistant. "Oh Stephie, you're a lifesaver," she said, as she snatched a Starbucks Caramel Latté from her hand.

Suddenly, Travis burst into the trailer. He looked pissed.

"He seems really mad," whispered Stephanie, out of the corner of her mouth.

Brianna stood from her chair, handed Stephanie back her latté and gave her a wink. She then walked up to Travis seductively and suddenly dropped to her knees. "Oh please, Travis, will you ever forgive me?" she pleaded with a slight giggle.

Travis let out a sarcastic laugh. "How fitting, Brianna Koe on her knees." He paused for a moment and stared down at her chest. "And wherever did you get that awful necklace?"

Brianna let out a yelp. She put her hand on the turquoise stones and stood to her feet. "It was a gift from my boyfriend."

The news of Brianna Koe having an actual boyfriend had the same effect as a needle scratching across a record album at a high school dance. Everyone in the trailer stopped what they were doing and looked in Brianna's direction. Even Stephanie, who had heard just about everything come out of her boss's mouth, gave her a look of amazement.

Brianna grinned. "You'd like him, Travis. He's got a really big cock."

Everyone broke out into nervous laughter and resumed what they were doing. Stephanie walked up to Travis and gave him a reassuring look. "We'll get her in makeup and give you a call, okay?"

Travis huffed. "Fine, but no more bloody delays!" he shouted, as he exited the trailer letting the door slam behind him.

Stephanie shook her head. She turned to Brianna and put her hand around her waist and led her back to the styling chair. "Come on, Brie, we have to get you in make-up. You can tell me about your boyfriend later."

Brianna relaxed into her seat. She gazed at herself in the mirror as her stylist began combing the knots from her hair. Once again she placed her hands over the turquoise stones and smiled. "Hey, where the heck is everyone?" she asked. "Have you been outside? This place is like a ghost town."

Stephanie nodded as she spoke to Brianna's reflection in the mirror. "Yeah, the F.B.I. has all media vans parked around the corner. I think there was a bomb threat or something. They're searching everyone, even the celebrity cars."

Brianna's smile vanished. "A bomb threat?"

"Yeah," replied the stylist. "I heard they think it's the same terrorists that blew up Paramount."

Brianna began to trouble her bottom lip with her teeth again. "Paramount?" she replied, sounding a bit nervous.

Stephanie looked at Brianna's reflection and detected a look of concern. "There's nothing to worry about. I'm sure the F.B.I. has everything under control. I mean, they wouldn't take any chances, right?"

Brianna didn't answer.

"Plus, I heard the F.B.I. guy in charge is really hot," said Stephanie, trying to get Brianna to focus.

"Yeah," volunteered the massage therapist, who was in the back of the trailer getting her table ready. "I saw him this morning," she said, as she walked up behind Brianna and began rubbing her shoulders. "He's rugged looking. Like a crusader. Reminds me of a young Indiana Jones."

"Yeah," interrupted the stylist. "But I heard he's married."

Stephanie let out a laugh. "Since when has that stopped Brianna?"

Brianna smiled. "Nope, not this time," she said. "I've finally met the man of my dreams and there's no room for anyone else." She then looked at herself in the mirror and once again rubbed her fingers over the smooth stones.

CHAPTER 53

IT WAS NEARLY 5:00 PM AND THE PRODUCER HAD TAKEN POSItion in a vacant apartment across from Radio City. Silently, he waited by an open window in the dark room and gazed down at the busy street below. He had a perfect view of the red carpet. He took a deep breath, reached for a pair of field glasses and brought them to his face. He could see paparazzi, camera crews and news reporters anxiously awaiting the arrival of their precious celebrities, and it made him sick.

He scanned the crowd, looking for the Hollywood Diaries camp. "Where are you, my little time bomb?" he said, gripping the field glasses so tightly that his fingers began to go numb. Then suddenly he found her. Brianna and her camera crew were setting up right outside the front door to the building. If she stayed in that location, he would be able to take out most of Radio City with a single blast. He steadied the field glasses by resting his elbows on the window ledge, zoomed in on Brianna's neck, and spotted the device. *Perfect.*

He then set the field glasses back down on the ledge and reached inside his blazer pocket. He took out the transmitter and placed it beside the binoculars. He checked his watch: 5:20 PM. Things should be rolling pretty soon. He had planned to set off the device at 7:00 PM. That would be right in the thick of things. Maximum devastation.

He took out a pack of Marlboro Lights and placed a cigarette between his lips. He lit it with an old butane lighter and inhaled the smoke deep into his lungs. He gazed down at the activity on 6th Avenue as he blew the smoke out through his nostrils like an angry bull. Taking another long drag on the cigarette, he began to wonder if he would ever feel vindicated. Would this be enough? Or would the killing need to go on?

He closed his eyes and rested the palm of his hand on his brow. *What has happened to me? How did it ever come to this?* he thought, as he crushed the remains of the cigarette beneath his boot.

He knew he would never return to Dubai, or the Cayman Islands for that matter. His thirst for revenge would never be quenched. He would keep killing until he was caught or until he was killed himself.

He checked his watch again, and then picked up the field glasses in one hand and the transmitter in the other. *It was almost time.*

CHAPTER 54

JAKE WALKED ALONG 51ST STREET, LISTENING INTENTLY through the small earbud hidden in his left ear. He looked down at his watch: 6:20. *So far so good.* He took a deep breath and then jogged across 6th Avenue. The sun was starting to set and it cast a blinding glare on the windows across from Radio City. He raised his hand against the sun and looked up to the top floors. Everyone was in place.

Chief Spota had been stationed at limo checkpoint one on 49th Street, and was busy playing air traffic controller with each of the five F.B.I. units that were scattered around the perimeter of Radio City. She was running a standard "go/no go" dialog, ensuring each team was ready and in position. "Field team one are you in position?"

"Field team one, that's a go, Chief Spota."

Jake listened as Spota ran down the same roll call with the remaining four field teams. As he stepped back onto the sidewalk, he noticed that the noise level had increased considerably. Hundreds of spectators had crowded into a segregated area in front of the building and were celebrating the arrival of their favorite stars. There had been a passageway cordoned off by a long velvet rope, that ran from 6th Avenue to the building entrance, where various entertainment media had set up interview posts.

Jake pushed the earbud further into his ear and struggled to hear over the commotion.

"Agent Chase, this is checkpoint one, do you copy?"

"Checkpoint one, this is Chase. What's up, Chief?" Jake shouted into the small microphone dangling by his cheek.

"Jake, we're sending the first limo in your direction."

Jake looked up 6th Avenue. "Roger that, Chief. How did it go?"

Spota chuckled. "Fine, Jake. I don't think Michael Bolton is going to pose any threat to national security tonight."

Jake watched the limo as it drove down the avenue and approached the Radio City Building. Slowly, the car came to a stop by the velvet ropes and, as the door opened, a huge cheer erupted from the crowd while hundreds of cameras flashed at the same time.

Michael Bolton stepped out of the car and waved to the crowd. His fans went wild and the paparazzi began snapping pictures and calling his name. Quickly, his people navigated him through the labyrinth of reporters, stopping only for the occasional interview. His final stop was at the entrance to the building. It was with a reporter from the entertainment show, Hollywood Diaries.

For the next half hour it was more of the same. Limos would pull up, celebrities would get out, and paparazzi would attack. By seven o'clock the place was packed. There was a line of limos that extended down 6th Avenue, and the number of fans in front of the building had doubled in size. Every few minutes Chief Spota would radio for updates from each of the designated F.B.I. units.

"Jake, anything out of the ordinary?"

Jake shook his head. "Nothing, unless you consider George Clooney getting out of a limo, wearing a police sergeant's cap, out of the ordinary."

"Roger that, Jake."

Jake sighed. He ran his fingers through his hair and tried to stay focused. The adrenaline was quickly wearing off and he was running out of steam. He looked down at the photo of Irgashev and shook his head. "Where do I know you from?" he muttered, as he glanced up at his sharpshooters again. His shoulders dropped. *Maybe I was wrong,* he thought. *Maybe I misread the whole situation.* He sighed again. But err on the side of caution. That's what they drill into your head at Quantico. Don't take any chances. As Jake looked over the huge crowd in front of Radio City, something told him he wasn't wrong.

CHAPTER 55

THE PRODUCER CRUSHED OUT HIS THIRD CIGARETTE ON THE floor beneath his boot and pulled up the antenna on the small, grey transmitter. He looked through the field glasses and could see Brianna still positioned close to the building entrance. For a brief moment he felt sorry for her. She had been so excited when he had given her the necklace. Her face had lit up like that of a child unwrapping a birthday present.

"Oh well, collateral damage. Can't be helped," he said angrily, as he switched the toggle to the "on" position. He gazed down at his watch: 7:05. He looked back through the field glasses and saw throngs of people crowded in front of the building and a long line of cars parading down the avenue. *Like lambs to the slaughter.*

He clenched the transmitter tightly and placed his thumb on the detonator button. "Goodbye, Brianna," he said, as he pressed his thumb down firmly and waited for the madness to begin. But nothing happened! He pushed the button a second time, then a third. Still nothing!

"Fuck!" he screamed, shaking the transmitter box and furiously pushing the detonator button repeatedly.

"No, no, no!" Something was wrong. Perhaps he was too far away. *Yes, that must be it,* he thought, as he ran for the stairs. *Just need to be a little closer, that's all. But not too close.*

As he darted out onto 6th Avenue, The Producer continued to frantically press the button and point the transmitter in the direction of the building. Still there was nothing. Suddenly, he stopped in the middle of the street and placed his hand on his forehead. A look of realization came across his face. His eyes narrowed and he threw the transmitter to the street smashing it to pieces. "Fuck,

Shavka, you have betrayed me!" he screamed, as he fell to his knees.

Pieces of the transmitter ricochet off the ground and hit a bystander in the back of the head. "Watch it, jerk!" yelled the man as he turned to face The Producer.

The Producer looked up at the man and smiled. He slowly stood to his feet and, without warning, pulled out his 9mm, pointed it at the man's head and began firing. BANG, BANG, BANG, BANG. Instantly, the man fell to the ground.

The sound of the gunfire echoed loudly off the buildings, sending everyone into a panic. Men and women were screaming and running for cover in every direction. Police barricades were knocked to the ground and people were trampled as everyone rushed toward Radio City for safety.

Immediately, Jake began running in the direction of the gunfire. "Get down! Get down!" he shouted, sprinting across 6th Avenue, with his 9mm clenched tightly in both hands. As he approached the middle of the street, he could see a man flailing about, waving a gun at innocent people as they ducked for cover. "Freeze!" Jake screamed, as he cautiously approached the gunman, pointing his Glock at the man's head. Instantly, Jake recognized the man's face from the photo Devasher had sent him. It was Nurillo Irgashev, the man responsible for the Paramount bombing. Shoot to kill!

"Put your weapon down," Jake commanded, holding his Glock steady between clenched fists. Jake could tell that Irgashev was completely unstable. He looked like a madman and was completely out of control.

Jake's eyes narrowed. "I said, put your weapon down or I will shoot you!"

The Producer looked at Jake and smiled. He cocked his head, considering. He then slowly began raising his hands as if to surrender.

Jake stepped toward the madman, leading the way with his gun fully extended in front of him. "I repeat, I will shoot you. Now, put down your…."

BANG!

Suddenly, Jake felt a sharp stinging sensation on the left side of his face. He had been hit. As he fell backwards to the pavement he managed to get off a shot. BANG. It hit the gunman in the shoulder and spun him around.

Jake landed on the street head-first, and everything went black.

CHAPTER 56

WHEN JAKE FINALLY CAME TO, HE WAS SPRAWLED OUT ON A stretcher in the back of a parked ambulance. His head was throbbing and he felt nauseous. He tried to remember how he had gotten there, but was drawing a complete blank. Slowly, he brought his hand to his face. There was a bandage covering his left cheek. Jake winced as he gently ran his fingers along the gauze. Carefully, he propped himself up into a sitting position and placed both feet on the floor. The rear doors were open and Jake gazed out onto 51st Street. Suddenly, he remembered. "Irgashev!" he screamed, as he attempted to stand but fell back onto the cot.

"Welcome back, Agent Chase," came a woman's voice from the front of the ambulance. "My name is Dr. Woerner," she said, shining a small pen light in each of his eyes and then looking at her watch. "You've been out almost an hour now."

Jake made another attempt to stand, but this time banged his head hard on the roof of the ambulance. The noise startled the driver as he looked over his shoulder and gave Jake a curious look. Jake closed his eyes and grinded his teeth angrily. He took a deep breath and slowly sat back down. "What's happened? Where's Irgashev?"

Woerner chuckled. "Easy does it, Agent Chase." She then placed two fingers on Jake's wrist and looked back down at her watch. "You were shot in the head," she said raising an eyebrow. "Lucky for you the bullet just grazed the side of your face. One inch to the right and we wouldn't be having this conversation."

"Or any conversation at all," interrupted the driver with a laugh.

Suddenly, Chief Spota came charging to the back of the ambulance. There were beads of sweat on her forehead and she was completely out of breath. "Jake, are you okay?" she asked, between gasps of air.

Jake nodded. "Irgashev?"

Spota shook her head. She was starting to breath normally again. "I'm sorry, Jake, we lost him in the crowd."

"Fuck!" shouted Jake.

Dr. Woerner gave him a disapproving stare and then made some notes on a clipboard.

"What about the marksmen?" he asked, as he stood up, paying close attention to the roof this time.

"Agent Chase, please, you have a concussion," pleaded Dr. Woerner, as she followed him out of the ambulance.

"Too many friendlys, Jake. It got pretty hairy out there. They couldn't risk taking the shot," replied Spota.

Once Jake was on the street, he began patting himself down. "My gun, where's my gun?" he asked frantically, and then turned to face Dr. Woerner.

She frowned. "Agent Chase, come back into the ambulance. Please, you have a concussion."

Jake peeled the bandage from his face and threw it to the street. "I'm fine, Doctor. Now, my weapon please?"

"I'll take responsibility for Agent Chase," interrupted Chief Spota, flashing her shield.

Doctor Woerner looked from Jake to Spota and then threw up her hands in defeat. "Fine," she said, shaking her head disapprovingly and called to the driver. "Jerry, please give Agent Chase his personal effects."

Jake took his Glock and shoulder holster from the ambulance driver and checked his ammo clip. He looked up at Spota. "I think I hit him," he said, and then paused for a moment. "Yes, I'm sure of it. Just before I blacked out, I got a shot off and I hit the bastard in the shoulder."

Spota looked pleased. "We'll get word out to all the local hospitals." Then she hesitated, a serious look settling across her face. "Jake, I'm sorry we lost him, but we're close. We're really close."

Jake was silent.

Spota sighed as she looked up and down 51st Street. It was quiet now. Although there was no longer an imminent threat, the awards ceremony had been terminated and every one had long since fled the area. She then turned her attention toward 6th Avenue. The medical examiner's office was finishing their investigation and a few reporters were snapping photos. She shook her head and turned to face Jake. "Why don't you let us get you a ride home? If anything turns up, I'll call you."

Jake checked his watch. It was almost nine and there really was nothing more he could do tonight. Plus, he needed to take a break from the case and try to get some sleep. He nodded at Spota. "Ok, Chief, we'll meet up again tomorrow morning."

Spota smiled and then radioed for one of the patrolmen. She then shook Jake's hand and made her way in the direction of the city coroner.

As Jake waited for the car to arrive, he typed a quick email to Devasher and briefed him on the recent events. He made sure to stress that Irgashev should be in custody within the next twenty-four to forty-eight hours. Then, it suddenly occurred to him that he hadn't heard from Ken all day. This was odd considering the number of emails they had been sending to one another over the past week. Jake sent the message, re-attached the PDA to his belt and tried to rub the tired from his eyes. As beat down as he was, Jake couldn't imagine how exhausted Ken must have been feeling in the Middle East. He suddenly felt sorry the old man. Once this case was over, Jake planned on having a little chat with his mentor about possibly slowing down a bit and letting him do most of the heavy lifting. It was the least he could do for his friend.

CHAPTER 57

IT WAS NEARLY 11:00 PM BY THE TIME JAKE ARRIVED BACK AT the house in Westchester. He had phoned Diane earlier and warned her about his injury, trying his best to tone down what had happened. But, no matter how you phrase it, "Honey, I got shot in the head," just comes across badly.

As the patrol car pulled up the driveway and approached the house, Jake immediately spotted Diane and Mike sitting on the front steps. Diane was smoking a cigarette.

Jake's shoulders dropped. "This can't be good," he said, as he shot the driver a nervous look. The policeman laughed as he brought the car to a stop. Jake let out a tired sigh. He grabbed his bag from the back seat and slowly exited the vehicle. He was still a bit nauseous and quite dizzy. Dr. Woerner was right. He probably did have a slight concussion. He gave Diane and Mike a wave and began walking in their direction

"Anything else I can do for you, Agent Chase?" asked the patrolman from the driver's side window.

Jake raised his arm and gave the driver an abbreviated wave but didn't bother to turn around.

"Okay then, good luck with the missus," he said, as he slowly turned the patrol car around and headed down the driveway.

As Jake approached the front door, Diane took a final drag on the cigarette, threw it to the ground and started walking in his direction.

"Here it comes," Jake mumbled, as he cautiously made his way toward the house. But to his surprise Diane wasn't upset at all. Instead she leaned in, gave him a kiss and rubbed her nose against his. She then let out a sigh of relief. Jake looked over her shoulder at Mike who just shrugged.

She then stepped back from him, put her hand on his chin and twisted his cheek to face her. She frowned. "I need to see this under the light," she said, as she took Jake by the hand and led him to where Mike was sitting.

Mike nodded. "How ya feeling, buddy?"

Jake slowly sat down on the step next to his friend and let out a groan. "Never better, buddy."

"I'll be the judge of that," interrupted Diane, as she knelt down beside Jake and examined the gash. Suddenly, her eyes widened. "Oh my God, who dressed this? And what the heck happened to the bandage?" she demanded, giving him a stern look.

Jake stayed silent.

Diane let out a huff. "I'm going to get my medical bag," she said, as she stood to her feet. "I'm pretty sure I have some Vitamin E cream and gauze. I'll be right back." And then she disappeared into the house.

Mike stood and stretched his arms over his head. "I think I'm going to be on my way."

Jake looked up at his friend. He thought about standing but then decided it would be too painful. "Don't be ridiculous, Mike. It's late."

Mike shook his head. "Thanks, Jake, but I really want to get home to see Anita. These few days with you two have been a revelation...puts things into perspective, man. I think I need to make some changes in a hurry."

Jake closed his eyes and let out a sigh. "We never really finished our conversation, did we?"

Mike chuckled. "Yes, well, you've kinda had your hands full, buddy," he said, as he headed down the steps to his BMW. Then he turned to face Jake and grinned. "And go easy on the Vitamin E. Chicks dig scars."

Jake's shoulders dropped. "Right. Scars," he repeated, as he traced the line across his cheek with his fingers. "Great."

He watched as Mike pulled down the driveway. When the beamer was finally out of sight, Jake took a deep breath and slowly made his way to his feet. He was still light-headed but at least the nausea was gone.

Jake entered the house and called out to Diane, but there was no answer. He shook his head. "This house is too fucking big," he muttered, as he made his way into Jack's office and fell backwards into the leather couch. "God, I need a vacation." He then reached inside his blazer, undid the snap on his shoulder holster and took out his 9mm, setting it down on the end table beside him.

He closed his eyes for a second, but as soon as he opened them he noticed it. He had to look twice to be sure, but outside the office was a trail of blood. Jake quickly raised his hand to his cheek. His face was dry. He thought for a moment but when he looked back at the door his heart nearly stopped. For a moment he thought he was dreaming. He blinked hard and tried to focus, but the image was very real. Standing in the doorway was Nurillo Irgashev, and he was holding Diane. His arm was around her neck in a tight choke-hold. His shirt was drenched in blood and there was a makeshift tourniquet tied around his shoulder. In his free hand he held a gun pressed firmly against Diane's head.

"Hello, Agent Chase. My name is Nurillo Irgashev. I believe you've been looking for me."

Immediately, Jake jumped up from the couch. His eyes narrowed and he clenched his teeth angrily. "I swear to God if you harm her I'll...."

The Producer laughed mockingly. "You'll do what, Agent Chase? I don't think you are in any position to be making threats. Do you?" he said as he tightened his hold around Diane's neck.

Jake paused for a moment. Then he smiled. "Look, take it easy, okay? You're right. You hold all the cards here. Now let's just talk this through. I'm sure...."

"Don't give me that fucking F.B.I. negotiation crap," screamed The Producer. He dragged Diane to Jack's writing table, bent her over and shoved her face down onto the desktop. Diane let out a cry as her face slammed into the hard leather surface. With one hand he pinned down her face, and with the other he clenched his gun, keeping it pressed hard against the back of her head. Diane struggled to get free, but it was no use. The Producer laughed and shoved her head further into the desk.

Suddenly, it occurred to Jake. The picture! That's where he recognized Irgashev from. He was the man with Jack in the picture at the Playboy Mansion. But how was that even possible? His mind was racing as he stared down at the photograph trying to make sense of it.

The Producer looked at Jake and followed his gaze down to the framed picture. He smiled. "Ah, starting to catch on, Agent Chase?"

"Jake, what is he talking about?" asked Diane, desperately struggling to get free.

"Let me explain, Doctor," said The Producer, as he grabbed Diane's shoulder and flipped her over to face him. Tightly he clenched her throat and rested the gun on her forehead. "Your father was a two-bit con man and a thief."

Diane looked confused. "My father? How do you know my father?"

The Producer tightened his grip on her throat. "Let's just say we were business associates." Then he paused and lowered his face inches from Diane's. His voice was low. "That is, until I killed him."

"What...what are you saying? Jake, what is he saying?"

Jake appeared calm and was slowly backing towards the table where he had left his 9mm. "Don't listen to him, Diane."

The Producer let out a sarcastic laugh. "No, listen to me, Doctor. Listen very carefully to me," he said angrily. "I put a bullet into your daddy's head, and now I'm going to do the same thing to you and Agent Chase."

Jake knew he was running out of time. He had to do something fast. He had positioned himself in front of the table and he could almost reach his Glock. "Look, it doesn't have to go down like this," he said, stalling for time.

The Producer let out a disappointing sigh. "Don't beg, Agent Chase. It's unbecoming. I expected more from a hero." Then, he looked down at Diane and his face became stern. "It was never about money. It was always about wrath!" He paused and looked back up at Jake. "Now, you and your lovely wife are going to die here tonight, Agent Chase, and there is nothing you can do about it."

"But I can!" screamed Diane. Suddenly, she grabbed Jack's ivory letter opener from the desk and drove it deep into Irgashev's scrotum.

The Producer let out a high-pitched scream, and with a look of horror on his face, he fell backwards off Diane, knocking her to the ground. He staggered and fell back into the wall. With a shaky hand he fired a shot, but the bullet missed Diane's head by inches. Before he could get off another shot, Jake grabbed his 9mm from the end table and fired four direct hits into his head. BANG, BANG, BANG, BANG.

Yippee Kayay, motherfucker!

CHAPTER 58

FOR THE SECOND TIME THAT WEEK, EVERY FIRE TRUCK, AMBULance and cop car in Bedford was stationed on Jake's driveway. It was nearly 4:00 AM and the place was swarming with cops. The city coroner's office had taken over Jack's study and was still going strong, even though Irgashev's dead body had been removed hours ago.

Jake was situated in the formal dining room and was busy giving testimony for the fifth time about the night's events. He was seated across from a uniformed police officer and was starting to grow impatient. Just then, the door swung open and in walked Detective Leary. Jake sighed.

"I'll take it from here, Sergeant," said Leary, as he sat across from Jake and began to tap out a beat on the table with his fingers.

Jake frowned. "Look Detective, I've been through this five times in the last hour. Get your hands on one of those notepads and you can read my statement." Jake paused and looked at the door. "I'd like to go and check on Diane. She twisted her ankle pretty bad when that creep fell on top of her."

Leary stopped drumming. "Relax, Jake, I just came in here to get that guy off your back and to offer you a handshake on a job well done."

Jake gave Leary a quizzical look. "For what, Detective?"

Leary started tapping again. "For solving the case involving your caretaker and his wife."

Jake leaned into the table. "What are you saying, Detective?"

Leary grinned. "I'm saying the prick you capped tonight was the same guy that killed Maria and Carlos." Leary paused. He took a deep breath and exhaled through his nostrils. "The DNA we got from Irgashev matches the DNA we found on Carlos' fist. Irgashev must have come looking for you guys and Carlos and Maria got in his way."

Just then, the dining room door swung open and Diane came limping into the room using a pair of crutches. "Jake, they want me to go for x-rays. I may have fractured my leg."

Jake stood from the table. "Detective, will you excuse us?"

Leary smiled and then looked over his shoulder at Jake who was helping Diane out of the room. "Of course, Agent Chase. Family always comes first."

"Yes, Detective, it absolutely does."

Once again, all was right with the world. The sun was shining, the birds were singing and it was a beautiful spring morning. Except of course, Jake and Diane were spending it in a hospital room with torn ligaments and a fractured fibula in Diane's right leg. On the bright side, perhaps now she would have some closure on her father's death.

She had just come out of surgery and her room at Northern Westchester Medical Center looked like a florist's shop. There was a beautiful bouquet from the Bedford Police with a very nice note from Detective Leary. Dr. Sinclair and Director Robbins had been phoning all morning and had sent a huge bundle of sunflowers. Even Jarvis had sent a stuffed bear holding colorful balloons.

"Jake, my leg is so itchy under this cast."

Jake grinned. "No problem. I grew up wearing one form of cast or another."

Diane tilted her head to one side and smiled. "I didn't know that."

Jake looked at her and nodded. "Sure," he said, allowing the word to linger on his tongue. "Between my brother Mattie and me, we should have had an orthopedic surgeon on retainer." He then reached over her and grabbed the bear Jarvis had sent. He gave her a wink, and then removed a balloon from one of the thin sticks in the bear's paw. "Here ya go," he said, handing her the stick. "Instant leg-scratcher."

Diane smiled. "You're a genius." She then she shoved the stick inside her cast and began scratching her leg furiously. Jake leaned over and kissed the top of her head.

Just then, the door to the room swung open and Mike and Anita walked in. They were holding hands and Mike was carrying a dozen sunflowers. He looked at Jake and grinned. "Just like I was saying, Anita. Kills the bad guy, saves the world and gets the girl. Jake Chase, superhero."

Jake laughed, and made his way to greet Mike and Anita. He kissed Anita on her cheek and then leaned in and gave Mike a tight squeeze.

Mike shook his head. "I'm serious, man, they should make Jake Chase action figures or at least a Jake Chase video game," he said, winking at Diane. He then interlocked both hands with his index fingers pointing in the air like a pretend gun. "Chase…Jake Chase," he said, imitating James Bond and then started cracking up.

Anita frowned and then made her way to the bed. "Oh you poor thing," she said, as she leaned over and gave Diane a big hug and kiss. "How are you feeling, sweetie?"

"Itchy," said Diane, who had begun scratching her leg with the stick again.

Mike approached the bed. He was no longer toting his mock Walther PPK. "And the baby?" he asked cautiously.

Diane gave a nervous smile as she set the stick down on the bed beside her. "They don't seem very concerned, but they're going to do a sonogram in about an hour, just to be on the safe side."

Anita sat down on the edge of the bed and placed her hand on Diane's leg. "Well you just rest, sweetie. Mike took the week off and booked us a room at a romantic inn in Pound Ridge." She then looked up at Mike and nodded. "We'll be right around the corner for the next ten days in case you need anything."

Diane raised her eyebrows and gave Anita a smile. "Jake and I are planning a little getaway too." She then glanced down at her cast. "That is, of course, when I'm finished with physical therapy."

Mike sat down in the corner of the room and began fiddling

with the remote control. "That sounds awesome," he said. Then he glanced over at Diane. "Mind if I put on the Yankees?"

Diane shrugged her shoulders and looked back at Anita. "Two weeks with no phones, no TV and best of all…no emails."

Jake smiled. He couldn't remember the last time he took a vacation. He was pretty sure the Bureau owed him something like thirty or forty weeks. But just as he was drifting off to a beach-side hammock, the door to the hospital room burst open and startled everyone. It was Martha, Devasher's ex-wife. She looked completely exhausted. Her eyes were red and she had been crying. Her usual sophisticated demeanor had been replaced by worry and fear.

Jake's first thought was that something horrible had happened in the Middle East. "Martha, what's wrong? Is it Ken?" he asked, as he jumped up from the corner of the bed and hurried to her side.

Martha began to cry. She pulled out a wad of tissues and brought them to her face. "Jake, I'm so sorry to bother you, but I didn't know who else to turn to."

Jake looked back at Diane, Anita and Mike who looked completely baffled. He then turned to face Martha and gently put his hands on her shoulders. "What is it, dear?" he asked softly, now fearing that his friend and mentor had been killed by Irgashev's henchmen in Dubai.

Mike stood from the chair and reached for a pitcher that was resting on a night stand beside the bed. He filled a plastic cup with water and walked it over to Martha. "Little sips, and breathe," he said, with a reassuring smile.

Martha looked up at Mike as he handed over the cup. "Yes, thank you," she said, and then took a sip of water. She then looked back at Jake. "I haven't heard from Ken in almost a week."

Jake looked confused. "I don't understand. He hasn't phoned?"

Martha shook her head. Her voice was shaky. "No, Jake, not a single call in over a week. We always speak. Every day." She paused and looked at the ground. "Even when he's out of the country," she said, as her voice trailed off.

Jake smiled. He felt a sense of relief. "Well, I'm sure he's just…."

Martha continued. "I got worried and went to his house this morning. I used the spare key he left me. He's gone, Jake."

Jake shook his head. "Martha, I think you're overreacting a bit. He's in Dubai. I just spoke to him a few days ago."

Martha's voice was more deliberate now. "No, Jake, you don't understand," she said. "The house is completely empty."

Jake's smile quickly vanished as a cold sweat began to form on the back of his neck. "What do you mean completely empty, Martha?"

Martha sighed. "I mean empty. Nothing, Jake. No furniture. No carpets. Nothing." She paused and then reached into her pocketbook and took out Ken's PDA. "I found this in the bushes by the front door," she said, staring down at the phone.

Jake glanced down at Martha's hands. They were trembling. "Yes, he told me he forgot it the morning he left for Dubai. It's probably why he hasn't called you in so long."

Martha stayed silent. She powered on the PDA and handed it over to Jake. He gave her a smile and looked down at the screen. Devasher hadn't erased any of his old emails. There must have been at least a year's worth stored on his PDA. Slowly, Jake began scrolling through the list, reading each one. "This can't be! No, this can't be right!" he exclaimed, as he began scrolling faster through Devasher's old emails.

"What is it, Jake? What's wrong?" asked Diane.

Jake put his hand on his forehead. He felt sick to his stomach. "No, no, this can't be," he repeated, as he reviewed the emails from the past two months, then the past six months, and then the past year. They were all signed DD: Deputy Director. Jake could feel his pulse quicken and his grip tighten around the PDA. He looked up at Diane. "It's Ken," Jake replied. "He was in on it. It was him the whole time!"

Diane looked worried. "What are you saying, Jake? He was in on what?"

Jake stared down at the emails and again fell silent as he continued to read in amazement. He was in complete shock. Paramount, Zurich Holding, Saudi Investments, Radio City. Devasher was in on it all…maybe even the murder of Diane's father.

"He's on Grand Cayman Island!" he screamed, startling everyone in the room.

"How do you know that?" asked Mike.

Jake pointed to the PDA. "This last email." He paused and started reading again. "They were planning to meet at the Hyatt on Grand Cayman Island the day after the Radio City bombing. That's where the money is!"

Jake looked up and scanned the room. His brain was racing and his heart nearly beating out of his chest. Finally, his eyes settled on Diane. She gave him a faint smile and suddenly the words of Detective Leary echoed through his head: "Family always comes first."

Suddenly, Jake deflated. His shoulders dropped as he stared into Diane's eyes. He sighed and turned to face Martha. "You need to get this to Director Robbins at the F.B.I. He will know what to do," Jake said, as he handed her the PDA.

He could feel the entire room staring at him in amazement.

Martha looked lost as she put Devasher's PDA back in her purse. "OK, Jake," she said, with tears welling up in her eyes again. "I just thought you would be the one who could help him. You know him better than anyone."

Jake turned up the palms of his hands. "Yes, but I need to be with…."

"Are you fucking kidding me?" interrupted Diane, who was attempting to get out of bed.

Jake turned to face her. "But I thought…."

"Give me a break. We've just been though the week from hell. Let me know if I'm leaving anything out, huh, Jake? A major Hollywood studio blew up, a building fell on top of you, your friend and mentor probably had something to do with it, you were shot in the face, I stabbed my father's murderer in places I care not to mention, who, you in turn, killed in our den, and, oh yeah, I'm pregnant with a broken leg. Plus, by my scorecard, there is still another Irgashev brother out there with a hundred and seventy-five million bucks!"

"What are you saying, Di Di?"

Diane raised her finger. "I'm not finished. Two days before this whole mess started, you blew up a Japanese helicopter and fell three stories into the East River!" she exhaled. "Didn't think I knew about that one, did ya?" Then she smiled. "Look Jake, you need to get on the next flight to Grand Cayman. You know, closure and all." She paused and smiled at Martha. "I know how you felt about Ken. If you don't confront him, you'll never have closure, Jake."

Jake was dumfounded. He shrugged his shoulders and blurted out the first thing that came to mind. "God, I love you, Diane."

"I know," she said, and then gave him a wink.

Jake's eyes narrowed as he quickly turned, grabbed the PDA back from Martha and bolted for the door.

Diane lay back on her pillow and carefully rested her foot on the bed. "And Jake, be careful," she yelled in his direction, and then blew the hair off her face.

"Always!" he yelled back. But before he could get through the door, he stopped dead in his tracks, turned around and made his way back to the bed. He leaned over and put a hand on Diane's tummy. He looked her in the eyes and said, "Always."

CHAPTER 59

FROM THE MOMENT JAKE ARRIVED ON GRAND CAYMAN ISLAND, his head was spinning. He found himself searching for excuses for what Devasher had done or at least trying to figure out a logical explanation for it all. But there was only one inescapable conclusion that he was able to arrive at: Ken Devasher was a criminal. Those five words swirled around in Jake's brain until it felt like his head was going to explode.

Devasher was his best friend and had become a father figure to Jake ever since his real father died on 9/11. The idea that he could have been involved in Paramount was completely unthinkable. Plus, if that wasn't bad enough, Devasher was leaving a trail a mile long, almost as if he wanted Jake to find him. Not only did he leave behind his BlackBerry and enough incriminating emails to put him away for life, but he had checked into the hotel on Grand Cayman under his real name. *Catch me if you can!*

"Yes, here you go, Ken Devasher," said the receptionist at the front desk of the Hyatt Hotel. "He's staying in one of our best rooms, Ocean View Suite 509." She smiled at Jake and pointed over his shoulder. "Just take the elevators at the end of the hallway."

Jake looked in the direction she was pointing and then returned the smile. He reached for his bag and headed for the elevators.

The receptionist leaned over the counter. "Um, Can I ask you a question?"

Jake let out a sigh, then turned to face her. He forced another smile. "Why not."

She leaned in closer. "Is he really an F.B.I. agent?"

"He is for now."

The long hallway was lined with large french doors, adorned

by white linen curtains. There was a cool ocean breeze that swept through the hotel and was blowing the curtains carelessly in and out of the open doors. Everywhere you looked palm-leaf ceiling fans were slowly spinning over dark rattan furniture. The effect was meant to be calming. In the distance, a cruise ship was anchored in crystal blue water, and wave runners and water-skiers were buzzing up and down the beach. Jake checked the ammo clip on his Glock 9.

Jake boarded the elevator. As the doors closed, he could feel the palms of his hands begin to sweat as he gripped the gun tightly between two fists. He couldn't believe what he was about to do. "Get it together, man," he said, as he watched the floor indicator above the elevator doors: 2…3…4. He clenched the gun tighter and could feel his pulse quicken as the indicator hit 5. *This is it.*

The doors slowly opened on the fifth floor and Jake stepped to the front of the elevator but was suddenly knocked back against the wall.

"AHHHH BEACH!" screamed a gaggle of bathing-suit-clad children as they all charged into the elevator at once. Jake let out a scream himself as he quickly hid the gun behind his back. He took a deep breath, forced a smile and carefully navigated his way through the army of kids, floaties and boogie boards. As the elevator door closed, he could hear the chant grow distant: Beach… beach…beach.

Jake took a second to regain his composure and looked around. More rattan furniture and palm-leaf ceiling fans. He was starting to feel light-headed; precipitated by a mix of nerves, adrenaline, sleep deprivation and a mild concussion. He dried the palms of his hands on his shirt and then began following the signs in the direction of Suite 509. He had absolutely no idea what he was going to say to Ken once he found him. "Hey, man, whatcha been up to?" just didn't seem appropriate.

What if he really had lost his mind? What if Ken pulled his weapon? Could he actually shoot Ken Devasher? *God, I hope it doesn't come to that*, Jake thought, as he leaned up against the wall beside the door to Devasher's hotel room. It was open mid-way. He looked around for a maid's cart, but none was in sight. "Fuck! Could this get any more stressful?" he muttered, as he nudged the door with his shoulder and peered into the room. He saw no one. With his gun clenched between his hands, he quietly entered Ocean View Suite 509. His heart was racing and in addition to all of his other ailments, his mouth had now become completely parched.

Jake made his way into the large main room of the suite. Empty. Not even a suitcase. No indication at all that anyone was staying there.

Don't let your guard down, Jake. Things aren't always how they appear. After all, it was Ken Devasher who taught him that.

The bathroom! The door to the bathroom was closed. "My god, is he in the bathroom?" Jake mumbled. He could already see the headlines:

DEPUTY DIRECTOR OF THE F.B.I.
ARRESTED DURING BOWEL MOVEMENT

Jake took a deep breath, and, with his 9mm pointed directly in front of him, kicked the door off its hinges and rushed into the bathroom. Empty. He exhaled.

As he started back through the door Jake suddenly froze. He felt every muscle in his body tighten as he slowly looked up at the bathroom mirror. It was a note hand written on the glass in black magic marker.

JAKE, SO GLAD YOU COULD MAKE IT.
THE WEATHER IS TERRIFIC!
POOL CABANA 9
DD

CHAPTER 60

THE POOL AT THE HYATT WAS A LIGHT SHADE OF BLUE AND THE sun which was hovering overhead in a cloudless sky, made the water sparkle. Teak lounge chairs were lined up like rows of soldiers standing side by side and ran four deep off the pool. Each chair came equipped with two neatly rolled beach towels and a colorful umbrella all bearing the Hyatt logo. It was paradise.

The shallow end was packed with dozens of families frolicking about, and it made Jake feel a little calmer. He figured that even if Ken had lost it, he probably wouldn't blow Jake's brains out all over a family on holiday. Or would he?

Cabana 9 was located by the deep end of the pool with the beach just behind it, far away from the happy families. It was a wooden structure covered by colorful stripped canvas. Inside, there was enough room for two chaise lounges, a small refrigerator, a sitting area and a plasma TV. Jake approached cautiously. He held his hand up and squinted against the glare of the sun. He was still a safe distance away but could see someone inside the cabana. It appeared to be a man about Devasher's build, lying carelessly on a lounge chair, reading a newspaper. Jake squinted harder, but the paper was blocking the man's face.

Jake grabbed a beach towel from a bin next to one of the lifeguard stands and folded it over his right hand, covering the gun clenched in his fist. He slowly walked along the poolside, completely focused on the man in the cabana as well as everyone around him. For all Jake knew, the last Irgashev brother was hiding behind a palm tree ready to cap him.

When he arrived at the cabana, Jake knew immediately that the man on the chaise lounge was Ken Devasher. Although Jake still couldn't see his face, he knew it was him. When you work that closely with someone for ten years you get to know pretty much everything about that person. Even the way they read the newspaper.

Jake stayed silent. He reached into his pocket and pulled out Ken's PDA and threw it down beside him.

Devasher let out a sigh and turned the page. "I expected something a little more dramatic from you, Agent Chase." He paused. "You know, maybe a little Shakespeare." Then he looked over the top of the paper and grinned. "Et tu, Brute?"

Jake dropped the beach towel and slowly raised his 9mm to the center of the newspaper. His eyes were narrow and beads of sweat were trickling down the sides of his face. He took a deep breath and spoke. "Deputy Director Kenneth Devasher, you are under arrest for murder."

Although the words were coming out of his mouth, Jake couldn't believe what he was saying. He had to steady the gun with both hands to keep it from shaking, and he was still expecting to be shot in the back at any moment.

Devasher began laughing and slowly lowered the paper. "Bravo, Jake, bravo," he said without the slightest bit of concern for the gun that was pointed at his head.

Jake took another breath. His voice was louder now and more deliberate. "I said you are under arrest. Now get up and keep your hands where I can see them."

"Hands where you can see them. Come on Jake! All I have on is this bathing suit. Where could I possibly hide a weapon?"

Jake looked around but kept the gun pointed at Devasher's head. "Irgashev?"

Ken laughed. "Oh, no need to worry about Shavka. There was an unfortunate scuba diving accident, you see."

Jake nodded and clenched his teeth. "All the same, Ken, hands up."

Devasher smiled. "Anything you say, Agent Chase," he replied, as he tossed the newspaper to a nearby lounge chair and slowly raised his hands.

Jake released the grip on his gun with his left hand and slowly reached into his back pocket for a pair of hand cuffs. "I can't believe what you've become."

Devasher turned his head slightly. "I've become wealthy, just like you."

Jake threw the cuffs to Devasher and re-gripped the gun with both hands. "You killed people for money, Ken."

"Well, it is an awful lot of money, Jake."

Jake shook his head in disgust. "Paramount. Innocent people lost their lives."

Suddenly, the smug look on Devasher's face turned to remorse. He sighed. "Paramount wasn't supposed to go down like that."

Jake gripped the gun so tightly that the veins in his forearms began to protrude from his skin. "And Diane's father?" he shouted.

Devasher looked dumfounded. "What about Diane's father?"

"Your partner murdered...."

Suddenly, a lifeguard let out a loud whistle and began yelling at some kids that were too far out in the ocean. The sound startled Jake and he looked over his shoulder for a second, but when he looked back there was only an empty chaise lounge and a crumpled copy of *USA Today*.

"Fuck!" Jake screamed, as he darted out through the canvas at the rear of the cabana. He emerged onto the crowded beach but, Devasher was nowhere in sight. He cupped his hand above his eyes and squinted against the bright sun that was reflecting off the sand. He ran several steps toward the ocean but then stopped. He turned in a complete circle desperately searching for some sign of the direction Devasher had fled. But it was useless. The beach was completely packed and Devasher had blended into the crowd and made his escape. He was gone with one hundred and seventy-five million dollars.

Jake's shoulders dropped. He gave one last look and then slowly turned and made his way back into the cabana. For a brief moment he was actually relieved that he didn't have to arrest his long-time friend and mentor.

"Fuck it," he said, as he fell back into the chaise lounge where Ken had been sitting moments ago. He closed his eyes and imagined Diane and what their new baby might look like. It made him smile. Jake thought again about what Detective Leary had said. *Family always comes first.*

He reached over, picked up the copy of *USA Today* and opened it to the sports page. Suddenly, Jake's eyes widened and his jaw dropped. Taped to the center of the page was a piece of the hotel stationery. Written in black magic marker were the words: *Good Luck, Deputy Director Chase.*

Jake shook his head. "Well I'll be damned," he said, as he tried to fight off a smile. He tore the note off the page and crumpled it into a ball. Under it, the headline read, "A-Rod Hits 500th Homerun!"

Well, at least Diane will be happy, Jake thought to himself. *About A-Rod, that is.* He then reached into his pocket and pulled out a pair of Ray-Ban Wayfarer sunglasses and slid them on his face. He relaxed into the lounge, and signaled to a cocktail waitress.

"Hey, can I get a Pina Colada over here!"

THE END

11/10

AUTHOR'S CHARITY

BLYTHEDALE CHILDREN'S HOSPITAL

FIFTY PERCENT OF ALL AUTHOR BOOK ROYALTIES WILL BE donated to Blythedale Children's Hospital.

Founded more than 100 years ago, Blythedale Children's Hospital in Valhalla, NY has been a leader in developing innovative, multi-disciplinary inpatient and ambulatory programs, as well as a community resource for children with a variety of medical concerns. Through its inpatient and day hospital programs, Blythedale Children's Hospital treats more than 300 children daily, making it one of the largest providers of children's health services in New York State. In addition, the Hospital provides diagnosis and treatment for hundreds of outpatients with a wide range of medical and rehabilitation needs. Because of the unique and comprehensive array of pediatric programs and services, children and families come to Blythedale from the tri-state region and beyond.

A child's catastrophic health problem turns a family's world inside out. For Blythedale's families—who are typically referred from the NICU or PICU of an acute care pediatric hospital, the Hospital offers individualized, round-the-clock medical care in a medically sophisticated, yet intensely child-centered environment. Blythedale prepares children to lead the most independent lives possible, and trains their caregivers to be confident providers for their children.

For more information please go to: www.blythedale.org